Eating Up the Evidence

A Sharp Investigations Novel

Book Four

BY: E. N. CRANE

EDITED BY: A. O. NEAL &
SUE SCOTT

Dedication

THANK YOU TO MY DOGS: PERRY AND PADFOOT.

THEIR SHENANIGANS, ANTICS AND BEHAVIOR ARE THE
MODEL FOR ALL THINGS WINNIE.

THANK YOU TO MY HUSBAND, BECAUSE HE KNOWS HOW
MANY "PEOPLE" LIVE IN MY HEAD AND HE'S NEVER HAD ME
COMMITTED. HE ALSO KEEPS ME IN COFFEE AND SNACKS
WHEN I START YELLING AT IMAGINARY PEOPLE.

SPECIAL THANKS TO JEFF NEAL FOR LENDING ME HIS ARTIS-
TIC EYE AND MILITARY KNOWLEDGE. MOST OF THIS IS MADE
UP, BUT I STRIVE FOR IMAGINATIVE ACCURACY.

Chapter One: Heat Wave

I t was eleven in the morning, I'd had 100 liters of water, and I was still thirsty. That's what I got for using the metric system and not having twenty-seven gallons like a real American.

On the ground beside me, Winnie was half under a shrub, trying desperately to get relief from the unrelenting sun. Despite four years in the Army together, the canine and I had never gotten used to the heat. Winnie, formerly Sgt. Winnifred Pupperson, was a German Shepherd Malinois mix that was only a working dog by breed. In terms of personality, she could best be described as an occasionally competent demolitions expert who preferred taking naps. Since that could also be used to describe me, we were the perfect team both before and after retirement.

The perfect team at completely destroying things people still wanted and/or needed. We didn't just occasionally start small dumpster fires or accidents that could be cleaned with a mop and some elbow grease. Nope, we indirectly caused the burning of a sports car and a newspaper office just over a month ago. Before that, we had destroyed the church event space, several walking aids and B-32 at a game of Bingo gone horribly wrong.

Though we'd foiled a gun heist, a Molotov cocktail exploded some munitions and shot people. We'd saved a school for women, but blew up a marketplace. Solved a murder and stopped a crime ring, but demolished a mobile home...

Suffice it to say, Winnie and I had earned our reputations and our lives weren't even half over.

I'm fairly certain that if heaven were like the principal's office, we wouldn't have a file folder.

We'd have at least a drawer... each.

We were never the bystanders of "little incidents". A fact that usually led us to getting assignments such as this: melting in the sun far away from people and buildings. I snatched a passing goat and examined its coat, hooves, and teeth. Before I could inspect his haunches, the goat bleated and attempted to impale me on his horns.

I let go and watched him leap off like Pepe le Pew chasing the cat in the Looney Tunes cartoons.

Sighing, I exchanged a look with Winnie and we both looked longingly at the barn.

There was a fan in the barn.

There was more water in the barn.

There were no goats in the barn.

Despite being in the first week of April, it was over ninety degrees. The dairy was doing killer business at the ice cream shop and no one wanted to be outside. No one, including me, but I didn't have much choice, given it was my job to "maintain animal welfare". I looked around the dirt landscape, void of anything that could harm the animals that lived there and cursed my boss under my breath.

There was nothing that would harm them... or offer shade to the world's most vile creatures and the unfortunate soul sent to check on them.

A goat bleated and I looked at the cloven hoofed devil. It was gray, with normal-sized horns, and a beard that was rather unimpressive for his five years of age. Berry was the reason we were out here, checking all the goats for injuries. Berry was the reason goats were my least favorite animal and those I anticipated being most likely to side with the robots in the robot apocalypse.

Berry was the reason I was considering trying aloo gosht.

The goat had barreled through a wooden fence and orchestrated a jail break into the horse enclosure. His reasons were unclear at first, but the horses made it clear he was unwelcome. It was a personal exile, the horses tolerated and appreciated the company of all the goats... except Berry. Berry gathered the goats into a herd and led them to what he expected was a greener pasture on the other side. True to his nature, Berry attempted to overthrow the horse hierarchy and become the unquestioned leader of the horse enclosure, which the grazing stallions... resented.

Immensely.

As it was neither greener, nor more of a pasture, Berry didn't have a leg to stand on.

The horses, however, had many legs to stand on. They used these to their advantage to send Berry back into exile by attempting to high-step stomp him back where he belonged... away from them. Berry deserved to be put in his place, but an actively lactating female goat fell into the line of fire. Since this was a dairy farm, her milk was far more important than Berry, his need for adventure, and the desire of the stallions to deprive him of it.

As the farm's animal technician, it was my job to make sure her milk was still suitable for consumption and none of the animals needed a visit from the local vet. When I suggested that this job could be done by murdering Berry and using him as an example to the other goats to shape up, and stand patiently in line for inspection or risk being tomorrow night's dinner, he told me that if I harmed a single hair on the stupid creature, I would be fired and brought up on charges.

When I told him it would be worth it, he threatened to tell my mother about the time he caught me necking in the back of the barn. When I told him only old people used the word necking... Well, now, here I was standing in the unrelenting heat with goats.

So, clearly, that conversation could have gone better.

"I hate you," I muttered at Berry, stuffing my dishwater blonde hair back under my ball cap after wiping a gallon of sweat off my forehead. I squinted my lavender eyes at him, trying for menacing, but even towering over him, I could see he was unimpressed.

"If we were in the Middle East, I could cook you and serve you to a hungry Army base with curry sauce and rice."

He bleated at me and I glared as he galloped away.

"Yeah, you better run!"

"Cynthia! Aren't you done yet?" I winced at the voice of my boss, Joseph, and my proper name spoken like a curse.

I glanced over and down at the short squat man in pristine work clothes. At six feet, I towered over his five foot something frame. He had on a cowboy hat in contrast to my ball cap, nearly new cowboy boots, and a flannel shirt stretched tight over his belly, the buttons looking more likely to pop than our cow who was currently in labor. I was no super model at size fourteen, but I was definitely not in danger of bursting out of my clothes. The t-shirt and cargos were sweat stained and stuck to every inch of my flesh like a second skin. Both were coated in dust, grass, and what might be manure, but I wasn't bursting out of them.

In fact, it was going to take a pry bar to get these clothes off.

"Cynthia Sharp, I asked you a question!"

Another Army flashback to hearing my name shouted in *that tone*. Every time we'd blown up a marketplace, crushed a pretzel statue, or set Florida on fire, someone would use my full name. Usually they'd include my rank, but since my "accidental" retirement when no one noticed my contract was up, I didn't have any rank.

Which was really a blessing and a curse. While I didn't miss the number of people allowed to yell at me in the Army, I really missed everyone being forced to admit I was special.

Well, a specialist.

Same thing.

"Joseph, it's hotter than a runway in Phoenix, Arizona, out here! I'm working on it!"

Winnie whimpered under the shrub and I gave her an apologetic look.

"It's only April, don't be a baby!" Joseph mopped sweat from his forehead as he shot daggers at me. I noted that much like the brim of his hat, his shirt was wilting fast and pools of sweat had formed under his arms. While I was uncomfortable, his face was a color that would be more at home on a tomato, and I tried to rein in my anger. "The men are done fixing the fence. You can't check a few goats in the same time it takes them to replace a whole ten foot section of fence?"

"There are ten men working on the fence, and they have tools! Also, it's not a few goats, it's two dozen and they won't stop moving around. Also, they all look the same!" I shouted and grasped the scruff of a goat as it passed and looked it over. His face went from tomato to something near eggplant and I acknowledged my plan not to send him into an early grave wasn't going well. "I can't tell if I've checked this one and you won't let me draw on them, so this is where we are, Joe!"

"Don't yell at me! I'm the boss!"

"Yeah, yeah," I grumbled and freed the goat. "They're all fine then I guess. Happy?"

"No!" He pulled his hat off to fan his face and his comb over fell into his eyes. "I want you to check the damn goats!"

"I did!"

Without a backward glance, I walked away from Joseph and the goats. Winnie jingled behind me and I looked down to see her panting in a pink camouflage collar with her name stuck to it in Velcro. The jingle was a Christmas bell Joseph made her wear after an incident with some sheep, food pellets, and the seat of his pants.

It had been hilarious, but now Winnie's presence required announcing.

We made it to the barn door, pausing to enjoy the blast of air from the fan. Winnie lifted her head and froze. Scenting the air, she let out an excited bark and took off toward the open-air paddock. My nose couldn't detect him, but I knew where she was going and a smile broke out over my face as well.

Larry had arrived to help birth the calf.

Larry, Dr. Lawrence Kirby, was the sexy commercial livestock vet, and the reason I was being blackmailed for "necking". He was tall, muscled like a nerd who walked into a gym and was too embarrassed to leave without working out, and funny in a way that was rarely on purpose. I rounded the corner to see Winnie easily leap the enclosure fence, run up to Larry and shove her nose into his testicles.

Just as the calf started to emerge, and he took hold of the legs.

Face pale, with a small but manly scream; he welcomed the calf into the world before collapsing in on himself in pain. For her part, Winnie licked his face and his arms as the farm hands arrived to remove the calf. I tried not to gag when I realized exactly *what* Winnie was licking off of him.

She'd definitely put worse in her mouth.

"Hey," I said, looking down at him. For the first time, he was the one coated in gunk and I... was coated in different gunk. So it was actually a SNAFU that didn't need acknowledgement. *Situation normal, all fluffed up.*

"Your dog is a jerk," he grumbled, ruffling her fur with affection.

"Yup," I said, looking down at both of them. "She said you missed your annual health exam and wanted to make sure you saw a proctologist."

"She checked my cavities this morning!" he complained, and I squatted beside him to kiss his nose.

"And you checked mine. What's your point?"

His smile was decidedly very male, and I determined he would live, so I offered him a hand up. With a tug, he was back upright and pressed against me.

"Should I check them again... just in case?" His face moved closer to mine, and he choked before taking a step back. "What is that smell?"

I sniffed the air and looked around.

"I don't smell anything."

Curious, I lifted my shirt and took a cautious sniff, gagging involuntarily.

"Goats. That smell is goats mixed with sweat and manure."

"Maybe I should help you check all your cavities in the shower, with soap." He waggled his eyebrows, but didn't get any closer.

A man cleared his throat behind me and we turned into my brother.

"Dude, I know you've had sex with my wife and everything, but don't remind me that you're doing my sister." Seth made a face, and I punched him. He grabbed my arm, put me in a rear wrist lock and held firm. Despite being nearly the same height and weight, Seth managed to maintain his grip while I struggled to get free. The nerdy structural engineer was either cheating or his muscles were cleverly concealed beneath pocket protectors and protractors.

"Geez you stink!"

I rolled my eyes and considered stomping on his foot or sending Winnie after his nuts, but smelling me was probably worse than both of those. It would also be embarrassing to admit that a trained soldier was incapable of freeing herself from a nerd.

A nerd who was also my brother, meaning fighting dirty was definitely on the table and I was still losing, even with my smell advantage

"If you don't want to smell me, get your butt off the farm, loser." I tried becoming dead weight, but the stupid twig somehow supported me anyway. "How are you holding me up right now? You don't go to the gym!"

"Carla and I need your help... with mom," he choked out the last and I shuddered, but continued trying to make myself the same weight as the Titanic. His wife Carla had been a honey trap government agent with an affinity for side gigs... including Larry. The one saving grace was that she hadn't had sex with my brother during the times she was hooking up with Larry, or I'd have needed a lobotomy to recover from the second-hand incest. She'd retired from that after one final mission to expose a corrupt council member that led to the death of a reporter, married Seth, and was now Sweet Pea, Ohio's chief of police. Despite the hate toward the way she got her experience, Carla was more than qualified to supervise Larry's brother, Daniel, and Barney Fife, no relation, who worked with him. My niece and nephew adored her and a few shots of tequila followed by a tell-all girl's night had made the lingering animosity about her screwing Larry fade.

Carla was a hot redheaded bombshell and turning her down would be hard for anyone. Larry was just a man, and she promised me she was more than done with him. We shook on it, had two more shots, then made Larry and my brother drive us home while we loudly discussed our sex lives and the penises of the men in question... which we took quite a bit of artistic liberty in comparing to the smallest things we could think of... alphabetically.

The woman was my new favorite sister.

My mom, on the other hand, was not exactly family friendly or easy on the faint of heart. While Lynn Sharp was not a drug user or an advocate of flag burning, the conservative community secretly wished she hadn't retired from academia and branched out into practical experimentation. Teaching sexual liberation and the historical repressions of female sensuality had been one thing, but insisting the senior citizens in the community explore theirs while teaching practical skills to the new adults of the community was another. No matter how hard Mrs. Kirby tried, she could not get the church to excommunicate my mom... or do more than to suggest that she herself could benefit from one of Lynn's "meetings".

The whole church was a bunch of closet sex fiends, and it would have been hilarious if half of them weren't ancient when I was born.

My mom's meetings were sex parties, where she encouraged swinging and sold pleasure toys. Toys that she was happy to demonstrate on herself and others, my dad included. The group had also hosted a live nude art in the park that featured my neighbor and her husband getting jiggy with it for the entire world to see. The basement was now the only guest bedroom in the house after Seth's was converted to a library for their ever-growing collection of research and my bedroom became a "playroom" modeled after those Fifty Shades books.

Books my sister Heidi gave her. My sister Molly supported this by sending them tips and tools for pleasure from around the world. The pair also cohosted and researched half of the "experiments" conducted in the house and had on more than one occasion, made sex tapes with their significant others for research.

Which was an assignment for my mom's class.

Hence, Carla was my new favorite sister.

"Not a chance, Sethany," I wriggled free and he let me go. "You are on your own with the Goddess of Giving."

I stuck my tongue out at him and he did it back.

"Let me rephrase that. Carla needs your help keeping mom happy so that I don't tell her about the time you used every glass Christmas ornament in the shed for target practice." He crossed his arms, and I hitched a shoulder.

11

"That was twenty years ago. She probably doesn't even remember the raccoon raid that shattered her family's Christmas Legacy Collection."

"She will when I remind her," he countered, and I narrowed my eyes. "Plus, there's the video."

"That video is garbage! No one will believe it's anything but a voyeur filming through frosted glass." He gave me an expression that screamed *try me,* so I made threats of my own.

"Show her that video and I'll tell her the real reason you were late coming from school on the day of Molly's wedding rehearsal was because you had to go to the ER for getting your penis stuck in a pottery wheel at school trying to make an impression for Dana Cummings." He turned a little pink in the ears. "An artistic rendering so she could satisfy herself at band camp without needing to resort to a flute."

"She played the clarinet! I couldn't compete with a clarinet!"

"You were suspended for a week and you made me lie that we were on 'different Spring Break' schedules!"

"You made me lie about eating your vegetables for years!"

"So, we agree. No one will know either of our misdeeds if you leave me out of this." I smiled in victory.

"If you tell her that, I'll tell her about the time you got drunk and taught a pole dancing class to junior high girls when you were supposed to be babysitting..."

"Enough," Larry said, coming up behind me but keeping his distance. "While hearing the end of that story sounds very promising for future blackmail, we do need to get back to work. What do you need help with?"

"Mom is pissed," he said, and I felt the hairs on my neck stand up. He should have opened with her being mad at him. I had friends all over the world, probably Carla and I together could get him into some sort of Engineers Without Borders program. Needing help with mom was a personal problem. Needing help with mom when she was angry was an international problem, and I started running through who I knew who would know where there were currently ongoing military campaigns I could send him off to.

"What did you do?" I whispered, trying to plan his evacuation and making a mental list of mercenaries I could hire to almost kill him so she'd feel too guilty to finish the job.

He *was* her only son.

"I got married!" He threw his hands in the air and my head dropped to the side, mimicking Winnie. "I got married in a barn and there was no party or decorations or fanfare. She never met Carla until after the ceremony. She didn't get to pass her anything symbolic and there wasn't even a cake, Cyn. Mom is pissed! She wants to throw her a party, get to know her and introduce her to the family."

I relaxed.

"Then let Ma throw her a party. Dad can cook, Mo will make a cake, no big deal. If it'll make Ma happy, just…"

"No! Not a party, a *party*. A pleasure party, with her toys, research group and her… methods of experimentation book…" Seth tried to emphasize all the crucial words and Larry gave a small chuckle.

13

"Has she met Carla? That woman is not a shrinking violet," Larry said, and I gave him a warning look. We may have worked through my jealousy, but I still did not need him to remind me of all that he *knew* about my sister-in-law in the biblical sense.

"Exactly! She said the reason Carla was so... diverse in her experiences was because she was exploring her pleasure. Ma said that if I want her to be happy, I needed to let her do a detailed analysis of the woman's pleasure and take excellent notes or some crap like that. She said it's a..." He shuddered, and I bit back a laugh.

"She said it's an Outgoing Orgasm Party, and we all need to be there."

"What do you want me to do? Doesn't sound like you have a choice," I smirked, and he shook his head. "Save me a piece of cake, though."

"I need you to demolish it in a way that only you can: accidentally and completely."

"Why would I do that, big brother? I'd hate for your wife to go unsatisfied after all she's been through... marrying you."

"You weren't listening, Cyn. I said *all* of us. Carla, me, Heidi, her husband, Larry and you are all expected to attend. Molly might even Skype in with her wife. It's family sex education night... with guest speakers and demonstrations." All the blood left my face and I looked between Larry and Seth in horror. One was laughing and trying to disguise it as a cough, and the other was pleading with me to get our whole family out of this.

14

"I'll think of something," I swore but the dread building in my gut said nothing short of an apocalyptic event would get any of us out of this.

Chapter Two:
Pleasure Party

"No way, Ma," I shoved the tie back hospital gown back at her. "There is no way I'm wearing that."

Behind me, Seth made a sound of agreement while Larry and Carla remained perfectly still. It was probably a positive sign for their future in this family that they didn't contradict my mom but didn't appear to side with her either. While they may be romantically linked to us, my mom was not one to be crossed... or denied.

Lynn Sharp was a short woman. She had perfectly straight grayish hair, pale blue eyes, and a few extra pounds that were a good indicator of her cooking. My dad was tall, gangly, and despite eating the same hearty and delicious cuisine, never gained a pound. They'd both worked at a university before retiring the day I graduated from high school and moved on to the research phase of their life.

I'd only learned recently that they had taught a sociology course and an anthropology course centered around sex and cultural development. Their research was encouraged by my sisters, not suitable for family dinner, and regularly haunted my nightmares.

"Don't be a prude, Cynthia! This is a safe space. Your sister and I," she gestured behind her to Heidi and her husband, already in their cloth gowns, "have found that without the confines of clothes and more discreet access to their partner, people can learn more. We'll be in a circle, no one will see your tushy."

Larry snickered at my mom's choice of words, and I elbowed him in the stomach. If he had any interest in touching my "tushy" again, he'd back me up.

"I'm not being a prude, Ma. If Larry is going to experiment with my erotic zones, we are doing it in a room that doesn't have members of my family in it!"

"Cynthia, I am a trained educator. As is your father, we can offer you insight and guidance. Your inability to relax in this situation is why Larry has such a hard time working you into pleasure. You need help dear, both of you."

Larry sucked in a breath behind me. Apparently, it was all fun and games until someone questioned his ability to provide satisfaction. It was Carla's turn to giggle and Seth turned bright red.

"Oh, come on, how many people have the opportunity to talk to their partner's past lovers? You are both in a unique position to learn more about..."

I clapped my hands over my ears and started humming. Larry pressed behind me and managed to keep his hands off his ears, but he moved us a foot farther away from Carla. My brother had gone from pink to red to sheet white and I knew covering my ears had been the right decision. He spoke, she raised a finger at him, he opened his mouth again and she responded with a sound.

Seth refused the gown she held up, issuing some sort of declaration that reminded me of Captain Underpants, and took Carla by the hand marching them into the living room.

"Honestly, the two of you are a family anomaly," she huffed and tossed the remaining hospital gowns on the floor when I finally took my hands off my ears. "At least take off your bras and put on sweatpants. You need to be comfortable."

Carla poked her head back out of the living room and we shared a look.

"I do hate my bra," she commented, and I checked out her impressive assets.

"Shoulder straps digging in?" She nodded and we agreed in silent understanding at the horrors of support garments. I personally was being attacked by a wayward underwire that needed to be sewn back into the lining. "Jeans are similarly pretty uncomfortable."

"I like sweatpants," Carla agreed, and I nodded. Grabbing the menfolk, we trooped to the basement to become appropriately attired for an orgasm exploration... with my parents, siblings, and the unfortunate fools who decided to love us.

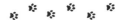

I woke up coated in glitter with a trash can beside me. Inside was saliva and bile, but no actual vomit.

Good deal.

My apartment sat above my office space on Main St. It was a quarter of the library's lot and was easily scanned in a single sweep. Couch, kitchenette, two barstools beside the counter... all of it was exactly as it had been before I left for my parents' house last night besides the damp towel on the floor, a pile of clothes, the trashcan next to my head and glitter.

So much glitter.

"What the hell, Winnie?" I whispered as the dog came to lick the sweat from my face. We looked around my apartment again, a pat to the other side of the bed and a glance at the open bathroom door indicated we were alone. My head was threatening to split in half, so I closed my eyes until it stopped. "When did a night at my parent's hit harder than a college kegger?"

When I leaned to grab my phone, tiny confetti penises rained down on my floor.

Winnie sneezed and two shot out of her nose.

My eyes scanned the floor and a trail of glitter penises led from the top landing of my stairs to the kitchen, from the kitchen to the bathroom and then finally my bed. The scent of coffee filled my nostrils and I staggered to the kitchen to find that I'd programmed the pot and left myself a post-it note.

Your mom gave you pot brownies.

Plot revenge after you rescue Larry.

Good news is we can work the coffee pot stoned.

Bad news, there might be glitter dicks in it.

Staring at the note, I grabbed a cup and poured coffee in it.

Except I missed and poured the hot coffee on my feet, turning them bright red with pre-blisters.

"Ow!" I screamed and then tried to rescue the falling coffee with my mouth and somehow ended up flat on my ass.

Winnie took the opportunity to jump on me, covering me in dog kisses and fur. I wrapped my arms around her and buried my face in her fur.

Then pushed her away.

"You stink, girl. Bath time is in your future."

She let out a low growl and I raised a finger in warning.

"No way. The groomers are on to you. They know you're all bark and no bite because then you won't get treats. You can't intimidate us," she let out another growl and nipped at my finger. "That all you got?"

Winnie opened her mouth wider and I took my hand back.

"Fine, you're big and bad and scary. But you're still getting a bath."

Shoving up from the floor, I threw a dish towel on the mess, vowing to actually clean it later. Then I took the cup and the pot and tried again. The liquid made it into the cup, the pot back on the warmer, and with a sense of urgency, I chugged the mug without altering the black, soulless water of vitality.

And choked on the bitter taste.

"That is disgusting. Why does anyone do that?"

Winnie's eyebrows danced in uncertainty.

"Yeah, I know. Big macho people who just want hot, bitter water."

Pouring a second cup, I doctored it to my liking and drank it much more slowly... so it took twenty seconds instead of five. Glitter penises floated in the lighter color and I contemplated if it was worth the energy to fish them out.

Winnie nosed her bowl under my feet and I decided to just drink the glitter.

I filled her bowl with kibble and a sprinkle of probiotics. I poured a third cup of coffee and watched the fluff monster eat voraciously while I tried to resemble a functioning human... while spitting glitter into the sink.

The bottom quarter of the pot was mostly glitter.

Tragic.

The dog nosed the bowl one direction, spun around, and attacked from a new angle. With every circle, I grew more mesmerized, wondering if this was what it felt like to live inside a Spirograph toy. She moved the bowl one last time for the last morsel, the coffee kicked in, and I wondered briefly if I should get her a bowl with a rubber bottom.

Then I snickered at the word rubber and killed my coffee, deciding I'd pay the price and poop rainbows later.

There was possibly still some THC in my system... that or I was incredibly immature.

Most likely it was both.

Satisfied for the moment, I meandered back to my bed and fished through the plastic drawers that held my clothes. There wasn't room for a dresser, there was no closet, so Larry had given me the three-drawer plastic rolling contraption after I spent two hours trying to find my clean underwear that I swore I'd brought home after borrowing his laundry machines. The search had been short and without fruition, ending in an activity that strictly dictated a no undergarment dress code.

We found them the next day when I took out the trash.

Apparently, I'd stored them in a plastic grocery bag that I'd accidentally thrown away and someone had dumped dog poop on the bag. Probably I could have cleaned them, but it seemed like too much work for something only mildly useful. Aside from one week a month, I was just as comfortable without them as I was wearing them.

A fact that the world discovered one week into going commando when the seat of my pants caught on barbed wire and I mooned half the farm. After tending to my wounds, Larry dropped me at home and arrived two hours later with the plastic chest and two-dozen underwear of varying styles. Also, varying pithy sayings, but I got the impression those were for him and not for me. Now the underwear, my socks, bras, and t-shirts all had a home. The rest lived in an under bed storage drawer after the metal rod I used as a closet met an untimely end.

Donning socks, a bra, some cargo pants, and a T-shirt with a squirrel on it declaring I was "too nuts", I grabbed my phone and searched for my wallet.

"Winnie, where's my wallet?" I asked her. She sniffed around, inhaling another dozen glitter penises, which she promptly sneezed across the room. "Never mind, we'll mooch coffee from my mom instead of bleeding Mo's coffee wells dry."

I clipped on her leash, stuffed my feet in the nearest shoes, and gathered my unruly hair under a ball cap. I carefully checked the trail of glitter for signs of my wallet one last time, but came up empty.

Winnie led me down the stairs and we each hissed at the bright sunlight when we opened the fire door to the alley. After a moment of agony, we trooped to the park where she did her morning business and I searched the square. It wasn't early, nearly ten, but the area was fairly quiet. Mo's was doing swift business, an older couple I didn't recognize were walking hand in hand past the shops, and the fire truck wasn't parked in its usual spot.

"Probably everyone ran off to watch them get a cat out of a tree," I sighed, watching the couple meander into the town's used appliance store. Winnie sneezed beside me and I watched a line of confetti penises disperse.

Apparently, we'd been here last night.

Sighing, I turned to follow the trail to my parents. A soft hum from my pocket showed an incoming call, and I answered Larry's picture.

"What the hell happened?" His voice was groggy and hoarse.

"I have no idea," I said back, and stared at the sidewalk. "I'm following a trail of glitter penises back to my mom's house and the apartment is littered with them."

"You know glitter is craft herpes, right? You're never going to be rid of them," he yawned into the phone and I laughed.

"Considering how many I've swallowed, I don't doubt that for a second. Plus, I don't own a vacuum."

He groaned and I assumed he'd just discovered the unfortunate limitations of standing. My eyes tracked to a small line of cars a street over from my parents. People milled around on the sidewalk, and the red lights of the fire truck were visible in the bright light of day. The ground looked wet, and there was a cruiser nearby, but I couldn't see Daniel or Barney.

Probably they'd parked the car and left for doughnuts.

"You coming back for me?" Larry asked, and I nodded. "Cyn, you there?"

"What? Yeah. I'm almost there, sorry."

Winnie pulled on my arm and I realized I had stopped to stare in the middle of the sidewalk, rubbernecking with the rest of the townsfolk.

"I think someone burnt a Marie Callender's pie near here and the whole town is out to watch," I said into the phone. Larry snorted and I heard the water running as he likely tried to rinse the rotten taste of bad decisions out of his mouth. "Where did you end up sleeping?"

"Bed in the basement. Why didn't you take me home with you?"

"I don't remember," I yawned and continued walking the hundred yards to my parent's house. "To be honest, based on the post-it I left myself, a lot of bad choices were made last night. Were you wearing underwear when you woke up?"

"Nope. You?"

I sighed.

"No. Should we maybe make a pact to avoid my parents at all costs?" My voice was hopeful, but the guilt that followed in my gut said no way that would happen.

"Nah, they might be the only ones who know what happened," he said just as both phones beeped, and I looked at the display.

"My phone's dying," I muttered at the same time Larry said, "Daniel's calling me."

We hung up and I trudged up my parent's front stoop and stared at the door. Inside, the house was already loud and chaotic. Through the door I could hear my niece and nephew shouting, smell breakfast cooking, and visualize my dad reading his paper without a care in the world. I knocked once and opened the door, cautiously stepping inside to see that their home had not escaped the glitter penis debacle, but had the added benefit of slime and children to spruce up the decor.

"Cynthia!" My mom said, marching toward me with a spatula and stroking Winnie's fur when she met her halfway. "I can't believe you!"

"Believe me?" I asked, trying to hold the pieces of my head together through the onslaught of noise. Apparently, Seth's kids were playing a game called loud and annoying and they were both winning. It was one of their favorite games when it was early, I was in pain, or on a Tuesday.

Why people procreated was beyond me.

"Leaving like that! You just ran out of the door screaming about freedom. You left behind Larry, your clothes, and your phone charger."

Which explained my phone.

"Did you find my wallet?" I asked and she furrowed her brow.

"No, you took that and your keys with you, dramatically screaming that you wouldn't let me rob you of your money like I robbed you of your sanity." Her lips pursed and I tried not to giggle. "Really, to your own mother?"

Stoned me was hilarious *and* honest. I tried to make a mental note to get together with her and swap stories. Maybe we could pull a Mrs. Maisel and get on some sort of circuit.

"Do you have coffee?" I asked, moving into the kitchen and plucking a piece of bacon off a plate on the way. My mom smacked my hand with the spatula but I ate the bacon anyway. In the kitchen was a full pot of coffee, which I poured into a cup. Behind me was the fridge and I started rummaging in it for something interesting to add to the cup.

"You don't get to have breakfast in this house after you left, judgmentally, and abandoned poor Larry." She tugged the cup out of my hand and chugged it. My mouth fell open and I stared, wide-eyed and horrified.

"You... took my... coffee."

Larry rounded the corner and froze. He looked from me to my mom, then down at the plate of bacon and contemplated his options. He liked the current arrangement of his face, but he also liked bacon.

"Mrs. Sharp?" he asked quietly, not daring to get closer. My mom whirled to face him, and the man visibly flinched.

"Yes, Larry?" She looked like she was trying to make her face less terrifying. To his credit, Larry didn't back away, but I'm certain his testicles shrank a little in his pants. My mom extended the plate of bacon out toward him and he ate a piece.

"Um... Cyn might need to leave and go to..."

The doorbell rang, followed by two sharp knocks and Winnie barked, claws clattering on the hard surface floor as she raced to the door. I took off after her, just in case one of Seth's kids made the mistake of getting in her way and I needed to rescue one of them from the other.

Fifty-fifty who would need my help more, but my money was on the dog if my shoe peeling off the floor was any indication. Those kids could have her coat superglued to her back and dyed orange faster than I could drink a triple shot espresso.

We arrived at the front door at the same time and I growled her into submission. Winnie sat, gave me a pathetic look, and flopped over on the floor.

I winced when I noticed her fur stuck to the surface.

Another knock and I gave her a warning glance before pulling open the door. On the other side was a perky looking Daniel Kirby and Carla wearing dark sunglasses, slacks, a polo, and an expression that said "please kill me".

Or maybe I imagined the please, and the "kill me" was actually "kill him".

Hard to say with the sunglasses and wishful thinking.

"Cyn," she began, and Daniel bounced excitedly on the balls of his feet. "I need..."

Her voice broke and her index fingers rubbed her temples. Larry came up behind me and handed both of us coffee.

"Thanks, Larry," she whispered into her cup, and we both drank quietly, the sun catching on her badge clipped to her belt.

"Are you... working?" I asked and Daniel pulled handcuffs from the back of his duty belt.

"You're under arrest." He took a step forward and Carla nearly clotheslined him.

"Shut up, Daniel. Cyn, you're not under arrest but we need you to come with us and answer some questions."

Daniel tried to slap a handcuff on my wrist when Winnie poked her head around the door and growled.

"What the hell? Muzzle your dog, Cyn!"

"No," I said. "Muzzle your mouth."

"Dude, dump her!" He shouted at his brother. Larry laughed and nuzzled my neck, sending little pings of happiness through me.

"Daniel, seriously! This is not an arrest. We need to talk to Cyn, on the record, then we can all go home and sleep. Maybe after we throw up." She pressed her hand to her stomach. "If I don't get this smell out of my hair soon, I will shove you down this staircase and let Winnie eat you. Cyn, please get in the car and come with us so we can talk."

"About... what?" My coffee was empty and Winnie was wagging her tail behind me while Seth's son Erich scrunched her ears.

I glanced at the floor and saw several clumps of fur in a residual patch of sticky.

Definitely needed to get her a bath.

"About the garage you burned to the ground last night!"

I blinked at Daniel and looked back at Carla, her face pained.

"Dude, I don't really remember last night, but I'm pretty sure Roger's chicken farm is the last thing I set on fire." I scrubbed a hand across my face and Larry rested a hand on the small of my back. "Actually, that was your cousin. Maybe Florida? Though I guess maybe the Fig's shed, but I remember more bleeding there than setting fire, Elliot burned his car..."

My brain wandered off and I stared blankly at Daniel when he cleared his throat.

"What were we talking about?"

"The fact that you're an arsonist!"

"Not... on purpose... I don't think... At the very least not recently!"

Daniel held up a clear bag, inside was a plain brown folding wallet with a dog on it.

"Then why was your wallet at the scene of an arson?"

Chapter Three:
Innocently Guilty

I t was a toss-up whether Carla or I wanted to be there less.

"What time did you leave Mr. and Mrs. Sharp's house?" Daniel asked for the tenth time.

"No idea," I huffed for the seventeenth time.

Carla banged her head against the wooden interview table. Given the size of the town and the police station, I was surprised it wasn't also the lunch table for the school and the stage at Pickles, an all-male review a half hour away. Yet here it sat, free of glitter, beer, and bologna on white.

"Where did you go when you left?" He insisted.

"Home," I answered. It was an educated guess since that's where I woke up.

"When did you arrive?"

"No clue," I yawned. "Must not have been early enough... Late enough? Enough of enough? I'm still tired, but I woke up there and I had programmed the coffee so I could rescue Winnie and feed Larry. Or... the other way around... Was I supposed to feed Larry or Winnie or one to the other? Do you think Larry would eat Winnie?"

I blinked at Daniel. He was scowling and the paunch in his midsection was more pronounced.

"You're not very attractive," I declared.

His jaw clenched and Carla gave me a subtle high five under the table with her index finger.

"Did you take a detour to the Jensen's house on your way?" Daniel crossed his arms, flexing so that his biceps would appear more impressive.

"Are you peacocking?" I asked and his chest puffed out.

"No, I'm accentuating my assets," he smirked and I had an urge to google peacocking for him, but it would be a waste of cell data. "Did you detour, start a fire, and then skip home to your filthy beast?"

"I. Don't. Remember."

I punctuated each word with a thump of my head against the wooden table. The idea was that if I hit my head hard enough, I might be able to forget this conversation... or lose consciousness for a nap.

Remembering the night before was not an option. A pithy remark about memories and vengeance for the "filthy beast" comment rolled around in my head, but nothing coherent came to mind so I moved on in silence. It was also very unlikely I skipped unless he found small piles of vomit on the route.

"How did your wallet get there?"

"No idea," I spoke with my face pressed into the table. "Does Larry know you call him a filthy beast?"

"When did you last see your wallet?"

"When you held it up in a plastic bag on my parent's stoop," I yawned. "How do you even know he's a beast?"

"Before that!"

"No idea," I repeated with another yawn. "Have you seen footage of him in action?"

"What did you bring home from Florida?"

"Sweat stained clothes and a dog." He was ignoring my references to his brother in bed... Probably for the best. I scratched my scalp and felt a chunk of something stuck in there, but it was too much work to get it back out again. I smoothed my hair over the chunk and tried to discreetly sniff my pits and check my breath.

Definitely needed a shower... and a toothbrush.

"Did you need something from Florida? I still maybe know some people there, possibly..." It seemed like a stretch to suggest I had friends there but a little too Godfather to imply there were people there who owed me a favor.

Especially when one of those "people" was possibly a cult.

"No, who needs something from Florida? What else did you bring home?" I pressed my cheek to the cool table and counted to five, but I couldn't remember any of the numbers after so I switched to humming nursery rhymes. "Cynthia?"

"What? Oh, from Florida... A bad attitude?" Carla snorted, but I couldn't move my head to see if she thought I was funny or sneezing.

"And?" He prompted.

"Uhh... sex for your brother? You know, the filthy beast."

Instead of waggling my eyebrows suggestively, I switched cheeks. Carla was definitely laughing.

"And?"

"The ability to ask after my dog in four languages?" I had no idea what use he would have for that though. As far as I knew, he didn't have a dog or a reason to leave the only country that would tolerate him.

A long-suffering sigh escaped his lips.

"As well as a book of matches from a bar in Florida?"

"Matches from Florida? It's too humid there for matches. Lighters tend to work better. They can't absorb moisture."

I glanced over at Carla, but she was leaning back against her chair with eyes half closed. After joining our ridiculous family, the woman deserved more than a nap... more than a nap but less than all the coffee in my house.

Even family had boundaries.

But if I had any Columbian cocaine connections, I'd hook her up.

Not like cocaine was coffee.

I could live without cocaine.

"Are you taking ownership of the matches?"

"What matches?" I asked, still staring at Carla. She had too perfect a nose to do cocaine. Maybe I could spare *some* of the coffee in my house.

"The matches from the bar in Florida I found near your wallet at the scene of a crime!" His face looked comically angry.

"No. Why would I have matches from a bar in Florida? I didn't go to any bars in Florida."

"Right. You were there for two years and you didn't go to a single bar?" His smug face grated more than his words.

"Nope. To go to a bar in Florida, you would have to go outside of your barracks. I went outside only when the Army made me and to walk Winnie. Otherwise, I stayed indoors with A/C, TV, and Winnie." I smiled at my rhyme, then scrunched my face. "OK, since I promised to tell the truth, I didn't have a TV. Sometimes I streamed shows on my phone, but mostly I read books and napped. TV tends to encourage people to visit, and I didn't want anyone in my room."

"So how did the matches from the Gator Gates Bar end up in Ohio?"

"Gator Gates?" I snickered and then stared at him when he didn't laugh. "Seriously? That's where the matches are from?"

"So you *have* been there?"

"No. I'm not allowed in there," I furrowed my brow and thought. "It's for seniors over 70. I guess my parents could go, but I'm not sure why they would need a swinger's club in Florida. The one they have here is way more promiscuous and free of charge, at least as far as I can tell. I've never seen anyone collecting money at the door, but they are encouraged to bring enough snacks to share."

Daniel choked on his spit and Carla lifted an eyelid at me.

"Why is Florida full of things I'd be fine never knowing about? Humidity, senior swinger's clubs, alligators, swamps..." She broke off on a yawn and I nodded my agreement.

"You haven't even seen the snakes and spiders."

The woman blanched and started to comment when Daniel interrupted.

"Could you stop being friendly with the suspect?" Officer Kirby glared at both of us and Carla flipped him off.

"Nope, I like her better than you. Here's the deal, Daniel. You're going to go outside of this trailer, find two very strong cups of coffee, and bring them in here. While you're gone, Cyn and I are going to talk crap about you and wonder how you managed to make children with a penis that small. When you return and we've had our coffee, we can try again."

Her voice left no room for disagreement and with a middle finger of his own, he stomped from the interview room and tried to slam the door on his way out. Unfortunately for him, it was an air release door so it just closed sadly while he stood there pissed.

"I really dislike him," Carla sighed. "But firing him is too much work."

"Did you look up how to do it?"

"No, I promised the former chief I wouldn't fire anyone for at least a year unless they murdered or raped someone. He said it takes that long for the idiots to grow on you and it would probably take me that long to frame Daniel for something good enough. Better off just waiting." Her sigh was legendary and I smiled. "You have no idea how much harder it is to be a married police chief than a slutty newspaper editor working for the government. I miss my old life."

"All the sex?"

"All the times I could have been shot and killed to avoid ever listening to these idiots." She scrubbed her face and blinked at me. "What were we talking about?"

"You were gonna tell me what's going on so I can try to actually help?"

"In a moment," she answered, pressing her index fingers to her temples and rubbing them in small circles while closing her eyes. I dropped my forehead to the table and rested my own eyes, embracing the silence and the whir of the air-cooling unit.

"OK," she exhaled slowly and I lifted my head. "Sometime after you left, I got a call about a suspected arson. The fire started at one or two in the morning. The Jensen's detached garage caught, but the fire didn't wake them. An emergency call got routed to Jenny, I think, the town's only dispatcher who was asleep in her bed. She called the fire department who went out to see if anything was really on fire, and Jenny... called the whole town. I've listened to the call, he said "small fire". Jenny put it out as the world was burning to the ground."

I nodded my understanding. Jenny had been a gossip since second grade. Hiring her as the town's only dispatcher was probably the worst decision the town had made since hiring Daniel, but the job was unpopular. No one wanted to be in charge of answering every one of the calls that came in, day or night. She was on-duty twenty-four seven since the town rolled up it's sidewalks at seven and stayed closed until seven the next morning. The only calls at night were barking dogs, lost drunkies, and bats in the attic, literal and figurative. It was her dream come true to know every juicy bit of gossip before the rest of the town and lord over the privilege of who would know first.

Sadly for everyone else, she'd refused to sign the confidentiality agreement, and they needed an employee more than they needed a good employee.

Which means her blabbering was not a violation of her contract or unexpected. Despite being a gossip, she was an honest gossip and she'd never failed to do her job.

At least not that anyone ever found out about.

"Which was it? Small or about to take Sweet Pea off the map?" Carla snorted.

"Sweet Pea isn't on any map and you know it. The fire was put out with a garden hose by a firefighter, but it was definitely not the small smolder the reporting party described. The Jensen's were woken up. After a quick walk-through of the garage, they determined nothing was definitively missing. Then... Hank, maybe, found the ignition point and there were matches and an accelerant not present anywhere else in the garage. When the sun came up, your wallet was found in the backyard with a possible secondary ignition point. Did you have any cash in your wallet?"

"I don't think so... if I did it was maybe ten dollars."

"There wasn't any when we found it. There are also only two access cards, your debit card and a credit card, your ID, and some dog fur. What else should be in there?" Carla was getting more alert and I tried not to be too jealous that the woman recovered quicker than I did, despite being older.

"No, I think that's all I ever really have in there. You think someone pick-pocketed me for ten dollars and then started a fire?"

It was far-fetched enough that it could be funny, and dumb enough to happen in this town.

"No idea what I think, other than that I can't picture you setting a fire on purpose. At least not a fire in some random stranger's garage in the middle of the night. You'd probably set an animal abuser's house on fire, but his murdered body would be inside. I could see you burning down a rapist's house, but again... murdered body."

"I would definitely do both of those things," I agreed.

"Any cameras in this town?"

"Not really in that part. They don't even have Ring cameras." I bit my lower lip and tried to think where in town cameras began but drew a blank. "Can you pull up any from Main Street to see when I was walking home?"

"We did, but nothing really pops up on your route. We can catch a few shadowy glimpses but I'm not sure if it's you or Jack the Ripper."

"I can see the resemblance." I sneezed and a glitter penis flew out of my nose. "I'm never going to be rid of these."

"Is that from the confetti cannon that old man was threatening people with?"

I stared at her, then back at the metallic phallus.

"Did you find any of those there?" I asked.

"At your mom's house or the scene of the fire?" She blinked. "How did that fit up your nose?"

"Heh heh, that's what she said," I snorted and Carla rolled her eyes.

"You're stupid. How did you get penis-shaped craft herpes?"

"A question for my mom, I think. You think if I show Daniel the dick trail from my parent's house to my apartment he'd let me look around the crime scene? I've never investigated arson before, but I know a lot about starting and causing fires."

"I think if you say 'dick trail', he'll plug his ears and run away, so it won't matter."

My grandma always taught us to not speak ill of the dead, but she never mentioned speaking ill of dead inanimate objects.

That garage had deserved to be burned.

At some point in its life, the Jensen's had painted it sunshine yellow and then allowed children to turn it into a mural. While most of the exterior was blackened and smoke-damaged on one side, what remained was a testament to why children's art was restricted to display *inside* the home. Circles with sticks and something that may have been a peapod or a spider without legs remained on the east side, while whatever existed on the west wall was gone forever beneath a layer of smoke and fire grime.

Inside were a soot-coated lawn mower, a snow blower, and gallons upon gallons of bottled water.

"What's with the water?" I asked no one in particular and Carla shuddered beside me.

"It isn't water," she shook her head and toed a bottle so I could see the label.

"Who needs this much hydrogen peroxide?" I asked in horror and she shrugged.

"When I asked, the answer made as much sense as the reason for the question, and I'd rather not repeat it. Suffice to say, the Jensen's are either survivalists, apocalypse preparers, or running a medical treatment facility for the mob."

"Is there even a mob anywhere near Sweet Pea?" I asked, kicking a metal tin lid and nearly falling into charred remnants of the shed's bottom corner.

The rotted out wood explained some of the soot and smoke, but still not fully.

"Does it really matter where you are? The mob will always find you." She spoke with such conviction I almost asked if she was in the mob but she shook her head to stem further questions and pressed a hand to her stomach.

Trusting her judgment, I studied the west wall. The ignition point was just beside the door, and a glance at the inside and the outside did nothing to indicate which side the initial blaze was on.

"Did someone swab this?" I asked, pointing to the wall.

"Yeah... we don't have chemical analysis, but we let a man called 'the nose' sniff it, and he said it was butane."

"Butane is odorless." I stared at her and she shrugged.

"There was also a can of butane in the trashcan up the street, so I decided it was good enough for now."

The majority of the burning was at ground level and I agreed. Butane was a heavy gas, all signs pointed to that being the culprit. "The nose" was also an old hippie from the 1970s who made YouTube videos on all the different ways to consume marijuana, including wax. If anyone could identify butane, the man who'd burned down half the wooded area behind his house making butane honey oil was probably it.

"Where's Daniel?" I asked, not really caring, but trying to distract myself from the sudden wave of nausea. I'd just gotten a whiff of something that had been singed or killed in the fire and it was not sitting well with the pot, booze, and sleep deprivation.

"Collecting glitter penises... I wanted to give him something even more annoying to do, but that was the only job that had overlap in the helpful and tedious circles of my crime solving Venn Diagram." She moved something on the ground with the toe of her shoe and I meandered over to take a look. It was a small slim pry bar, and the teeth on the end were snapped off.

"Is this the Jensen's slim jim?" I asked and Carla shook her head.

"They haven't opened this shed in six years. Not only can the Mr. and Mrs. not confirm if anything is missing, they can't tell me whether there was butane in here before the fire started. Honestly, they were pretty rude for people who had a fire that could have destroyed their home. I'm not asking for a parade or anything, but the level of hostility at having their slumber

41

disturbed was borderline criminal. They acted like I was waking them up to watch something obscene or grotesque instead of questioning their safety and the desire of strangers to set them on fire. When they saw your mom's borrowed T-shirt, they couldn't close the door on me fast enough."

"Do you think they're hiding something?" I asked her, taking in the shed as a whole. It didn't look like a criminal enterprise, but my imagination was lacking at the moment. If they were stitching up foot soldiers for the mob, they weren't doing it in this shed... or while sleeping in their beds. The first was unsanitary and the second just impossible.

One cannot sleep and stitch bloody people without constantly needing to do laundry.

They'd need a bug out van to have any credibility as survivalists preparing for the apocalypse. My eyes tracked to the mini van in the front drive and I couldn't picture it combat capable. Maybe they had an off-site storage unit? I opened my mouth to ask, but Carla was muttering to herself.

"I think they're just assholes," she grumbled. That was also reasonable. She prepared to add something to the thought when her phone rang and she answered it with a grunt.

I half listened as I circled the ten square foot shed and tried to decide if this was even a crime. It could have been an accident, stupid teens, or the Kirby kids who clearly endeavored to a life of crime and destruction. Despite the amount of smoke and volume of gawkers the fire had generated, most of the exterior damage was limited to the front corner where the accelerant and matches had been found and everything the smoke plumes touched.

I crouched down and saw the metal tin I'd kicked. It was a perfect circle with indents around the edges and a gooey blue substance in the middle. The area around the goo was slightly blackened, but overall the metal circle was unharmed. Small bits of cardboard and a nearly complete match were stuck in... I sniffed the goo.

Paint?

The disc was the right size to be a paint can lid... had the fire been started on the lid? If the goal was to prevent spreading, why use an accelerant?

"Are you kidding me?" Carla's voice brought me back and I tilted my head. "I'm on my way."

She stuffed the phone back in her pocket and dug out car keys.

"We need to go." She gestured to the passenger side door and I followed her to the Chevy Malibu with spotlights.

"What's going on?" I asked and she rolled her eyes.

"Someone set Amber's Shoe Ambrosia on fire, and she's blaming you."

Chapter Four:
Dumpster Fire

"Well... "Well... that was an exaggeration," I grumbled when we pulled up behind the still intact Amber's Shoe Ambrosia. The building sat mid-block on Main Street and was clearly neither on fire nor in danger of catching fire. The owner in question was standing behind the building speaking to Barney, when Carla parked the car along the back fence and studied the scene of the crime.

Or... alleged crime as I saw zero evidence of a fire... or murder.

Which was confirmed when Amber's voice got louder and no one fell over dead or slit her throat. The shrill voice could kill, I didn't doubt that, but it was hard to believe no one had killed her yet.

It was still early though, and if I stayed in the car, I wouldn't have to testify when someone finally snapped.

Sitting in a courtroom waiting to dime out people was my least favorite part of being an Army police canine handler. Slightly above it was cleaning up the canine's poop.

My favorite part was the canine herself, give or take a few tooth marks.

"Does she have an off button?" Carla winced as Amber Carter's voice permeated the sanctity of the car before she had even opened the door. "Or a bottle of meds to take the crazy down a notch?"

"None that I've found. If she's not playing the victim, she's actively the villain. I think in school she tried to be both the cop, the robber, and the bank owner, just so she didn't have to share roles in the one woman show of her life. It was mildly entertaining for anyone lucky enough to see two children fight over a ski mask and a sack with dollar signs drawn on it. If they didn't prescribe her anything then, it's probably too late now."

Another wail of emotional turmoil cut through the car and I reclined my seat. Amber Carter was a year older than me, but we'd graduated the same year. It was unclear if she was held back in Kindergarten or she'd talked her dad out of registering her when she was five, but however it happened, the girl and then the woman remain the bane of my existence. For thirteen years, she'd crushed my cookies, started rumors that I was an alien experiment sent to destroy the Earth with my overgrown feet, and smeared chocolate pudding on my pants so people would think I'd gotten diarrhea.

She was also loud, self-centered, and too stupid to be of much interest to me today.

"What are you doing?" Carla asked, reaching across the seat and levering it back into the upright position.

"I was going to nap, but I guess I'm close enough to my apartment that I could go nap there if you want me out of the car." I let out a wide yawn and stretched my arms over my head.

"Oh, no," she shook her head and unbuckled both our seatbelts. "You are going out there and helping me or I will read you the poem I was forced to write about your brother's penis while stoned."

"You wouldn't!"

"I would. It's called *Mushroom Member* and my rhyme scheme puts the *ick* in limerick," she raised a threatening finger at me, and I surrendered.

"Geez! Fine, how do you know about rhyme schemes and types of poetry after last night? I think every part of my brain not required for survival died."

Carla shrugged at me and I eyed the scene again.

"You should know that my being here will only make this worse and I might throw up on your crime scene."

Another shrug, she'd decided we were going down together.

Climbing out, I scanned the area for anything that could potentially have been on fire or used as a weapon when Amber tried to set me on fire. While the shoe store was still erect and undamaged, someone had ignited the dumpster that sits behind it. Most of Main Street's shop owners had gathered, as well as most of the town's residents who'd been recently released from church. I turned back to the car and pulled some aviator sunglasses off of the sun visor before shutting the car door.

"Arrest her!" Amber screamed, and I decided to ignore her in favor of cataloging the guests in attendance at her performance. Even with the shades, the sun was too bright. Every citizen's face seemed to reflect the light of a thousand suns, each stabbing a spot behind my left eye like a white hot poker.

Deep breath, I encouraged myself before checking out the masses a second time.

Most of the gathered populace seemed to be gawking at the shoe store owner, but a fair amount looked hopeful that the dumpster may flare up again and resume its fiery rampage on the public space. I tried to note the names of those looking a little too in love with fire but gave up on the fourth guy named Earl. The commonalities linked back to a more primal need to wreck than an actual desire to set fire to any part of town.

Ever since the local fair was forced to cancel the demolition derby a decade ago, the town's thirst for metallic bloodlust was at an all-time high. The town's Earls were desperate to see something melted and mangled in the name of entertainment.

"This is ridiculous," Chris muttered, and I turned to see the man who is dating my best friend standing with his hands on hips looking irritated and useless. Chris was a volunteer EMS firefighter who also worked as an actual nurse two towns over. I'd learned that only a month ago and I was very annoyed when he refused to treat my wounds after an unfortunate incident with barbed wire. Rather than help me in the privacy of my own home, he made me go to the medical clinic where there is still a picture of my injuries on the wall of the nurse's breakroom for levity.

Which is why Larry now treats all my wounds.

"Why are you here? Was someone injured?" I looked at Amber and her employee, Terrance, but both looked free of blood, burns, and bandages. In fact, they were practically camera ready and I considered asking for the contact number of their cosmetician.

I wanted the option to powder my nose before being videoed doing something stupid... er than normal.

"No, they just needed an extra body on the truck and I was nearby," he shrugged and looked up at me. I was only an inch taller than him, but it seemed so much more when I found him annoying. Though today I found the world annoying, so it wasn't exactly personal. As far as bodies went, his was perfectly acceptable for sitting on a truck. It had muscles where muscles were needed and eyes the color of a spring sky and lips Mo was more than happy to kiss.

At the moment though, his body was just one more thing in my personal space bubble that I wanted gone.

"Nice to know you refuse to treat everyone's wounds and not just mine," I grumbled and he straightened himself to appear taller.

"The laceration was on your ass, Cyn! I don't want to see my girlfriend's best friend's ass. Or sew it. Or touch it," he shuddered, and I rolled my eyes. While his point was valid, the rejection stung my sleep-deprived post-drug brain and reaffirmed that the public was not equipped to deal with me.

Nor me with them.

"Guess you're not a professional, then. And for the record, my ass is fantastic and you should be so lucky! Just ask Mo!"

I stomped off toward the burned-up dumpster and slipped in the water, going down to one knee with enough force to send a shockwave of pain up my leg. While my jeans managed to not get ripped, I swore with the careless abandon of a newly minted eighteen year old in college. No matter that there was a fire and water is how fires are put out, the universe had betrayed me.

Satisfied by my tantrum, my eyes met the dumpster which was now above me. It was dark green with black plastic lids, flipped open and tucked behind it... fifteen inches from the back of the building. Standing carefully, I moved closer and noticed it was closer to three feet from the wall. With effort, I crouched back down to ground level and studied the area behind it. There were four divots in the asphalt, perfectly in line with the wheels. If the dumpster were seated in them, it would be flush against the wall with the lid closed.

Taking care not to touch the green dumpster, I studied the gap and the wall. Whoever had set it on fire had taken the time to pull it away from the wall and protect the lids. There was no soot, scorch marks, or debris on the wall or the area around it. The rubber flip back lids were equally unharmed and the fire damage concentrated toward the front.

"What did she throw away in here?" I asked, peering over the side at cardboard boxes and tissue paper. Despite being a rhetorical question, I was curious what could be beneath the obvious.

"Mostly paper," Carla answered, using a gloved hand to shift aside the layers to reveal more of the same. Much like the proprietor of the dumpster, there wasn't anything more under the surface.

"Why is most of it stacked near the front?" Behind me was an overgrown shrub and I snapped off a branch before poking at the charred remains inside after visual approval from Carla. Beneath the top layer of shoe paper, I'd spotted something familiar. A few more pokes and I unearthed a cup from Mary's Muffins and More that looked to be mostly intact.

"Interesting," I said, poking the cup.

"Not really," she sighed, taking my stick and removing more layers of paper until we reached the bottom. Amidst the damp ash and pooling water was an incinerated book of matches.

"Wonder if those used to be from the same club," I asked as Carla reached a gloved hand in to collect the matchbook.

"Might as well see if someone in the area can tell me."

"Works for me. I need coffee," I pointed to the cup and then hitched a thumb in Chris's direction. "Also, I need to talk to my friend about her horrible taste in men."

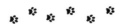

Nearly every shop on the way to Mo's was deserted. Mary's Muffins and More, a boutique pastry and coffee house, was owned and operated by Mary O'Connor, aka Mo. Mo was an average height, curly haired, red-headed baker with above aver-age coffee skills and genius level baking ability and intelligence. When I left to join the Army, she left to Teach for America and we arrived back in town a few months apart. She'd chosen baking over working with children, and I chose... Well, I hadn't actually chosen anything besides having a dog. My mom had gotten me the job of animal technician behind my back and investigating the town's problems was a bartering gig by Mrs. Margot in ex-change for no longer having to live in my parent's basement.

I walked into the bakery dejected that I wasn't actually an arsonist. At least being an arsonist would have been a choice, a declaration of my non-conformity. Instead, I'd fallen in line just as I had every day for four and a half years.

"Mo... I think I need a new life."

"Can you wait a second?" she said, roasting some espresso beans.

"Yeah, I guess. It's not like I have anything in my life worth getting to," I grumbled. Maybe I should join the Peace Corps , or Teach for America. Were you allowed to bring your dog on those things? Maybe a security detail for Doctors Without Borders? If they didn't have borders, they needed someone to protect them, didn't they?

"Oh no, you're wearing that face," Mo said, stepping away from a handful of waiting customers to put a cup of coffee in my right hand and a cookie in my left. "Sit on that stool and I will be with you in a minute."

Mo hurried through customer service and then casually locked the door behind the last customer. A harried looking man threatened to bang on the door, but Mo gave him a look that sent him on his way before pulling up a stool of her own and sitting beside me.

I was still holding the coffee and cookie, not having consumed any of either. Though I was impressed at her ability to serve so many customers so quickly, I was more impressed by the command presence she'd pulled out of nowhere.

"What's wrong?"

"Chris insulted my ass," I grumbled and she had the good grace to mask her laugh as a cough. "Also, people keep accusing me of being an arsonist and now I wish I was one just to have done something on purpose with my life. I couldn't even try to blow up Florida on purpose. Nearly everything worth mentioning in my life was an accident. Do you think Doctors Without Borders needs an armed security detail? Winnie and I could protect some doctors, probably. We wouldn't have to look at needles, I'm sure."

"Drink the coffee before I hit you," she said and my eyes snapped to her. "Now, or I will hold you down and pour it in your mouth."

Mildly alarmed, I complied and chugged the whole cup in a few minutes.

"Now eat your cookie," and once again I complied. It was some sort of frosted sugar cookie and as the sugar hit my tongue, I felt my mood brighten. "You know that you are not allowed to leave the house without eating or having sugar filled coffee. This whole thing could have been avoided if you stopped in this morning instead of walking past."

"I had sugar filled coffee," I protested, but she was probably right. After last night, a normal amount was not enough to stop the existential crisis of examining my life. I'd need half the supply of Columbia to combat my dread at being an international disaster. "But thank you. You looked busy and I didn't have my wallet."

"I'm always busy, but never too busy to save you from yourself. Also, I promised you free coffee for the month after you came to the rescue-" I held up my hand before she could speak the words. The free coffee had come with a promise I would also never have to talk about how I earned it.

Suffice to say, there were handcuffs, something old, something red and something blue.

"Right, sorry. Now tell me about the fire."

"Which one?" I asked, taking the replacement cup of coffee she handed me.

"How many have there been?" She looked puzzled and I realized with gratitude that my friend was neither a rubbernecker nor a news junkie. Godzilla could be stomping down the highway, but if she couldn't see it from her shop, she'd go about her day like nothing strange had happened.

Gotta love a woman with tunnel vision and a work ethic.

"Two. Jensen's shed and Amber's dumpster. Though neither burned as effectively nor as completely as most of my accidents, they were certainly unsightly and inconvenient with the gathered crowds. Seriously, what's wrong with the people in this town? I thought streaming and HBO were finally available here."

"They are, but Reality TV and True Crime are the highest grossers , and since you're both, you're S.O.L. until you learn to stop Hurricane Cyn before she touches down. Do they still think you started them?" she asked and I shook my head, marveling that I was shit out of luck for convincing the town to get a group rate on a satellite dish and hoping it would buy me some privacy. Also a little annoyed she brought back my nickname from the Army.

Hurricane Cyn was so... off the coast of Florida. This was the Midwest.

I should be Cyn-nado.

"No, I was cleared of the first one by glitter penises and the second by being in police custody over the first." I drank the coffee in my hand and pictured both fires. "I think the people in this town need to build a community theater. Nearly every townsperson congregates at the scene of disasters. Honestly, they weren't even spectacular fires. I think the small incident you had with your oven was more spectacular, and that never hit YouTube."

"Yeah, because no one is allowed in my kitchen. Your incidents are always in public. Besides, I heard the town had a sad eight fire-free years while you were in college and then the Army. Maybe they're playing catch-up," she teased and I frowned.

"No one started any accidental fires while I was gone? What about Crazy Carrie? She was obsessed with that California Firefighter... John Orr? I was sure she'd do some decent work with matches after I left. OK, not matches, that woman practically screamed 'flamethrower enthusiast'."

"Carrie became a novelist who commits arson on paper. Though I think she used to practice in secret in her backyard with accelerants because James told Kelly who told Chris that there was a massive cloud of smoke at her old house two years ago."

"She moved?" I was surprised. Small towns were excellent fodder for novelists... and arsonists. To leave would be to give up a gold mine of material and unusual names.

"Kind of..."

"Kind of? How do you kind of move?"

"She went to prison for tax evasion and fraud. Personally, I think she did it on purpose so she could write novels and let someone else oversee paying her bills and giving her food. She wasn't making a ton of money, and since none of her novels are centered around fraud, she's allowed to profit off of them. I think being in prison gives her more street cred."

I shuddered at the thought. If prison food was anything like Army food, she was better off going hungry and earning her street cred as a vigilante... or a hooker.

We all make choices, I guess.

"Hey, I found a cup in Amber's dumpster. Did you sell any coffee to an arsonist this morning? Probably a man or a woman without lipstick." I pictured the cup and she gave me a deadpan stare. "What?"

"Aside from you, how the hell would I know if anyone started a fire? People don't just tell me these things."

"I don't know... accelerant smells? Soot on their shoes? No eyebrows?"

It had been a long shot, but she looked to give the question proper consideration. Mo's willingness to take me seriously was one of the reasons we continued to be friends. A normal person who served morning patrons wouldn't have tried to remember the hundreds of faces she served.

I, personally, would try to actively forget to avoid any future issues should they murder anyone.

"Honestly, with the morning rush, all of you caffeine junkies look like hypes on the verge of a breakdown. I try to avoid eye contact with anyone who comes in before noon. Sometimes even after noon, depending on when *you* get up. I gauge my customer's potential for violence by how much they resemble you while waiting for coffee which has made me alarmingly aware that my life would be in great danger if we weren't friends."

"Hey! I'm a freaking delight and I've never killed anyone before coffee."

"What about that man whose hand you shot off in my kitchen?"

"That was at night! Well after coffee!" I argued and she lifted a red eyebrow.

"Weren't you drinking coffee when those men insisted you follow them and leave the coffee?"

I sighed with heavy resignation.

"Point taken. Keep an eye on your shop and your dumpster and people who smell like accelerants," I said, hopping off the stool and offering her a fist bump.

"Should I know what accelerant smells like?" She bumped fists with mine and I shrugged.

"Anything flammable? Gasses, oils, alcohols? You have fry oil here, so maybe ignore that smell?"

"Fry oil doesn't catch fire!"

"It does if you put a bomb in it! Don't you remember that Stephanie Plum book?"

"Nerd alert! Nerd Alert! Bookworms are so gross!" She laughed and I tried to feign insult before heading to the door.

"I need to get back to Larry before my mom convinces him to write a poem about my lady garden."

"Please tell me you're joking?" Her face was looking pale under her freckles and I shuddered.

"If only I were."

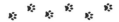

Two hours later, Larry and I lay naked in his bed. Winnie was asleep on our feet, and if I were a kitten I'd purr. After retrieving my dog and man from my mother, I had a lot of apologizing to do. Since I wasn't great with words, I decided to get on my knees and beg for forgiveness. Then he returned the favor and we were both settled in for a cozy evening of not doing much.

"How much of last night do you remember?" he asked, stroking my hair from my face and sending a jolt of electricity to my happy place.

"Virtually nothing after sweatpants. Why?"

Larry tugged his lower lip into his mouth. The fingers of his left hand beat an unsteady tune on my shoulder and the muscles in his neck tensed as he carefully avoided eye contact with me.

"Why are you eating your face?" I tugged his chin down to meet my gaze and he seemed to flinch as he let out a breath.

"Do you remember who was at the party last night?"

"Uhh... not really. My parent's sex club friends, my sister and her husband... My other sister video called with her girl-friend... I think you and I were the only two people under forty, so I hadn't put much thought into studying the guest list. Why? Did you do something stupid? Did I do something stupid?"

I tried to work up a trace amount of alarm, but doing stupid things was the nature of my existence and Larry doing something stupid would be a nice role reversal. The man remained quiet and I studied his face. He was nervous, un-comfortable, and I couldn't help smiling at his discomfort.

"Yes! It was you this time! What did you do?" I did a small happy dance and he shifted against me. Winnie let out an annoyed grumble from the foot of the bed.

"You weren't there! I know it wasn't you," I said to the dog. She crawled up the bed and licked my face before settling beside me.

"Come on, spill!" I demanded and poked him in the ribs. "Please tell me it was stupid and someone got it on camera! I'd kill for a photo proving I'm not the only one who gets awkwardly groped by old ladies."

"You... what? Never mind, the Jensens were at your mom's party..." he rubbed his jaw, the stubble scraping against his palm and I shrugged.

"So... what?"

"Not the ones who own the house, their parents. They are visiting for a week and that was the first night of their trip. I think they are old friends of either your parents or one of their... group members, maybe? They were definitely not new to the scene, the expectations, or the chemical methods of persuasion used to gain compliance."

"That was very scientifically put, but you could have just said getting stoned and banging each other. Did you see them naked? Did you get them naked? What did they need your *compliance* with? Good dog, man, did they tie you up? Did you tie them up?"

My eyes were getting wider and I couldn't figure out if it was with horror, excitement, or just anticipation of someone else's embarrassment. While I was just as jealous as the next woman, if the man wanted to throw down with a member of my mom's club, it was hard to be mad.

Everyone wanted to dabble in aged scotch at some point and I'd rather he get it out now than during a midlife crisis.

"No, nothing like that. Jeez! What's wrong with you?"

"What's wrong with you, Mr. Vague and Ominous. If it's not that, what is it? Did you try a toy in a new part of your body?"

"Could you... ugh! It's just... the older Jensen's live in Florida, and I think I saw one of them take something out of your pants.

Chapter Five: Test and Detest

Time Kirby brothers were on my list.

Not the good kind of list that gets presents, sex, and cookies.

Nope, they were on the Winnie porch poop list, maybe even flaming, with bullet points and exclamation points. They were on the air horn at two in the morning and eggs flung at their windows list. The list for people who would be punished severely if The Purge ever became a real thing.

In Larry's case, there was probably also sex still on his list, but maybe I'd cheat him out of cuddles and cupcakes.

Daniel's crime was refusing to give me back my wallet, ID, or debit card. He claimed they were evidence until the crime was solved, but his stupid grin made me think it was personal. No matter how hard I insisted that depriving me of my property was a crime, he insisted harder that it was evidence that had narrowly escaped being eaten by the fire.

Carla showed up to murder one of us for ten seconds of quiet. She agreed with him and offered me twenty dollars to leave the station, keeping her name off the list, but only just.

Instead of going home, I'd gone back to the Jensen's. If their parents admitted to "accidentally" taking the wallet, I could have it back. If they admitted to arson, I could have my wallet *and* get to rub Daniel's face in the fact he was wrong. There was no downside, and I practically skipped the two blocks to their house anticipating the opportunity to show off my "I'm Awesome, You Stink" dance in Daniel's stupid face.

In ten minutes, I rounded the corner to see the last of the looky-loos had left. All that remained was a few empty coffee cups and gum wrappers beside water puddles. I scanned the neighborhood, preparing my questions when I came up short.

The Jensen's house was deserted.

Winnie and I circled the property three times, every time stopping just short of the crime scene tape on the shed. A gray minivan had been in the drive that morning, but it was gone and all the doors were locked. None of the neighbors had answered when I knocked, and then Daniel arrived to shoo me like a raccoon digging in his garbage. It was demeaning, rude, and frankly made assaulting an officer seem worth the temporary vacation in an orange jumpsuit.

Except Daniel's brother, the good-ish Kirby, showed up and carried me away like a responsible adult who was dating a child trapped in a woman's body. This, however, was not the reason he wasn't getting cupcakes and cuddles. Larry was on the list because he'd refused to steal his brother's keys for me so I could get my wallet back. It wasn't as though I regularly asked him to help me commit minor felonies.

He owed me!

His counter argument that I did regularly ask him to commit felonies, like breaking and entering and mail fraud, seemed a bit exaggerated. The mail fraud thing was only once, and I think having a free sample of adult diapers sent to his brother at the station barely qualified. It's not like he had to pay for anything.

Instead, he'd driven me to the local branch of my credit union to have my debit card re-printed, the nearby outlets for a new, boring, wallet, and made me an appointment at the DMV for Monday morning.

Which had arrived and there was no escaping the bureaucracy. Larry had followed me in his truck to the building, waited until I'd parked the Jeep, leaned in for a kiss, and then abandoned me.

Two freaking hours ago.

"Seriously? I know you can't print it on-site, but why won't you just take my money and send me a new one in the mail?"

The woman resembled Roz in Monsters Inc. and moved like Flash in Zootopia. If she had been any more of a stereotype, Disney would have made a movie about her.

Disney or Quentin Tarantino, because the chick was an inefficiency horror movie.

"My supervisor is checking something. Your license has been flagged." She seemed like she was bored with me. A metal spoon sat inside a white cup and she gently stirred the tea inside. Then she lifted and lowered the tea bag, stirred again, and picked dust out of her keyboard while I stood awkwardly in front of her with numb feet and zero patience.

"Should I go sit down?" I asked, inclining my head to the bank of chairs behind me. Winnie was sitting on my foot, her full ninety pounds pressed against my leg and a stream of drool pooling at the corners of her jowls.

"If you leave, you'll need to get back in line and we'll have to start over," she sipped her tea and then clicked the mouse. "Just have some patience, Ms. Sharp."

She made duck lips at her phone and snapped a selfie. Then tipped her chin up and down, snapping another from each angle and then appearing to inspect them before snapping her fingers at a passing mail deliverer and insisting her photo was a work of genius.

The poor mail woman looked terrified to say no.

"Is your phone just full of selfies and duck lips?"

The woman turned and the mail cart scurried away. At least I did one good thing today, but the young woman was not free forever. It was but a temporary stay of execution.

"I'm sure your camera roll is just pictures of your dog. If you had a face like mine, you'd want pictures of it too. Instead, you have... that," her upper lip curled. "Have you never heard of eyebrows and contouring?"

Her phone buzzed before I could rip the tea bag from her cup and throw it against the eye exam board. The thick splat of the wet leaves hitting something would have been so satisfying, even if it wasn't her self-voted superior face. The DMV employee, Vivian if you believe nameplates, was bored and zoning out with her cell phone pressed to her face. She grunted, picked at fingernails that were as unnecessary in length as they were impractical for a woman whose job it was to type, picked up her desk phone, hung it up, and stared at nothing.

I gave her a minute in case it was a stroke, but the vacant expression and lack of sincerity lead me to assume that was just her face. Desperate to be free, I cleared my throat, but she continued to ignore me.

"Ma'am?"

"He's coming out to speak with you."

Vivian picked an imaginary fleck off of her sweater and pressed a button on her keyboard. With the device's glow she snapped two more selfies and then pulled out a two-sided mirror to study her face even closer. Satisfied with what she saw, the self-possessed government employee clicked play on a video I could watch in the reflection of her mirror.

The woman was now ignoring me to watch an eyebrow tutorial on YouTube while a hundred people waited. The man who appeared behind her glanced at the woman, the screen, and after a discreet eye roll, waved me around to a new section of the waiting area. She made no move to help another patron or answer the ringing phones that blared throughout the office.

"You need to re-take your behind the wheel."

I tore my eyes from the world's most useless government employee.

"I'm sorry, what? My license isn't expired."

"There's a note here about an accident where a Jeep rolled over and some... incidents in the Army. Your record was flagged to retake the practical driving portion of the exam." His eyes dropped to Winnie who had collapsed onto the floor. "We don't allow dogs in here."

"She's a veteran," I said, as though that would suffice. To his credit, the man chose to roll his eyes rather than point out that being in the service doesn't make her a service dog. "Why do I need to retake an exam if my license isn't expired? I'm not renewing it, I'm just replacing it!"

"You can't replace it without extending the expiration and we can't extend the expiration unless you re-test." His flat voice tested my nerves and my patience.

"I didn't ask for the expiration to be extended, can't you just reprint my old one?"

"No."

"Why not?" The whine in my voice hurt my soul, but I had barely passed the behind the wheel ten years ago. Now that I'd had a taste of driving a vehicle through a wall, there was no way I was going to be able to drive normally. I'd been tainted and no one would give me a license if they knew I was saving to have a roll cage installed in my Jeep.

Maybe I could get a guest spot on The Grand Tour, filling in for Richard Hammond the next time he broke something or blew it up. Aside from being twice his height and a woman, probably no one would notice the temporary exchange.

"Because." He shrugged and his eyes darted back to the woman at the counter and he sighed the sigh of a man desperate to end his own misery. "This is the government, Ms. Sharp. This is how we do things."

"Slow, inefficient, and wasteful?" I said, following his line of sight.

"Never hire someone dating your boss's kid. They think she's a goddess and no amount of evidence will let you get rid of her. She's the office herpes." His pained expression brought a smidgeon of pity until I remembered I couldn't actually drive away from this building legally.

"So, what? I wasted two hours, now I need to make an appointment to take a test to get back something that was perfectly valid until the police took it?"

"I mean, if the police took it then it probably wasn't valid," he countered.

"No, it was just at the scene of an arson they think I committed." My arms crossed my chest defensively.

"Um..." he glanced at the hundreds of people waiting, a bead of sweat dripping down his soft baby face. His eyes looked to be assessing the area for potentially flammable items and I made no move to clear his assumptions.

Being suspected of arson may be useful after all.

"Usually yes, but I'd like to get this over with. Where is your car?"

I pointed to my gray Jeep and he gestured to a line of cars outside.

"Pull it around and we'll get you out as quickly as possible."

Four hours later, Larry pulled to the curb with Seth in his passenger seat.

"Don't say a word, Sethany," I grumbled, passing him my keys. The sun had set, the office was closed, and I was no longer a licensed driver. He patted me on the top of my head like a child and walked to my Jeep, sliding easily behind the wheel and turning over the engine.

He rolled down the window as he drove past us and turned up the volume on the radio.

"I would walk five hundred miles, and I would walk five hundred more..." before flooring it out of the lot with a cackle. Valuing his bedroom privileges, Larry climbed out and wrapped me in a hug.

"It's OK. I can give you a ride to work for two weeks until you can test again."

"This is stupid," I grumbled rubbing my cheek against the soft red T-shirt he wore. "I can drive."

Larry did not agree with me.

"You don't think I can drive?" My eyes bored into him, but he gave me crickets so I poked him in the belly. "Why won't you tell me I can drive?"

"I promised never to lie to you at some point... if I didn't, I promise now. Your driving is terrifying."

"Whatever." I pushed away and slumped into the passenger seat. Winnie climbed in the back and sprawled across the bench seat, falling asleep almost immediately. Larry slid behind the wheel and squeezed my thigh. "There is nothing wrong with my driving."

"Besides your questionable relationship with speed limits, roadway signs, and turn signals?"

"None of that existed in Afghanistan." My grumble earned me a chuckle and he raised his hands in surrender.

"You didn't learn to drive in Afghanistan, Cyn." His voice was joking but his face said he meant it.

"So? Most of my adult driving was done there."

"No, it wasn't! You were there for eight months!"

"I didn't drive much besides there," I lied. During college I'd driven repeatedly from Colorado to Ohio and to the states neighboring Colorado in a misguided attempt to see the nation's natural wonders.

Instead, I saw a lot of freeways and was conned into giving more than one free ride when I refused to accept grass or ass as forms of payment. The nineteen seventies ruined the transportation bartering system.

"Want to practice in a deserted parking lot so you can remember how things work in America? I can teach you what the dial in the center means, where the turn signals are, show you pictures of road markings, and after you ignore all of that, we can do what Alicia Silverstone and Benicio del Toro did in Excess Baggage."

I suspected he was wiggling his eyebrows at me, but I elected to ignore him and his smutty suggestion.

Instead, I watched Seth make a left out of the driveway, taking my Jeep to his house so I wouldn't be tempted to drive without a license. The only people who complained about my driving were men. As though they had cornered the market on defensive driving and were now experts qualified to teach us all things. Sulking, I stared straight ahead and waited for Larry to start the car and take me home.

"We can take turns being the driver?"

I shivered and narrowed my eyes at him.

"Are you trying to cheer me up or get laid?"

"Both," he leaned in and pressed a hard kiss against my mouth, nipping my lip before he pulled away and dropped the car into gear. We drove quietly back to Main Street, Winnie's snores mixing with the pop music playing in the background. The cab was intimate, the lack of regular street lights making the whole town appear dark and tempting. It was just past nightfall, nothing near the middle of the night, but it still felt like a blanket wrapped around me in comfort when I looked up at the moonless sky. I'd always thrived in night and darkness, but there was something about this evening that brought to mind bonfires, camping, and a desire to live like a mountain woman.

"Do you think whoever burned the garage and the dumpster were the same person?" I asked and felt Larry shrug beside me.

"I think it's a big coincidence if they weren't, but after knowing you, random fires aren't impossible."

I punched him in the arm and he caught my hand, brushing a kiss on the knuckles.

"Daniel will figure it out."

"You don't really believe..." I broke off as we turned on Main Street and I noticed a small figure hunched on the sidewalk in front of my building. Larry's eyes cut to the curb and he pulled slowly beside the figure, showering the woman in light.

She hurried to her feet and I struggled to pull her name from the recesses of my brain. Nothing came to me, but I got out of the car and offered her a hand. We managed to get her upright while she focused on getting her oversized tote onto her shoulder.

"Hi," her voice rasped into the night. Larry killed the lights and engine while I unlocked the door to my office.

"Hi... Do I know you?"

She hurried inside and I flipped on the light but left the heavy curtain across the front window closed. My hope was that no one would see us down here and I could take my disgraced former automotive operator ass to bed at what some would argue was barely nighttime.

After a pint of dark chocolate cherry ice cream to cheer myself up.

"Yes... sort of. My name is Amy Howard. We met briefly at a game of Bingo."

A sea of angry senior citizens threatening me with bodily harm came to mind and I took a step back.

"Look, I know that we caused quite the scene but I bought you a new B32!"

She waved me off and set her bag beside the guest chair. Without seeking permission, she bustled to the coffee pot in the corner and got to work. The woman needed no guidance as she filled the water, added a filter and coffee grounds, worked the brew settings, and stabbed the button in the middle with a glossy red fingernail. Once the pot was on, she turned around and started tidying my coffee cart.

It was like being a child watching your parents clean your room. It would probably look better, but it would never feel like my space again. There was something sacred about a teenager's room and a woman's coffee cart that was being stomped all over, but the idea she'd impale me with a lacquered red fingernail kept me from forcing her to stop.

"I'm sorry, Amy, but... can I help you?"

My nose pricked at the scent of coffee and I inhaled. The scent woke up my brain cells, and I plucked Amy's face from my memory. Her blue-gray hair, the raspy voice, it all came back. She had accused a man in a Hawaiian shirt of being a cheater when I passed my Bingo cards to him. There was spilled punch, ink everywhere, and Winnie had tried to steal her quad cane's tennis balls, sending her face first into the mess.

"Where's your cane?"

Her eyes flicked to me and she nodded.

"Good, you remember me. I don't need it anymore. I had the surgery to replace my hip and I'm good as new. Well, good is a relative term. I'm... walking normally. I heard you needed to buy a replacement punch bowl, table, and pay restitution to the church."

I nodded, trying to swallow the groan at having this woman in my office.

"Well, let's get to it then. I need your help."

"Is this related to Bingo, cheating or...?" I trailed off, grateful when the pot signaled completion and I moved her aside to pour two cups. Amy took hers, pouring a small amount of milk and taking a dainty drink as she stepped away from my sacred space. My coffee need was more dessert oriented this evening, so I dumped marshmallow flavored syrup suspended in a non-dairy solution into my mug and swallowed it in three gulps.

Then poured another and repeated the sequence again, taking smaller drinks.

Behind me, the door squeaked open and I turned to see Larry, looking worn out but curious.

"What's up?" He ventured to the cart and made himself a cup. Since four cups was the pot's limit, he started drinking his while preparing a new pot.

My hero.

"This is a private meeting between Ms. Sharp and myself," she sniped at him, but Winnie lifted her lip in warning. "Oh, fine. I'm not sure it's possible to keep this a secret anyway."

Mrs. Howard drank slowly and took in the small office.

"I need your help with the fires."

"I didn't start the fires!" I protested, wondering if being falsely accused was how Billy Joel really came to write that song, and now it was stuck in my head. Larry smirked behind her and I gave him a warning finger. "I started some fires, but I didn't start *those* fires."

"Enough. I'm certain you likely did not, but I'm afraid I might know who did and I'm not sure what to do about it."

"What? Did you tell the police?"

"No. I don't want to involve them until I'm certain, but it's tricky," she chewed on her lower lip and meandered back to the coffee pot for more. "You see, I was a bit annoyed to have been uninvited from your mother's gatherings when my husband passed. She said I was welcome as soon as I remarried or started dating, but you needed a partner for the activities."

My hands got clammy, and despite my semi-professional nature, I gagged.

"Please, Amy, I can't get you a date or my mother to make an exception." She huffed and stared down her nose at me.

"Mrs. Howard, thank you. I don't want your help getting back in your mother's club, I want your help figuring out who started the fires." Her eyes were a severe shade of blue that mirrored her hair.

"You said you thought you knew who did it?" The conversation had left me as exhausted as the 6 hours I'd spent at the DMV, and she was too busy holding back her secrets to let me help in any genuinely helpful way.

"I do. But the trouble is, I take Ambien and medicinal marijuana, so I can't quite be certain if anything I recall in the night hours is real or imagined." Amy wrung her hands in front of her and I relented, plopping into my chair and pulling out a notebook.

"Who do you think committed the arsons?" I asked, pen poised on the lined sheet.

"Well... I think I did," Amy Howard sighed, and I dropped my pen.

Chapter Six:
Self-Imposed

"Now, why do you think you committed the arsons?"

The man in front of me was shrunken and balding. His skin appeared averse to sunlight, moisturizer, and showering. He wore stretchy pants and a Metallica shirt with more holes than fabric covering his rail thin frame and small, pointy nipples. The soul patch on his chin was either ironic or the product of misplaced marketing, because aside from his waistband, he could have owned a comic book shop in The Simpsons.

As it was, he probably owned a comic book shop in his mother's basement... a comic book shop or a little shop of horrors.

"Well, I can't be sure..." he launched into what sounded like a Dungeons and Dragons campaign and I took careful notes.

On top of my desk were seven filled spiral notebooks, outside stood fifteen more people, and the last of my ninth pot of coffee was in the mug beside me. The mug featured a White German Shepherd, a standard tan one, and a black and brown, declaring a woman needed one in every color. Behind me, Winnie was letting out small whimpers as her paws twitched and I wondered what she was chasing in her dream.

"How did you start the fire?" I asked when he paused to breathe.

"Flamethrower," his sincerity floored me.

"Pete Ressnal?" I confirmed his name from the top of the page, and he nodded. "Congratulations, you probably did not commit arson, but you have issues distinguishing fantasy from reality that a licensed professional should examine."

"You're... not licensed?" Pete appeared to see the office for the first time, eyes landing on Winnie. "When did that dog get here?"

"She... you..." I glanced between the two and Winnie lifted her lip with a grumble.

"I think I should go, but like... you'll tell the cops it was me if everything matches the crime?"

There was no other response than to nod as he shuffled out the door.

Next in line was Stephanie from the local nursery and I couldn't hear another story. Two months ago, everyone was standing outside demanding I prove they weren't criminals. Now, they were all standing there to confess, feeling guilty for littering, enjoying fires, or in the case of a five-year-old boy, burning leaves with a magnifying glass on the sidewalk six miles from the site of either fire.

None of them had wanted to confess to the cops "just in case".

No one could tell me what that case was, or why they trusted me with their fire-loving secrets. After seventeen hours, I was going to be late for work if I had to hear one more story and sleep was a non-existent dream on the horizon.

"Stephanie, I'm going to ask you two questions and then I'll ask everyone outside, then I'm going to get ready for work and turn relevant information over to Carla. When were you last in Florida?"

"Ew, who would go to Florida?" She looked appalled and I nodded.

"How did you start the fire?"

"Improper chemical storage."

"Cool, thanks. I'll let you know if any fires start that way."

I pushed back from the desk and felt half my body pop and creak. My left foot was asleep, and I limped to the front door, holding up a hand before the next person could enter and launch into their confession. A silence fell over the crowd as I walked outside, and I addressed the people.

This must be what it feels like to be a messiah.

"Raise your hand if you've been to Florida?"

No one raised a hand.

"Raise your hand if you take Ambien or another sleep aid?"

Every hand went up. I waved them back down.

"Finally, raise your hand if you believe you started the fire with matches?"

No one put their hand up.

"Congratulations! None of you set the Jensen's shed or Amber's dumpster on fire. Please go about your day." I spun on my heel and locked the door before they could register my statement and protest. Winnie and I marched to the rear of the building, up the stairs, and into my apartment. My bed, perfectly made and un-slept in, called to me but instead I turned right and went into the small bathroom.

Stripping, I turned the shower on full heat and let the water beat my muscles. I wasn't tired, but mentally I needed a break and a snack. Grabbing soap, I tried to concentrate on just washing, forcing my mind into the moment and trying desperately to let all the thoughts fall out of my head and breathe.

I made it ten seconds before my phone blared from my pants on the floor.

"I'll just ignore it," I told myself, the ringtone ending as the call rolled to voicemail. Lather, scrub, rinse. Lather, scrub, rinse.

The device went off again.

"Uhn…" I grumbled and shut off the water to fish through the items on the floor for my phone. The display was an unknown caller and I questioned whether or not I wanted to risk being offered a renewal on my auto warranty. "Hello?"

"Cynthia Sharp?"

"You called me and you're not sure?" A yawn escaped my lips and the woman on the other end inhaled in annoyance.

"I'm calling from the hospital in Yellow Springs. Your parents are here." A page came in from the background.

"Are they OK?" I ran out of the bathroom naked, trying to listen and put on underwear at the same time. "How did they get injured? Are they sick?"

"Ms. Sharp, I am not a medical professional. I work with the county Sheriff's Office. We need you to come pick them up and bring money to pay their citations." As another page was heard in the background, I heard the two-way radio I imagined clipped to her shirt squawk.

"You... how much do I need to bring?"

"Two hundred dollars and pants for both of them," she hung up and I spent a long moment considering the ramifications of leaving them there. Winnie let out a soft whimper and I nodded.

Family was family, no matter what weird crap they did without pants on.

I called Larry.

"I need a favor."

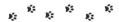

Nothing could have prepared me for what awaited me when we arrived.

While being told my parents were in the hospital was debilitating, being told they were in police custody gave me a panic attack. Being in police custody in the hospital and in need of pants was grounds for a complete psychiatric evaluation and a strong desire to request a lobotomy while in attendance at the facility.

A uniformed officer met me at the entrance to Emergency and guided me into an elevator just beyond the nurse's area. I anticipated we were headed to the secure wing of the hospital or a private interview room, but he selected the button for the basement.

"What specialty unit is in the basement?" I asked, watching the light flick to B, and he gestured for me to precede him out. Larry followed both of us in a silence that threatened to break into laughter.

"Just the morgue. Follow me." Deputy O'Hare led the way to a severe Latina with high cheekbones, piercing eyes, and a pixie cut that showed off both. Her uniform was flawless, her make-up free face the envy of gods, and beside her sat... my parents.

"You..." I stared at my parents, seated on a gurney outside the cold storage unit for bodies. Each was wearing a paper hospital gown covering their fronts, but their naked ankles revealed the reason I was asked to bring them pants. "You..."

The sentence was impossible to finish.

If I asked how they lost their pants, they might tell me.

"Really, after I picked you up from that house when you thought a Furry Party was for pet lovers, you could at least look me in the eyes," my mother spoke regally.

"I could, but I won't because when you picked me up I had all my clothes on," I hissed and raised a warning finger.

"You'd been there for an hour and we both know you weren't wearing hair gel when you left the house."

I opened my mouth, gaping and stammering in silence until the deputy interceded.

"Ms. Sharp, can you sign here that you are paying the fine and we are releasing them into your custody?" the deputy spoke and held out a citation. The charge was listed as public indecency and a sinking feeling filled my gut.

"Definitely not the same, ma!" I handed them the pants I brought and reached into my pocket to grab my wallet and the cash.

My back pockets were empty.

I patted down my front pockets and came up empty.

"Where's my wallet?"

"You got it out of the car..." Larry offered.

"I..." Stuffing my hand to the very bottom of my back pocket, I felt a breeze on my fingers. "This pocket isn't sewn at the bottom, is it?"

"It is not," he confirmed, and I looked helplessly at the deputy.

"I'll be right back." Larry started to follow but she halted him with a finger.

"You're staying here," Deputy Pixie Cut ordered and I held out my hand for the car keys. Her name badge said Montalvo and her face said she would cuff him to my mom if he challenged her.

"You don't have a license," he said when it dawned on him what I wanted.

"I don't need to drive the car to unlock it, Larry," I countered and he hesitated with the keys in his hand. "I promise I won't abandon you here. I'll just go get my wallet and then come back."

"I'm going to need more than a promise." His eyes went wide and I let out a groan.

"Why is everyone I know a pain in the ass?" I yanked the keys from his hand. "You all need to have your heads examined."

"Cynthia, you are so unnecessarily tense. Larry, dear, did you not pay attention the other night to my lesson on the importance of making her relax? The key is to..."

I growled and ran for the elevator like the basement was about to catch fire and explode in an action movie.

Retracing my steps, I had to re-walk Emergency twice as my brain worked overtime to make what had just happened normal. My parents were being fined for doing the deed where dead bodies were stored.

A man with a screwdriver through his eye was wheeled past me and I stared at the perfectly ordinary trauma.

"Why couldn't they be here for something normal?" I groaned to myself and walked Emergency a third time before exiting into the parking lot and scanning the lot for where Larry had left his car.

Laying on the ground beside Larry's blue two-door car was my plain wallet and I sighed in relief, moving toward it. An SUV screeched to a halt and I froze, watching a frantic man unload a pregnant woman. Two nurses rushed out with a wheelchair, whisked her away, and the man dumbly got back in and tore through the lot looking for a parking space. He narrowly avoided two people shuffling up the aisle by Larry's car.

One dropped and I started to run, worried I'd just witnessed a hit and run. The figure righted itself and the pair moved to an old red hatchback. They climbed in and I slowed, deciding there was no reason to run until I came level with Larry's car and looked at the ground.

My wallet was gone.

"Hey!" I shouted, waving toward the hatchback. A flash of green eyes, and the red car gunned it through the lot. Frantic, I climbed behind the wheel of Larry's car and lurched after the red car. They took a turn on two wheels through the exit, and I memorized the license plate as I followed suit onto the main highway. The car turned toward Sweet Pea and I called Carla through the car's Bluetooth.

"Someone stole my wallet!"

"We didn't steal it, Cyn-"

"No, not that one. The new one. It fell in the parking lot, and I thought the person was hit by a pregnant man but they stole the wallet and when I tried to flag them down, the pair took off in a red car. I'm following them."

I read her the plate and she sucked in a breath.

"Pull over, now."

"What? Why? Is it stolen? Are they hardened criminals? We're on the highway headed toward town." Red and blue lights filled the interior of Larry's car and I pulled to the shoulder to let it pass.

Instead, the cruiser pulled up behind me and I frowned at the uniformed figure that got out.

"Carla, the officer isn't chasing the suspect, he pulled up behind me."

I gestured wildly at the retreating red car, rolling down the window and coming nose to nose with Daniel Kirby.

"They stole my wallet!"

"Sure *they* did," he drawled and pulled the car's door handle.

"Daniel," Carla warned through the car but he pushed the end call button on the steering wheel.

"What are you doing?" I shoved his chest as he reached across my lap and unhooked the seatbelt. "I need to get my wallet and then get my parent's citation paid and..."

He pulled me out of the car and spun me around. With deft movements, he kicked my legs apart and patted me down.

"You're going to need to send someone else to rescue the public fornicators."

The snap of metal cuffs clapped onto my wrists and I strained to get away.

"What the hell, Daniel? We aren't that kind of friends." My elbow failed to make contact with his gut but my foot found his instep to stomp. "Let me go!"

"Can't." I could hear his smile. Kirby pulled me up and shoved me toward his car. He popped the back door and shoved me into the seat, leaning in to stare at me down the tip of his nose.

"Driving without a license is a crime, Ms. Sharp."

Chapter Seven: Interviewing Disaster

I I was once again seated at the wooden table, waiting for the world to make sense.

Carla had arrived with Seth, who delighted in photographing me in the back seat of the police car. He took Larry's car back to the hospital, a fresh wad of cash in his pocket to pay for our parents' freedom. While I begged and pleaded for the same treatment, it was in vain.

Neither Seth nor the police offered me monetary liberation. No one offered me water or my one phone call either. Carla and Daniel argued for twenty minutes outside of the car, and she stormed off while he sat against the hood and ate an apple.

Then he ate a carrot.

Out of food, I expected him to chew on a piece of wheat or play the harmonica, but he just sat there. Picking food out of his teeth with a dental stick before pulling out his phone to blast aliens while I slowly melted to death.

First, I resorted to bouncing in the back seat to shake the car, nothing.

Then, when I played a drumline sequence on the window, he rolled them down and carried on.

When I started singing It's A Small World at the top of my lungs, he decided it was time to drive me back to the station for my statement.

A statement he'd yet to collect since abandoning me here an hour ago.

My phone rang and I flinched at the display. Joseph, my boss at the farm, was calling for the fifth time and I had no reason to answer. Until Daniel came back and did... something... I had nothing to tell him. After yesterday's unplanned day off to get my license in order, he'd been irritated but understanding. If I told him I was in police custody, he would have a fit and threaten to fire me.

We both knew he wouldn't. As much of a pain as I was to have as an employee, finding someone to replace me was both more difficult and a bigger headache than keeping me.

Also, I had dirt on him that I could wield to my advantage but hopefully it wouldn't come to blackmail. I was still uncomfortable with the idea of blackmail. Especially after that murder a few month's back.

Bludgeoned to death for blackmail was not an attractive death.

The phone rolled to voicemail and started ringing again almost immediately.

This was now my mom's fifth call and if I wasn't speaking to Joseph, I really wasn't speaking to her. While the first would involve yelling, the second would have yelling, guilt, and mentally scarring images.

We both knew my arrest was my fault, but there was no need to discuss it.

When that call rolled to voicemail, the phone lit up with a text message.

Larry: *You owe me.*

Since he was right, and I had no interest in admitting that to his face, I responded with a thumbs up emoji and leaned back to stare at the ceiling. The gray tiles reminded me of high school, as did the pencil sized holes punched into them. I'd never understood the urge to use pencils and rubber bands as a bow and arrows with the aim of getting it stuck in the ceiling, but it apparently didn't end with high school.

The trailer door creaked open, bathing the space in sunlight that brought the dank interior into sharp relief. In the bright light, the wood showed its age, the carpet showed its filth, and the walls were yellowed with age.

"Your grouping sucks," I hadn't bothered to look at who entered. "You have neither accuracy nor precision. These shots are all over the place. How did you pass range days in the academy?"

"Hard to believe you are a trained soldier," a soft voice filled the room and my eyes snapped to a suited man leaning against the frame between the entryway and the portion designated for interviews. He had dark hair, medium brown eyes, and a mouth that looked like it never learned how to smile.

"I don't know you," I said and went back to staring at the ceiling. "Where's Daniel? Or Carla? Or... anyone with the power to take my statement so I can leave?"

"I asked to speak with you first," he said, pulling out the chair and sitting down with a grace that belied his size. He was easily two inches taller than me, wore his muscle in hard-packed bulk, and had a buzzcut that looked terrified of disobeying the head it sat on.

"Marine?" I asked and he raised a brow.

"Former," he answered when I remained quiet. "Heard you were Army."

I shrugged before offering a single incline of my head.

We sat in silence, the click and hum of the air conditioner kicking in filling the void. Mr. Marine shifted in his seat, stuck out his leg and leaned back. His posture was a mirror of my own, but he looked uncomfortable.

Career military turned Law Enforcement had a notoriously animosity - filled relationship with slouching. I had a notoriously bad habit of slouching and not giving a fluff. We were destined not to be friends even before I noticed his stiff, almost disturbing visual assessment of me.

Men of his background also struggled with silence and patience, so I waited him out while my phone danced across the table with incoming calls.

"You going to answer that?"

"No."

"Why not?" Curiosity got the better of him and he leaned over the table to study the device. "You don't want to talk to your mom?"

"Not right now."

"Why not?"

I just stared at him in response. The chances he was here to discuss my family were slim enough that I needn't bother with this question. He'd either give up and move on, or we'd sit here in silence until the room collapsed around us. Either option was fine with me, as I had no desire to share information about my family with a stranger.

Especially not one who grew more and more uncomfortable the longer he sat in the room. I was fairly certain I didn't smell, but I did a quick sniff test just in case.

Pumpkin-y fresh.

"Fine, none of my business." He raised his hands and I snorted my agreement. "I'm here because of the fires. This is the tenth small town where random fires have been popping up. While not a federal case in itself, we found it suspicious and had a hunch we were missing something. Reached out to Gretchen Harpole, told her the fires were now happening in Sweet Pea, and she recommended I work with you. Apparently, you helped her with a money laundering/drug scheme and I checked your record..."

His face showed something that would live in a family with horror and envy.

"Hard to believe you're still alive."

I declined to comment. If he thought surviving was my biggest accomplishment, he wouldn't care much that it hardly registered when my life was in jeopardy anymore. That or saying it out loud might invite the universe to try harder.

"I need help with these arsons. We are headed into fire season and a wildfire would devastate the federal resources if we can't put a stop to them."

A rehearsed speech, but it looked like his first time delivering it. Either someone had forced him to ask for help, he had to practice speaking to strangers or he was lying.

None of which really mattered to me.

"What makes you sure they're connected? The country is full of children and immature people who think playing with matches and magnifying glasses is fun. Small towns are no exception. There's a deputy here whose kids are in line to join the ranks of America's Dumbest Criminals as soon as they lose their juvenile status." I looked at the man who'd birthed the hooligans as he walked in during my statement.

"Watch it, Sharp. I could have you put behind bars." He gave me a threatening finger point and my phone went off again before my witty retort could blossom into words.

For the best, really. I was running low on witty and was teetering into immature and childish.

"Are you going to answer that?" Marine Man asked again, and I shook my head.

"It's rude to answer your phone in the middle of a conversation."

Daniel rolled his eyes and stabbed the answer button.

"Cynthia's phone," he thrust the phone out and activated speaker.

"Where the hell are you?" Joseph roared on the other end of the line.

"Police station. Daniel wanted to see me in handcuffs cuz his brother wouldn't share the pictures from the other night." I smirked and then my face paled.

I'd just made an explicit joke to my boss.

Made an explicit joke to my boss in front of a stranger.

An explicit joke, to my boss, while in front of a stranger, and in police custody.

That was it, I was never going to my mother's house again. She would hear about her rotten influence, maybe get grounded from hanging out with her friends, and be sent to bed without a narcotics laced dessert...

Joseph remained silent on the other end of the line, and Daniel's slack-jaw expression was proof I'd messed up. Marine man... was laughing quietly with a full set of perfect teeth. Some of his serious military demeanor had rubbed off, making him look like a regular person... almost.

The hair on his head was still terrified.

"Cynthia..." Joseph began but fell silent again. "You..."

He stalled out a third time and I threw him a bone.

"I lost my license. Daniel saw me driving Larry's car and detained me. I've been sitting here all afternoon."

"When you get out, I expect you here doing rounds," he hung up and I shuddered.

Yup, I was going to get my ass handed to me... probably by the goats.

"I thought you were a private investigator," Marine man spoke, and I cut my eyes to him. His veneer had broken another notch.

"That's more of a part-time gig to pay my rent." I didn't think mentioning that the act itself is what covered my rent in the apartment above the office, was relevant. "What makes you think all of this is connected?"

"The car. It has appeared and been reported in every town during the fires in connection with a petty theft. A candy bar, or a scarf... stuff that most people wouldn't notice, but when they did, the thief got into a car with the same plate as the one you read to Carla."

"Did the thief get in the driver's side or passenger?"

He seemed to puzzle over the question.

"Were there any thefts without fire?" Perhaps that first question was too hard.

"You... what?" Marine Man and Daniel stared at me.

"You connected the thefts to the car, the car appears everywhere there was a fire. Did the car appear anywhere without a fire? Did the thief get in the driver's or passenger side? Could there be more than one person as I saw in the car or is the second person a recent addition? Could it just be a road tripping Klepto who was unfortunate enough to be following the same path as an arsonist ? Do the two only occur simultaneously?"

A lot of blinking occurred, and the men remained silent.

"So you have no idea?" They nodded and I smirked at Daniel. "Guess now you believe that my wallet was stolen? You owe me an apology!"

He held up my wallet in a plastic bag.

"Sorry you dropped your wallet in a parking lot and someone picked it up and you committed a crime to get it back." His lifted lip sneer sent fire through my veins.

"Whatever, at least I won't need a new bank card. Where did you find it?" I reached for the baggy but he withdrew the wallet from my reach. "What are you doing?"

"It was on the side of the road three miles from where I stopped you. We collected it, but then we got word that it was possibly connected to the fires and now we are holding it as evidence for prints. You'll be able to retrieve it after the investigation is closed." He smiled wide and I showed him my teeth.

"Daniel, I hate to do your job for you, but things booked in plastic can't be printed. Do you even watch TV? That's CSI 101." I threw myself against the back of my chair and crossed my arms. "OK, Marine Man, what do you want me to do?"

"Martin," he said, extending a hand which I shook without enthusiasm.

"Probably still going to call you Marine Man."

He seemed to think a moment before nodding.

"Guess that's fine. I need your help putting an end to this before the country catches fire and we can't put it out. Legally, in most of the places the pair started fires, it's vandalism or criminal mischief which isn't a big deal, but with summer... we can't risk it."

I let out a long sigh.

"Fine, whatever. Give me what you have and I'll look it over tonight," I held out my hand but he just looked confused. "You have files, right? From the other towns that were 'hit'?"

"Well, not *on* me..."

"Are you kidding? I've been sitting here for hours waiting for you to come talk to me and you didn't bring *anything*? Did you think I'd just Google it and know as much as you?"

Tired and cranky were not a good combination on me, but I couldn't get my mouth under control as it berated the man in the suit.

"No, just... Daniel said you weren't stable and I wasn't allowed to bring paper in here because you would use it to slit my wrist... which now sounds ridiculous. Maybe we can meet for dinner and work on it together?"

Daniel made a gagging face and I looked for paper to slit his wrists but came up snake eyes.

"Whatever, Marine Man, but you better bring pizza and dessert. I'm unpleasant without dessert."

"She's always unpleasant," Daniel laughed, and I stomped on his foot as I passed, feeling satisfied when he screamed in pain. "Proving my point! I'm telling Larry to dump you."

"I'm telling Larry to give your kids loud and obnoxious presents for Christmas. Indestructible ones that would be an environmental hazard for you to throw away." I stuck my tongue out at him and he did it back while Martin chuckled behind us and gently pushed me toward the door with a hand on my lower back.

I shoved his hand away and let him go in front of me.

He pushed the door open and I hissed at the bright sunshine.

"You two hook up at some point and it go badly?" he asked, sliding on sunglasses and tugging me toward the exit.

"Ewww! No. He just... annoys me," I huffed out and felt some of the tension leave my shoulders now that we were outside. "I had a crush on him and I think some of the embarrassment of my poor judgment from back then lingers. His level of cocky makes me want to take him down a peg."

"I'll give you that last, but I think you guys still want to bang each other. You need a ride?" he asked, following me through the public entrance and out to the parking slots situated in front. Next to the police cruiser was Daniel's truck, Carla's unmarked Chevy Malibu, and a black SUV with DC plates.

"Yeah... do you mind stopping at my place first? I need to pick something up to get back at you for that last comment."

Chapter Eight:
Baled Out

"D amn-it Winnie, stop!" I ran at full speed after my errant partner as she tried to swallow the hardened lump of fat and maintain speed at the same time. The dog glanced at me once, slipped under the wooden posts of a fence, and crouched low to finish her treat.

"I'm sending you to the pound!" I shouted, trying to jump the fence posts.

The left side of the pasture had lost its wooden posts in a storm last month and the farm hands hadn't had the opportunity to permanently correct it. In their place were a temporary series of metal posts with barbed wire looped between at four separate heights. Winnie stood, noticing for the first time where she'd run with her snack... and coming nose to nose with a black steer sporting an inch long tuft of hair on his chin.

"Winnie! Back out slowly," I tried to remain calm as I approached the pair. My partner tilted her head left, the steer let out a soft snort. The dog tilted her head right and the steer... charged.

"Out! Leave it! Play Dead!" None of my commands made it through the dog's sudden panic as a beast ten times her size came after her. Lacking directional sense, the dog beelined it for the temporary section of fence and cleared the wire in a single leap, landing gracefully on the other side. With her head high, tail even higher, she pranced the width of the paddock in a victory lap. Flashing her regal red bandana.

To the bull who lived in *this* pen.

The thundering of hooves preceded a loud howl and the fur missile flew back over the wire, cleared the fence behind me, and made tracks to the barn. Without the grace or muscles, the bull elected to charge through all of it, taking a length of wire and a metal post along with a herd of liberated steers toward the ice cream parlor.

The dog crawled into a small hole dug for a tortoise who had passed, leaving only her nose peeking out above ground. Barty the Bull had no real sense of direction and after stabbing a groove in the entire length of the barn, slowed down his charge as he came to the end of the thankfully blue building.

And into sight of the bright red ice cream parlor.

"Watch out!"

My voice was lost under the sound of fourteen farm hands trying to grab the raging bull. Recently freed, the steers grazed heedless of the rampaging bull or the men and women chasing it. I kept running, coming even with the far side of the barn just fast enough to see Joseph standing with his phone pressed against his ear. One second he looked alarmed, the next second his pants were gone and the bull's horns were stuck in the side of the building.

I stood transfixed as my boss took a moment to register the sudden breeze on his nether parts.

His almost completely nude nether parts, the neon green thong the only fabric between his manhood and my nightmares.

"Are you OK?" I asked, strategically approaching him from the front and looking anywhere but directly toward his person.

"This is your fault, isn't it?"

"Not... I mean... Winnie... Yes, sir," I spoke to my tan work boots and didn't make eye contact with Joseph.

I would look at his eyes, but to get there I'd have to pass his man thong and I just couldn't do it. I was about to be fired and I had every intention of getting fired without having a permanent mental scar of seeing the outline of his man bits.

"Explain!" he snapped, as Barty Cowch fought the four hands trying to remove his horns from the building. The blissfully ignorant steers were still grazing nearby and I questioned whether or not all men could be tamed with castration. Could mandatory castration be a thing?

I mean, if people without uterus's could vote on abortion, the world should get to vote on castration.

"Damn-it, Cynthia! I said explain!" His shriek pulled me back into myself and I told the story to the spot over his left ear. As the saga continued, his face grew more red. From red it went to a near purple and I decided it was best to stop before he had a myocardial infarction.

Spit flew from his mouth when he opened it, and I tried to make myself as small as possible.

"First you show up three hours late, then you tell me that half the product has gone bad because a fridge went out overnight and no one noticed. Then you drop a bucket of fat, lose some to that damn dog, who then pisses off the steers? Frees them, and then a bull rips off my pants and you... you...."

The farm hand brought the denim colored material to Joseph who inspected the pants for damage. As he turned, a metal snap glinted in the sun and I snatched them from his hand.

"These are tear away pants! Why are you wearing tear away pants with a thong on a freaking farm?"

My boss pulled the pants out of my hands, deftly snapped the side seams and stepped into them with only the ankles flapping open to accommodate his boots.

"It doesn't matter what kind of pants I wear, Cynthia! I can wear yoga pants if I want to! None of it would matter if you and your dog weren't a damn disaster!"

My response stuck in my throat as the truth of his words hit.

"I'll go get my things," my voice broke a little, but it was the only responsible thing to do. No need to make him say the words that I was fired, it was implied. Maybe there was a traveling circus I could join... Winnie would be the ringleader, ordering me about alongside goats and the man with four nipples.

"Go get your stuff? Go get... and leave me here? With a bull stuck in my building, demolished fences, and no one to perform output maintenance? No. No way are you getting off that easy. Finish your rounds, then you are going to make up the three hours you missed repairing the fence. Tomorrow, your dog goes back to work modeling for pictures in front of the ice cream parlor, and you will shovel every last animal dropping in the barn. After that... after that I'm going to find five hundred other laborious and unpleasant things for you to do until you're old enough that it's considered harassment and illegal!"

Joseph stomped off toward his shack of an office and the silence was deafening.

Though still stuck, Barty Cowch was now still. The steers paused in their grazing to give me narrowed eyes and every other farm employee was choking back a laugh. At a loss for what to do, I turned on my heel, grabbed a steer by his horn, and led him back to what had once been his home. Winnie slunk in beside me and I gave her the evilest eye I could manage.

"You. Are. Never. Getting. A. Puppuccino. Again."

A small whimper escaped her throat and I pointed toward the employee dirt parking lot a half-mile away.

"Go wait for Larry," she tried to lick my hand but I growled at her.

"You are not forgiven."

Tail tucked between her legs, she made the slow trudge to the lot as I messaged Larry to come pick her up and informed him I wouldn't be getting off any time soon.

Larry responded with a link to a YouTube video and I watched in horror as the events replayed in front of me. It hadn't been five minutes since the event and we were already trending.

Larry: *I'll save you some ice cream.*

Despite several of the guys offering to stay and help me, I had turned them all down in favor of solitary labor. It was my mess and I would clean it up, I insisted to each one and in turn they all shook their heads at me in disapproval before shuffling off to the parking lot and heading home.

Only three cars remained, and I knew the owner of at least one of the vehicles was Joseph.

Despite the break in the heat, it was still mid-eighties and the sweat pooling on my back and underarms had turned the olive green shirt nearly black. Everything stuck and squelched as I fought my anger and frustration. Neither were productive... and neither made the sledgehammer any lighter as I swung it down onto the last post needed to seal in the steers.

My hammer missed and lodged itself into the ground for a full minute until I could convince my arms to pull it free. My eyes traveled around, seeing Joseph head to his truck in the tear away pants. The ice cream shop was sealed up tight, and Barty Cowch had been tied off to the far end of what was once an enclosure and soon would be again. Someone had patched the side of the barn and the shop, filling the digs in the wood with some sort of wood adjacent polymer that would need to be painted.

With a sigh, I raised the hammer again and tried to line it up with the fence post.

"Need help?" A man reached out, holding the post steady just in time for the hammer to drive the post home.

"Thanks. That's the last one of those so I should be good."

"You're not an island, Cyn," Jessie said, trying and failing to take my hammer but handing me some water. "No one wants you to get hurt. Let me help."

I accepted his water but retained my hammer as the sun slipped below the horizon.

"Appreciate the offer, but I've got this," I told him, bringing the head of the hammer down hard on a metal rail and driving it into place. "You should get home to Katie."

"It'll get done faster with the two of us," he tried to slide in and position the next rail.

"It's not supposed to get done faster. It's supposed to get done by me as retribution for what my dog did."

"Does it matter how? If it gets done, then it's done."

"It matters to me, Jessie," I chugged the rest of the water he brought me and blinked into the darkening sky. "This is my punishment, and I don't cheat when it comes to work."

He handed me two more water bottles and tugged the hem of my soaked through shirt.

"Sun's gone down. You can ditch that now that everyone's gone home and you won't get sunburned."

I nodded at his suggestion, and with a clap on my shoulder, he strode off toward the lot and started his truck.

A quick glance showed Jessie had, in fact, been the last and with a long, deep breath, I ditched my shirt and kept working in my sports bra. Every muscle ached, fire raced through my lower back, but in three hours it was done, and I leaned back against the cart I'd moved my supplies in.

Just after ten, I stared at the taut wire and the smooth wooden posts I'd unearthed and pounded into the ground. Relieved, I raised my arms, feeling the stretch through my whole body. A long yawn escaped and before I could stifle another, a soft voice carried through the night.

"Larry?" I said quietly, but either he was too far away, or it wasn't him because the sound carried on. Carefully, I maneuvered around the scrapped remains of the old fence and tread lightly to the barn.

"Larry?" I asked again, just a bit louder.

A second voice joined the first. Neither loud enough to make out, but both conveying displeasure at something. My ears strained toward the barn, but I couldn't hear any more.

My feet led me back to the pen and a bright light filled the area behind the ice cream parlor as an engine roared to life. Moving quickly, I did my best to ignore the burning in my lungs as I ran to see who had come out to the farm in the middle of the night. A door slammed shut, the voices arguing once again.

"Hello?" I called out, hearing the tailgate of a truck bounce on the lower bumper. "Larry?"

Something slammed into the bed of the truck, two doors opened and shut, before the engine revved and the truck took off down the road and disappeared into the night. As my eyes adjusted to the returned darkness, I felt my phone vibrate in my pocket and I answered it without looking.

"Cynthia, there is a strange man loitering outside your house," Mrs. Charles let out a long, wet, round of coughing and I pulled the phone away to study the tire tracks. There wasn't a lot behind the ice cream parlor, mostly metal buckets, trash cans, and coiled hose. I used the dim glow from my phone's screen to try and see what, if anything, could have been taken.

"Are you listening?" she rasped into the receiver and I chewed my lip, trying to think what Joseph kept back here.

"No," I answered honestly, trying to spit out the salty bits of sand that had been caked to my face.

"Cynthia, there is a man standing outside where you live and when I asked him what he was doing with pizza and cookies outside your home, he informed me you were having dinner with him. It's not that I'm against a woman getting hers, but how could you do that to Larry? And if Larry knows, how could you let such a fine specimen just stand here and wait? Men have a short attention span, Cynthia. A man like that probably has options..."

I tuned out her rant, the man was probably lost. If he was there for me, that pizza box probably held a subpoena.

A rectangular outline sat in the soft sand and I moved in closer to see the long horizontal lines in the dirt. It was just over a yard in length, and there were three vertical lines cut through the horizontal ones.

"Cynthia! Does Larry know?"

"I'm sorry, Mrs. Charles, but I need to go."

Without waiting for a response, I hung up, took a photo and sent it to Larry before calling him.

"Is stealing a bale of hay a crime?" I asked when he yawned his hello after four rings.

"Yeah... I think. Why?"

"I think someone in a truck just stole some from behind the ice cream parlor."

Chapter Nine:
Night Terrors

I t was nearly midnight when Daniel dropped me off in front of Sharp Investigations.

He had taken thirty minutes to arrive, looked at the empty space for two minutes, and declared it was nothing. When I'd called Joseph, he said the hay was old and if someone wanted to steal it, he wasn't going to waste energy filing a report.

"Next time you witness a petty crime, do us all a favor and turn the other cheek," Daniel remarked as I closed the door to his car and stared at the front of my building.

In lieu of replying, I gave him a stiff middle finger and started searching for my keys as he drove away from the curb.

"Are you sure the two of you never..." I turned to see Marine Man inserting his pointer finger into a ring created by his thumb and index on the opposite hand.

"What do you want?" I yawned, watching him open the back door to his SUV that sat parked against the curb. He pulled out a large pizza box, a container of frosted sugar cookies, and a six-pack of beer. On top of the pile was a thick binder and my brain struggled to remember if I'd accepted another man's offer to be my boyfriend.

"Is there a subpoena in that box?" I yawned again and wondered why he was playing a process server long game. He could have served me at the jail, or at my work... or...

"We were having dinner to discuss the cases? I know it's late, I meant to be here a lot earlier, but thankfully you're later than I am. I didn't figure you'd be too far in front of me after I saw the video, but I didn't anticipate you arriving after twenty-three hundred," he was using twenty-four-hour time for eleven in the evening and I tried to clear the fatigue and cobwebs.

"I forgot when my dog destroyed half a farm and got a bull stuck in a wall." I found my keys, put them in the heavy wooden front door and pushed it open. The downstairs office was blissfully cool, the heavy curtain on the front window blocking the ambient light from outside. Winnie's dog bed lay empty in the corner and I considered curling up in it for a nap.

Marine Man snapped on the light as though he read my thoughts.

I blinked in the light and caught a glimpse of his face taking in my appearance. Something resembling disappointment mingled with confusion that faded into a blank expression.

Apparently tired and sweaty women were unattractive.

Thank dog, because if he made a pass my body was too tired to punch him in the face.

"Pizza's a little cold now, but if you have a microwave..." He trailed off as I stumbled toward the coffee cart and popped a single-use pod in one machine while collecting supplies to make a full pot with the other. Two of the jugs of water I kept under the counter were full of sink water, but two more needed to be refilled upstairs to fuel my addiction. "Are you making coffee while you wait for your coffee?"

"Mmmhmm," I said into the cup as I drank deeply. "Isn't that why single-use dispensers exist?"

"I mean.... I have beer so you don't really need to make a full pot," he said and I watched him set all the items he'd brought in on my desk. "You really only need a cup for yourself."

"First, you don't know what I need, buddy. Second, I didn't offer you any coffee, so it's safe to assume none of this is for you. Third, if you value your physical well-being, do not stand between me and my coffee." I raised a warning finger as the coffee maker beeped and I refilled the mug stating I was a dinosaur trainer with the Jurassic Park logo and the silhouette of a woman in front of working dogs with her hands out.

"Rrrright," his sarcasm turned to alarm when I finished that cup and poured another. "Should you be drinking that much coffee this late?"

"You are one more comment about my caffeine addiction away from getting thrown out with your pizza and beer and your untouched files, Marine Man."

"Martin," he corrected, and I raised an eyebrow in a *what makes you think I care* gesture. "Fine, whatever. Do you have plates?"

I inclined my head toward an out of the way cabinet with a microwave and a neat stack of paper plates and cups underneath it. Martin went about putting slices on plates and heating them while I finished my third cup and plopped heavily onto the seat of my ratty pink desk chair. Beside me was the plastic clam shell of cookies and the thick blue binder. Deciding dessert first was an excellent motto, I broke into the cookies and took a bite while flipping through the binder.

The first page was a list of dates and locations. I scanned the oldest to the most recent, noting that there were roughly five fires per location beginning nine months ago. Aside from dates and locations, there was a brief reference to what had been set on fire in a shorthand that would make the Unabomber proud.

As a tired ex-soldier covered with dried sweat who'd eaten 2 cookies, I just found it annoying.

Pizza appeared on top of the file folder and I offered Marine Man a grunt of thanks. Moving the plate to the arm of my chair, I picked off a pepperoni while I looked at the names of the towns across the country. Cucumber Crescent, Blueberry Meadows, Sunnyhill... it was like the whole country was filled with small towns who named themselves something beautiful to make up for their lack of actual marketable features.

"What do you think?" Martin asked and I ripped the crust off my pizza to eat it. Despite what people say, the crust is my least favorite part. If I eat it first, all that's left is cheesy topping goodness. It's like vegetables. Eat them first and the only stuff left on your plate is what you actually wanted in the first place.

"About the pizza? I live here, so I mean... I've had it and it's always good," I chewed the crust thoughtfully looking at the states. New Mexico, Colorado, Northern Texas, Kansas, Nebraska...

"I meant about the case," I could hear his implied eye roll, but I elected to ignore him. Like all men, he seemed to assume I was a mind reader who would just interpret his questions seamlessly.

"This is the summary list of the arsons. Where are the petty thefts?"

He moved over and flipped to a page halfway through the binder with the list of petty thefts.

"They aren't on the list because they are just sort of mingled between the fires in remote areas with no name," he shrugged and I wiggled my nose looking at what was stolen. "I looked for any other reports that mention the red car, there's a search running. So far there have been a couple hits between the towns, but there were only courtesy reports without much detail. No one wanted to press charges over nail clippers and Jiffy Pop, so it was more a 'just in case' report."

"Have you plotted all these on a map?" I flipped through the book for a Thomas Guide page or a map printed from the internet with a crayon line playing connect the dots.

"No. The general trend was west to east, why would I need a map?" I picked up my slice of pizza and ate cheesy, pepperoni, olive goodness. I stuffed my face while I fired up the CPU that lived in my office. The desk unit in the office was donated by a "customer" who needed my help getting to the bottom of the censorship on his porn website.

Turns out it was his mom, and after she learned he was the webmaster, she threatened to cut him off from chocolate lava cake at family functions if he didn't shut it down. The mini unit had been being used as a backup to his main drive due to the volume of viruses inherent in collecting material for his line of work. Once he'd scrubbed it of porn, he gifted it to me for use in the office.

Apparently my twelve-year-old Dell laptop belonged in a museum beside dinosaur bones and Giga pets.

"Why is there a naked man as the background image on your computer?" He looked appalled and I smiled at the chiseled abs and bronzed skin. There was a folder Mr. Colvin hadn't deleted and I liked to rotate through the images as my background just to make Larry a little jealous.

Keeps his ego in check.

"Why is there anything anywhere?" I countered, opening a mapping program and entering the cities as way points on the way to Sweet Pea. The starting point was nearest... "There's a Las Vegas, New Mexico?"

"What?" Marine Man crowded my air space and zoomed in on the dot. "Why are the biggest points of interest a Walmart and a McDonalds?"

"Well, we don't have either here, so it's definitely a step closer to a thriving metropolis." I nudged him over so I could get another slice of pizza. He tried to take my plate and I growled.

"I was going to heat it up!"

"Mine!" I barked, stuffing the room temperature pizza into my mouth.

"You have issues," he grumbled, moving away from the computer and back to the guest chair. He cracked open a beer and I decided it was a great time to refill my coffee mug. "So, anything of interest?"

Every joint in my body popped on the way up and I couldn't move my legs enough to do more than shuffle.

"Well, the map defaults to fastest, and it looks like a lot of back-tracking to get on major highways after stopping in these towns. If we assume they don't, then the potential criminal duo avoids major roadways to have better access to small roadside towns and regional law enforcement. Seems reasonable if the car is less than legally registered." My arm shook as I tried to raise the coffee cup to my face. Either my tolerance had dropped or every muscle in my body had reached its limit for the night.

Rather than risk it, I fished out a straw and dropped it into the cup.

"What makes you think it's less than legally registered? Also I followed up on which side of the car they saw the suspect get in. It alternated, so there were two all along."

"So definitely a crime duo. If the car were legally registered, you'd know the identity of the arsonists and I would be sleeping right now. Either the car is stolen, the registration is out of date after the vehicle was sold, or... I don't know. It was purchased off the side of the road with cash and no one had a stamp to mail in paperwork."

Another cookie appeared in my hand and I stuffed it in my mouth. I could only hope it would somehow stop the onslaught of words before I started spouting conspiracy theories about aliens and Dracula.

"You're not wrong," Marine Man conceded, taking a cookie of his own. "Registered owner filed a cash transfer to a fake shell corporation. Man was legally blind and couldn't describe the buyers. He said he only communicated with them digitally, and aside from one male and one female voice on the day of the transfer, he can't tell us more. He's also not completely sold on the one male and one female voice either... I get the impression he didn't like me asking questions."

"In New Mexico?" I tried to picture the plate from the red car. It had been from Arizona.

"Yeah, man lived in Arizona, moved in with his kid when he couldn't see anymore. The car had been sitting a couple years, but the kid kept it operational and decent mechanically." He looked so confident and while I wanted to challenge that people lie about used cars and the thing could die any day now, it was too much effort.

Unless you personally look under the hood of a car, you don't know crap about its condition.

Unless you knew squat about cars, then looking under the hood meant watching the seller for a sign they didn't want you to see something. Which I knew from personal experience was hit or miss, and the man in front of me was probably in the same boat.

"Who's the man's kid?" I asked, not caring much.

"Mechanic in the area. Hires ex-cons and gives them a purpose." Marine Man made a face and I shrugged.

"Hire a bunch of former car jackers, and they already know more than the average joe. Seems like a solid strategy for labor and probably you don't have to be as competitive with wages." He made the face again. "What? I didn't say it was right, I just said as a business strategy it wasn't bad for profits. As a human, it kind of makes you a jerk unless you pass the savings on to your customers and give the guys decent benefits to stay clean. It would actually make you a good person as long as you kept the wage to the national average and helped with housing."

I stared at my wall and wondered if Joseph would hire ex-cons to work at the dairy. Maybe he did and no one had told me, which might actually explain his leniency in keeping me around. Though none of them would fear me or Winnie after the mistaken snack incident.

Deadly or not, no one is forgetting the time a grown woman ate a Milk Bone, decided it was better than not having a cookie and polished off the whole thing. Then the trained military canine took a nap so deep she fell off a bale of hay, farted and startled herself into a barking contest with the neighbor's rooster.

Turning back to the computer, I picked a small town at random and typed Blueberry Hill fire into the browser window. It would be interesting to see what the local's take on the event was. I pressed enter and my eyes moved to my desktop background.

That would be a nice view to wake up to. Sleep would be a nice thing to do before waking up to that.

"Cyn!" Marine Man snapped me back and I blinked at him.

"Right, investigation into arsons. Talked to any of the kid's employees, see if they heard anything through their old life?"

"No."

"Why not?" I ate the cheese and toppings off a slice of pizza and abandoned the bread. I didn't need the calories, but I wanted the cheese.

He shrugged and shifted awkwardly. I scanned the results... warehouse fire? My eye's tracked to the case summary but I couldn't tell if any of that was code for warehouse fire or just a rough sketch of two stick figures having sex. I read through the headline on the computer screen. A warehouse of a business that was operating in the red burned to the ground. Mysteriously cleared of inventory...

"Cyn!" I snapped awake again and blinked at him.

"Why didn't you question the kids' employees?" He shrugged. "You hadn't thought of it?"

Martin nearly nodded, as much of a confirmation as I would get. With a sigh, I put the suggestion on a sticky note and set it down in front of him. The book in my lap suddenly felt a thousand pounds, and I had still only looked at the arson and theft summary pages. It was a three-inch binder that was nearly full, but my eyes were drooping and my brain declared giving the man a suggestion had earned my pizza and cookies, so I could call it a night.

"Warehouse?"

My gaze fell to my empty coffee cup, then lower and lower...

"Cyn?" My eyes snapped open and I saw Martin an inch from my face. His light brown eyes flecked with amber were staring into mine. The curve of his mouth, mildly appealing with a touch of frosting in the corner of his lips. Marine Man's nose had three bumps. Likely the product of being broken a few too many times, and his jaw had just the right amount of scruff to be rugged but not bearded.

"Yeah?" I blinked, trying to remember if I should kick him for being this close or kiss him. *Where was I?*

"Thanks." He didn't move back. Broad hands were resting on the armrests at either of my sides, he smelled like stale coffee and sweat... or maybe I did. My eyes stuck to his lips and I tried to picture them making words and... other things... The other things made a cold sweat trickle down my back.

Definitely no to the other things.

His hand brushed my arm as he closed the browser window beside me and seemed to inhale my scent.

"For?" I asked, my brain was feeling a little floaty with the need for sleep and the proximity of a man.

A fairly attractive one.

Maybe the other things could work out after all.

"I-"

The door to the office swung open and I heard the clatter of dog claws before Martin let out a masculine scream.

"Am I interrupting something?" Larry's voice was harsh, and my eyes drifted over to him. "You look like you need a shower."

"Smells like it too," the federal investigator spoke while holding himself upright with the assistance of my desk. Winnie shoved her head into his testicles a couple more times and then trotted back over to give me slobbery kisses.

"Wish you'd done that in the reverse order," I yawned into her fur and hugged her close. Her soft fur felt amazing against my face and I leaned against her like a fluffy but mobile pillow. "You gave her a bath."

"Why does she do that?"

"Do what?" Larry asked and I was grateful. My brain was foggy with sleep, and I didn't know if the *her* Martin referenced was me or Winnie. Neither of us was especially transparent in our reasoning nor in our execution, so it was a toss-up.

"Stick her head up there." He pushed himself upright and tried to gather his dignity. "My brother said half the guys in Afghanistan were scared of a dog making them infertile."

"Brother?" I yawned, sliding off the chair and crawling on all fours to Winnie's bed. The dog followed and we both curled up.

"Yeah. My twin was a Ranger. He told me stories about a female K-9 and her handler. The dog liked to greet people by shoving her nose into their unmentionables and the handler was more likely to shoot you for being an idiot than the insurgents. But he said she showed up and saved his team's ass more than once. He never mentioned you by name, but the dots line up for it to have been you."

I blinked at him and shrugged.

"I never shot anyone." Larry looked at the binder on the desk, the food, and back to me. "At least not until after I retired. Making the Rangers infertile probably would have been a blessing."

"Believe it or not, when he demanded the handler reprimand her dog, she said something similar and threw a plastic bag of poop at him."

"Oh yeah? Steve is your brother?" I yawned again.

"What? You... you throw poop at people?"

I'd only been inclined to throw dog poop at one man. He'd been leering at a friend of mine when Winnie took her shot. Steve hadn't so much as demanded I reprimand Winnie as threaten to shoot her, which is when the plastic bag of poop hit the side of his head with a splat.

"Not people, just a person. Steve Bermudez... your last name is Bermudez?"

"No... I mean... You throw poop at people?"

The man was surprisingly indignant for someone who wasn't hearing the story for the first time. If Steve really was his brother, he had to know his brother was more likely to downplay than exaggerate the incident.

Machismo jerk-wad.

Larry cleared his throat and I looked over at him, still assessing the food and beverage situation for signs we were on a date.

"What is all this?"

"He wanted my help, promised dinner and cookies," I shrugged. "I'd have given him help in the police station, but your brother told him I could commit murder with paper."

"Can you?" Martin asked with a touch of alarm. He was look-ing at me like it was the first time he'd ever seen me, studying and apprehensive. Who knew confirming a story about throwing poop would do that? If I hadn't been so tired, I'd have tried to mess with him. Regale him with tales of paper, salt and lemon... but it was too much work.

So I chose silence.

"She can't. It looked like..." Larry scratched the back of his head with his left hand, and I licked my lips at the smooth skin that the movement of his shirt exposed. His eyes darkened and we shared a glance that was all business. "Never mind."

"Will you bring me a blankie?" I asked and the door banged open. "Also lock the door so the wind can't blow it open."

"Not the wind," an angry man said and I tried to lift an eyelid but it weighed more than my furry pillow.

"Okay, Not The Wind, will you lock the door and bring me a blankie? Quite a name by the way," Winnie let out a soft fart and I sputtered upright from the smell and locked eyes with Deputy O'Hare. "Did you arrest my parents again?"

"No. I'm here to ask for your alibi." he crossed his arms and tried to flex his muscles. "A bale of hay just took out half the crops in Cartersville."

Chapter Ten: Hay There

C artersville made Sweet Pea look like New York... or at the very least Cincinnati.

The town had been founded by Amber Carter's dad. He'd named himself the mayor, was sleazy and slimy, and contributed greatly to her mistaken belief that she was royalty. While the dumpster fire behind Amber's Shoe Ambrosia was vandalism at best, destroying the crops of a small town could be detrimental to the economy and warranted a much bigger response. Though I knew I hadn't started the fire, the people of Cartersville deserved to know who had.

At least until I arrived and realized that "half the town's crops" was code for a marijuana grow in the town founder's backyard.

Then, well, then it sounded like someone else's problem because I had zero interest in the devil's lettuce.

If someone wanted to burn fresh weed, who was I to judge?

This was not worth leaving Winnie's bed for, but I tried to ask a helpful question.

"Do you think this is your arsonist?" Marine Man shrugged.

Not helpful.

"Does it match the pattern?" He waggled a flat hand in a *kind of* gesture.

That wasn't helpful either, so I gave up.

"I don't really have a purpose here, got it," I said into the gator I pulled over my face. Marijuana being smoked smelled disgusting. Fresh marijuana being burned smelled like the seventh ring of hell. A fact I just learned today that I'd have happily carried on without ever having knowledge of.

Winnie flopped on the ground beside me and I wondered if the air was safe for her... or really anyone besides Cheech and Chong.

"Why *am* I here? I was with actual law enforcement the whole night."

Winnie grumbled in agreement and sneezed dirt from her nose, a glitter penis landing in the sand. My gaze drifted back up to the men beside me. Deputy O'Hare, Marine Man, and Larry all shrugged and I decided men were stupid.

"I'm going to take a nap in the car," I made it four steps when Daniel Kirby grabbed me and dragged me back toward the chaotic lightshow. Winnie hadn't quite made it to standing yet but she let out a soft growl and I whole-heartedly agreed.

"Where do you think you're going?" He demanded as I twisted my bicep out of his grasp.

"Ow, you Neanderthal!" I made an exaggerated show of how much my arm hurt, but the muscles had gone numb from pain hours ago. "No one said you could manhandle innocent bystanders!"

"You're not innocent!" he declared.

"Why are you here? You don't work here!"

"I was asked to consult," Daniel crossed his arms, a smirk plastered on his face that I considered punching.

Amber sauntered into the scene in impractical shoes and insufficient clothing.

"I knew it was her," she jutted out a hip and a half dozen plastic bracelets bounced on her wrist. Winnie sneezed on the cloud of perfume that wafted off of her, and I was pretty sure she was going to need a saline rinse to find bombs after everything that went up her nose tonight.

My eyes landed on a second metallic penis... her poor nose.

"Check your facts, losers. I was with Daniel until he dropped me off at home where this federal agent took custody of me. I have nothing to do with this!"

For the second time I made to stomp off to the car only to be grabbed and brought back by a Kirby brother.

"Larry," I growled, and he pinned my arms to my side and held me close. "I'm tired, cranky, and in pain. Let me go."

His arms dropped to my hips, fingers digging into the sore muscles and tendons until a gasp of pleasure slipped from my mouth. I leaned into him, quietly begging his hands to take on the knots in my shoulders and glutes. If I could sleep standing up in the Army, I guess I could sleep standing up against Larry.

Especially if it meant I got a deep tissue massage.

Winnie leaned against my leg and I offered her ears the same affection my sad muscles were getting.

"Maybe you didn't start the fire, but I'm sure you arranged for it," Amber simpered, trying to get Marine Man to take in her rose-colored short shorts and tank top in soft velvet. He seemed less than interested as she pressed her breasts in his direction, so she gave up and sulked. "I mean, you work on a farm. Farms have hay and *that* is burning hay. First my store and now this? You're such a jelly bean..."

"No, that is burning marijuana near the smoldering remains of hay. No one would be jealous of you and your-"

A few scathing comments came to mind, but Larry's thumb landed on a pressure point. I melted like the polar ice caps due to global warming and decided I didn't *need* to insult her.

"So, you admit it? You brought this hay here?" It occurred to me that this might be Amber's version of pajamas. Her messy bun on top of her head and hastily applied lip gloss indicated she may have been in bed, but the shoes and the bracelets said she'd been engaged in horizontal cardio and he'd asked her to leave on the shoes.

A little much, but as established, men were idiots.

I scanned the area for a potential sucker and stopped short at a man speaking animatedly to the female officer with the pixie haircut. He was wearing overalls with nothing underneath, sporting strawberry blonde hair and freckles across his nose that didn't look quite natural.

Winnie scented Amber's direction and then the man, looking at me last. Whether her nose had confirmed my suspicions or she was just looking for treats was impossible to know unless I went and asked someone.

Reluctantly, I stepped away from Larry and moved toward Deputy Montalvo. They were maybe a football field away, but even at this distance, the deputy was clearly ready to tase the man. As I got closer, I could make out his voice before the words. It was deep with polished diction, and subtly British. All at odds with his outfit and demeanor.

When I was within ten feet, it became clear that the hair was as fake as the freckles and the man's muscles were from the gym and not laboring in the fields.

"Can I... help?" The deputy looked pained at seeing me.

She did not apparently believe I could be helpful.

"Yes, you can help. You can explain to me how this rental truck was stolen and returned with hay in the back! It's a rental. How am I supposed to return a rented truck when it is filled with hay? How does one even get hay out of a truck bed?"

"Broom?" He snarled at my suggestion. He was either un-familiar with the household tool, or he thought using one was beneath him. "Wooden handle? Straw bristles at the bottom?"

The man lunged and Montalvo gripped his arm in warning.

Ignoring the look of murder Deputy Montalvo shot me, I walked over to the truck and studied the headlights. Even off, they weren't anything remarkable. The treads in the dirt road that lead to the rear of the Carter property looked the same as the ones on the farm, but all tire treads looked the same when you knew nothing about tires... or cars...

I had no business being here.

The man had rented a silver Ford F-250, the interior black with what must have looked like a Starship Enterprise console when turned on. Plastic floor mats smeared with a bit of mud sat in the foot wells, and the keys were dangling in the ignition.

"How did they start the truck to steal it?"

"With the keys. Honestly, you Americans and..."

"How did they get the keys?" Deputy Montalvo's sharp voice cut through the night and I had an urge to singsong "*somebody's in trouble*".

"They were in the truck. It wasn't to be unattended for long," he shoved his arms across his chest, and I snickered at the exposed nipple of his pec. There was nothing unusual about it aside from serving no biological purpose. I just decided nipples were hilarious.

Geez I needed sleep.

"So, you... donned that disguise, parked your truck out here, and walked away intending to come back soonish, found the truck missing, and then... did what?" I squinted into the night, but aside from a yellow barn, the burning pot plants, and a corn field that was untouched by fire, there was nothing out here. "I mean, it should have been immediately obvious that the truck went missing, why didn't you call immediately?"

Overall man huffed out a breath and tried to cross his arms tighter.

"I was otherwise engaged, madam."

"Doing... what? That outfit is not suitable for field work," Deputy Montalvo snickered at my comment and I tried not to pat myself on the back at having broken her tough girl exterior.

"If you must know, Ms. Nosey Pants, I am an actor. I solicited Ms. Carter for assistance in preparing for a role. The character is a farm hand who wants to win over a city girl and Ms. Carter herself needs to prepare for her part in a survivalist project. She gets stranded in the country and there is a scene where they meet in the barn and then go stargaze in the bed of the truck before the evening concludes with a literal roll in the hay."

"So... it's an adult film?"

"It has a plot!" he argued with belligerence.

"Is the sex on screen?" Overall man remained silent. "That's what I thought. You're acting in a porn. Is Amber also in this porn?"

"No, she's participating in a documentary on cross-country travel and small-town crime." He actually looked jealous and I considered pointing out that hiring actors sort of disqualified it as a documentary and she was just as much there for people to look at as he was. Considered and dismissed the idea when he sneered down his nose at me.

He deserved to feel inferior to Amber.

"Right, so... you park the truck, go into the barn, Amber stumbles out in her heels, you get out to the truck and it's gone... why didn't you call then?" My face held more than just skepticism that he was telling the truth.

I was also concerned he would answer the question honestly and I'd never be able to unhear it.

"Launch sequence was initiated. It was to be a chaste kiss before looking at the stars but she got carried away and I hadn't the inclination to say no. The star gazing was to be an outdoor encounter, but when I couldn't find the truck, we skipped to the barn scene." No color rose on his cheeks as he confessed to being too horny to concern himself with grand theft auto.

I gave him a few brownie points that made him somewhere close to anchovies on my "Disgusting Things" list.

"What time did you arrive here at Ms. Carter's barn?" The deputy seemed to have found her official capacity to investigate now that the crime was more than a dirty truck.

"At ten in the evening." He sniffed and tried to look down his nose at us again, but he and I were the same height. A fact that I emphasized by rolling to the balls of my feet to look down at him.

Petty vengeance, thy name is Cyn.

"We were in front of the barn getting to know each other for fifteen minutes before we returned to the truck."

"Did you hear the engine start?"

"No. I wasn't listening for it."

"Did you hear any voices or humans moving around?" I followed up to my last question without much faith or enthusiasm.

"If I had heard anyone, I would have mentioned it earlier. Who are you anyway?"

"At this point? I'm just an unfortunate farm worker dragged out in the middle of the night. Other days, I'm a private investigator and retired military police K-9 handler." Without permission, I climbed into the bed of the truck. "To you, I'm the woman who is grossed out that you boinked Amber in a barn instead of reporting a stolen vehicle and are too inconsiderate to put a shirt on and cover yourself."

"I am covered!"

"Then why can I see your nipple, man?" His eye roll was nearly audible. "I'm just saying, *other* Brits would have covered themselves. There were no nipples in Harry Potter. Not even when they went swimming in the murky lake."

Mingled with the loose hay was dirt, a few pebbles, and smears of shoeprints in mud. Looking for anything to link this truck and the burning bale of hay to the dairy, I crouched low and studied the mess. Both shoe prints were similar in size to my own, so the owners were either tall or circus clowns.

Some days I was both, so *or* wasn't really required but it made me feel better.

"What are you looking for?" Deputy Montalvo was leaning against the side of the truck watching me. Her voice held genuine curiosity and I nearly swelled with pride that she took me seriously.

Even I didn't have the audacity to take myself seriously.

"I don't know exactly... Something to indicate where the hay came from?" It wasn't really a question, but I was questioning my sanity. The whole area was filled with hay and the dairy farm was forty minutes in the opposite direction of Sweet Pea from Cartersville. Who would take the time and energy to go to the dairy farm to pilfer a bale of hay to drive it all the way back here?

Then set the stupid thing on fire?

A splotch on a few pieces of straw caught my eye. The splotch was blue and a little flaky, forming a circle spot when lined up with a neighboring piece of hay. I sniffed and detected sugar. A few more pieces nearby had additional spots, flecked with multi-colored flecks... sprinkles maybe?

"This was the hay behind the ice cream parlor." I looked at Amber's date and then at the deputy. "Who drives forty minutes to steal hay and set it on fire? There are literally hundreds of hay bales between here and there."

Winnie let out a soft bark. My eyes dropped to her and followed the focus of her eyes and ears.

A shadow skirted the edge of the yellow barn and I tried to shine my phone flashlight on it, but the battery was dead. Montalvo had a Maglite at her hip and I gestured to borrow it. Intrigued, she handed it over and I jumped lightly from the truck, ambling closer to the barn with no visible purpose. Winnie had remained in place with a gesture, but I could hear the restless moving of her paws. When the corner was three feet away, I leapt forward and snapped on the flashlight at the same time I called out.

"Winnie!"

Two boys fell over each other, startled and trying to run away while lying on the ground. Winnie bounded around the corner, blocking their escape with a soft growl and a flash of teeth.

"Stop," I said, grabbing one by the blue plaid shirt and hauling him to his feet. The Deputy arrived to pick up the other one and we looked between the pair of boys skeptically.

"Explain," I ordered, noting that neither had made it to the facial hair portion of puberty yet but they weren't shorter than me by much.

"We don't know what you're talking about, we were home the whole night!" The mousy brown-haired kid in Montalvo's grasp spouted the words as though he'd practiced them.

"Home? The whole night?" The deputy smirked, and he nodded enthusiastically.

"Yeah, we were nowhere near the barn outside the Carter's property. We don't know what you're talking about! You should ask Cyn. I bet the hay was from where she worked and then she brought it here because she's super jealous of Amber and wanted to frame her for a crime. You should be talking to her!"

Blue plaid shirt dropped his face into his hands and scrubbed the pathetic scruff that graced his young face. If it weren't for the sound, I wouldn't have believed he could grow anything more than corn from his ears.

"Jack, shut up," he grumbled, and the other kid stared at him.

"You said when they asked to tell them we don't know what they're talking about and we were home the whole night!"

"That doesn't work if we're not standing in our house when they ask, idiot. How are we even related?" He jerked himself out of my grasp and straightened his shirt to look between us. While normally that constituted resisting arrest, he was just too adorable to reprimand with any sincerity. "Seriously, you accused Cyn to her damn face. I told mom I was better off being an only child and she should have adopted a dog when she remarried instead of having you."

Jack's eyes widened as he stared at me and his mouth fell open.

"You're Cyn? Amber said you looked like Godzilla with blonde hair and an over-sized butt." his brother choked, as he craned his neck around to look at my backside. Apparently, saying he shouldn't have been born was old news to the younger brother, but my ass was new territory he'd yet to examine. "You knew she looked like this, Matt?"

"Jack, shut up!" Matt looked ready to eliminate a sibling and I instinctively moved slightly between them.

"But she's kinda hot in a chubby, old lady way!"

Now I turned on Jack, deciding maybe I'd let Matt prune his family tree. Winnie's tail twitched in anticipation, and I remembered we were technically adults trained in combat and legally we wouldn't stand a chance in court.

But he'd called me chubby and old... I heard myself growl in sync with Winnie.

"OK, OK." Montalvo redirected the kids back toward the crime scene and dropped the tailgate on the truck. The boys were encouraged to sit, and she pulled out a notebook. Winnie sat at my feet and I checked my pockets, coming up with a treat for her hard work. "Let's start from the beginning. What is your last name?"

"Carter," Matt said at the same time Jack said, "Chandler."

The Deputy gave them a look that probably had serial killers confessing, but neither boy retracted their statement.

Kids these days. They were either indifferent liars or had two different last names.

"OK, let's try a different question, how old are you?"

"17."

"14."

That looked on par with their faces.

"Call your mom," she held out her phone and they exchanged a look. "Now!"

"I don't know the number!" the younger boy whined to an audible eye roll from his brother.

"Then use your own phone, kid," I spit the words at him. He'd called me old and chubby, I was so not being nice to him.

Jack pulled his cell phone out and worked the keys, holding out the device for everyone to hear.

"Jack? Where the hell are you?" A woman growled into the phone after four rings. "You better not be with Matt and those damn Carter cousins. You both-"

"Ma'am," Montalvo interrupted, and charged on hoping their mother would stop talking. "Your sons are at the scene of a fire, where marijuana was grown and now it's burning."

"We didn't start the fire!"

"We only stole the hay!"

They shouted together before the venomous voice of their mother came through the line.

"Matt you-" I plugged my ears and moved away quietly. Whatever the boys knew or the reason they'd done it, none of this seemed to require my chubby, old lady presence. I reached Larry and poked him in the ribs.

"Can we leave?" I whispered and he nodded, backing away from his brother and the federal officer slowly until we were far enough away to turn and run.

"Larry!" Daniel shouted, but we dove into his car and locked the doors.

"Drive! Drive!" I begged and he gave me a wide smile.

"What's in it for me?" He let Daniel get closer and I panicked.

"Anything you want! Please?" He leaned in and kissed me, our tongues touched, and heat filled my body as I fisted my hands into his shirt. With reluctance, he pulled back and kissed my nose.

"Your wish is my command, but remember this the next time you have secret meetings with men in the middle of the night."

"Remember what?" I asked as he pulled the car onto the road and the lights started to fade behind us. "It wasn't really a secret, Daniel knew."

"If you want me to be your getaway driver, you won't have any more midnight meetings with men bearing cookies, unless the cookies are yours, the man is me, and I get an all-access taste test."

Oh boy.

Chapter Eleven: Rubbernecking

"No," I whispered to my cell phone, having seizures beside the bed. "Please, no."

My eyelids wouldn't open. There was simply no amount of sound that could convince my eyelids to open.

"Cyn," Larry whispered, and the scent of coffee filled my nose. "Cyn, you need to get up."

A tear rolled down my cheek and he sucked in a breath.

"Please, don't cry. I'm sorry, but you have to wake up. You made me promise." A few more tears slid down my cheeks and he pushed a straw between my lips. Instinctively, my tongue and throat worked, letting coffee slowly filter into my system. One more tear sneaked out before I wiped my face and sat up to face the day.

"Why did I make you promise?" I sniffled into my arm. We were in his house, sunlight streamed through the window and cast the room in a beautiful yellow glow. Winnie lay, four paws in the air, at my feet, her tan fur turning an auburn in the direct light. Larry had a cornflower blue comforter that made me think of fields of wheat swaying in the wind.

"Because you said you needed to go home to read the file and I said you needed sleep and my bed is more comfortable." He passed me another cup of coffee, plucking the straw from the first and placing it in the second. "So I said if you spent the night and actually rested, I would wake you up with enough time to look at the file before you had to go to work on the farm."

I glanced behind him and saw two more steaming mugs of coffee on his dresser.

The man had come prepared and I felt another tear slip between my lashes.

"OK, so I hadn't promised you. You fell asleep without objecting, please stop crying!"

His begging forced a smile onto my face and I downed the second cup of coffee. Larry replaced it with mug number three and lifted my chin to look at him. He tilted my face left, then right before dropping a kiss on my forehead.

"I bought breakfast burritos when you're ready to stand." He extended his thumbs from my chin and rubbed back and forth beneath my left eye. "I also got the binder from your office and hung an illegible sign stating you'd decided to take up being Sasquatch of the Midwest, but Mo made me take it down."

"What? Why?" He dropped his lips to mine and lingered for a minute.

"The fact you are offended she made me take down the sign is one of the reasons I'm certain I love you." He took a step back, folding his hands in front of his...

"You... have a different breakfast in mind?" All my tears were gone now and what took their place was heat, desire, and... my stomach rumbled.

"Yeah... I know better than to make you do cardio before feeding you. Come on." He tugged the hand not wrapped around a coffee mug and pulled me out of the bed. The sheet fell to the floor and I looked down at the pink dancing skeleton underwear covering me.

"Guess I should put on pants," I sighed, and he tugged me out of the room.

"No way. In this house, there are no pants at breakfast time." To prove his point, he undid the tie of his sweats and kicked them off into the hallway. He was wearing red boxers with the image of a green alien saying *Yoda One I Love*.

"Where did you get those?" I laughed and he tilted his head to look at me in a move that mirrored Winnie. "What?"

"You don't remember?" He pulled two plates from the cabinet and placed a wax paper wrapped roll on each, then two containers of red sauce, two of green, and four cups of guacamole divided evenly on each.

"Remember what?" I asked, pulling the burrito to me and uncapping all of the containers to finger paint with food. The burrito was egg, bacon, cheese, and some green leafy stuff that I accepted because of the bacon and the cheese.

"At your mom's party, we were instructed to find underwear that represents our partner. I picked those for you, you must have picked these for me, because they arrived in the same box yesterday."

I looked again at the pink skeletons I had paired with a too tight white tee that likely belonged to Larry.

"I remind you of dancing pink death?"

"I remind you of Star Wars. A movie you've never even seen, I might add."

I closed my eyes to savor the oversized mouthful of burrito and think. Larry seemed to remember way more of that night at my mom's house than I did. While knowing might bring comfort, not knowing kept me below the threshold for being committed into a psychiatric ward.

I decided I did not need to ask him for any other details I might have "forgotten".

"Pretty sure it was just the nerdiest thing I could think of under the influence," I said around the half-swallowed wad of food in my mouth. I swallowed again as I stared at the message. "Was I trying to say I love you; I love what's in your pants, or what's in your pants loves me?"

"No way to know." He bit into his burrito, and I poked the three-ring binder with the arson reports and petty thefts. While I was supposed to be reading it, it held about as much appeal as remembering that night at my mom's house.

I sighed and he tilted my chin to look at him and tapped the tip of my nose.

"But you should probably know the last one is definitely true."

I smiled as I watched Yoda's face.

"Is there such a thing as breakfast dessert?"

Larry caught my eye and grinned.

"Second breakfast?"

"Elevensies?" I countered, wiggling my eyebrows.

"And you call me a nerd. Innuendo with Lord of the Rings..."

"Are you... declining?" I asked and he shook his head.

"You have a full morning planned." He wrapped up the second half of our burritos and put them in the fridge with the salsa. "We should get started."

I slid off the chair and took his hand as we moved back to the bedroom.

"Hopefully you've brought enough food." I tugged his T-shirt over his head and threw it on the floor. "I'm starving."

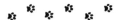

"Crap!" I grabbed the binder, Winnie's leash, the rest of my burrito, and pinched Larry's ass. "We're late, Joseph is going to kill us!"

"I can drive you to your apartment," he yawned and I shook my head.

"No, you have to get dressed to drive me to work because you're supposed to be there in ten minutes!" I bent over to check that I was wearing some version of pants and a shirt.

Larry startled and looked at his phone.

"Crap! Leave Winnie, you'll get done faster."

I dropped her leash and the binder since I wasn't reading it in the next ten minutes, kept hold of my burrito, and dashed through the front door. My feet slapped the concrete and I dropped my shoes to stuff them inside, bending down the heel like a toddler. Shuffling, I dragged my laces around the corner and froze at the crowd in front of Mo's bakery.

The air was devoid of the usual sweet smells of caramelized sugar and baked cinnamon. In its place was the acrid stench of burnt popcorn and fresh foliage. I pushed through crowds of people, desperate to find my friend and confirm the smell was not a delectable batch of baked goods she'd murdered by accident.

"Mo!" I called out, but no one so much as looked in my direction as I arrived at the scorched metal tub being doused with water.

"Mo!"

Still nothing. My eyes scanned the group for her red hair, coming up shorter than her five-foot nothing frame.

"Mo!"

"Cyn!" A voice squealed behind me, and I turned to see Mo waving at me from between the buildings.

"Are you OK?" I gasped after running to her. Grabbing her forcefully into a hug, I took the opportunity to physically check her for injuries, my hands roving in what might be considered inappropriate areas of her body. "What burned? Are the cupcakes OK?"

"I'm fine, the cupcakes and cakes are all fine," she shook her head surveying the crowd. "I was inside, preparing for the late morning crowd, listening to Avril Lavigne and singing when a metallic scrape pulled me from the back room. I walked to the front and didn't see anything so I went back to work. Chris ran into the back door and pulled me out, shouting about a fire and needing to evacuate."

"What caught fire?" I asked again, trying to peer around the corner while sniffing her. "None of you smells like it was on fire."

"You know those hideous 'repurposed' horse troughs that are being used as flower beds but the only thing the flowers are doing is taking a dirt nap because no one waters them and the sun is too direct for the varietals-"

"Mo!" I poked her in the ribs to end the gardener tangent. While I could appreciate the woman's green thumb, I needed to verify that no one was trying to murder her.

"Right. Someone pulled one of those horse trough planters in front of my shop, only I didn't see it because of the pastry counter. Then I guess someone else must have come by and set it on fire and the crowd gathered and..."

I tuned out her recount of how hot and heroic Chris had been. The first responders cleared the trough and while Mo was mid-sentence, I walked away back to the front of her building. A thinning crowd stood circled around a slightly rusted alloy trough, the top edges smeared with black soot. It was still half-full of soil, the remnants of what may have once been plants, burnt paper, and a shiny coat of something oily.

"Accelerant?" Martin appeared beside me, studying the rainbow effect of the residue. It was hard to tell if he'd just arrived or had been out canvassing and just gotten back.

"Guess you'll have to tell me," I shrugged, and the clock chimed one o' clock.

"Crap!"

I took off toward my apartment, shoes flapping. The curb came too soon, my toe caught, and I plowed face first into the concrete sidewalk.

"Geez!" A rasped voice spoke beside me and I looked up at a woman with bright green eyes in a weather worn face, holding a heavily weighted shopping tote. "Quite the fall."

My forearm swiped across my face and came away with blood. My palms were similarly afflicted, but nothing hurt bad enough to require medical attention.

"Yup," I climbed to my feet like a newborn deer and casually looked the woman over. She'd worn shapeless clothing, her hair concealed under a floral bandana, a large tote slung on her arm. Sitting at the top of the bag was an elongated glass "tree stump" from the local novelty shop, Curious Courtship. "Did you buy..."

But I couldn't finish the sentence without asking an old woman if she'd intentionally purchased a glass dildo. I firmly believed people should be comfortable talking openly about sex and purchasing exploratory aids, I just didn't want them talking about it openly with me.

My phone alarmed and I remembered the time.

"Crap. Have a good day!"

I dropped my keys twice trying to insert them into the lock. Blood smeared from the scrapes on my palms, and a trail of blood followed me into the building, up the stairs, and through the door to my living space. Stuck for time, I stripped, rinsed in the shower for two minutes with soap, grabbed the nearest clean clothes, threw snacks and water in my backpack, and was back in front of my building when Larry pulled up in his truck with Winnie.

"Are you bleeding?" he asked when I climbed in, Winnie set about licking my face clean of the newest hemoglobin deposits like the velociraptor she pretended not to be.

"I had a gravitational incident, it's fine. We need to go." I gestured for him to get moving and he accelerated slowly past the remnants of the crowd still gathered in front of Mo's. "Who would burn a planter full of soil?"

My voice came out quiet. Larry didn't seem to have heard me, so I watched Martin work as we passed. Behind him, admiring the view was...

"What the hell?" Larry looked over at me, but he didn't slow. "How is Phil standing there?"

"What do you mean? Despite his interest in crafting for the boudoir, he's as much of a gawker as the rest of this town." Larry turned left, and I lost sight of Phil ogling the federal agents' assets.

"Yeah, but he owns the novelty shop." I shifted in my seat to face out of the windshield as Larry accelerated. "Does anyone work for him?"

"Who would work for him? And why?"

It was a valid question, but I couldn't move past the curiosity.

If Phil was in front of Mo's, how did that old lady have one of his "tree stumps"?

Chapter Twelve: Adjusting Focus

I banged my head against the door and let out a small sob.

"Come on! This is ridiculous!" My hand wrapped around the door handle and I pulled with my full weight, but it didn't move. The door stayed put as I pulled harder and harder, lost my grip, and landed flat on my ass in front of the Sweet Pea Credit Union. Sitting in the window was a handwritten sign that said they were closed so Kelsey could run an errand.

"Do you really think sitting there is a worthwhile use of your time?"

A man in his mid-thirties stood there, looking down at me. Despite having been born and raised here, I'd made it a point not to learn everyone's name and face. So, while the man was probably not a stranger, I wouldn't have picked him out of a line-up even if given his name, rank, and serial number.

"I don't think my time is worth as much as you think, but I appreciate the vote of confidence. Can I help you?"

The last two days had been a blur. While my plan had been to study the arson binder, there had been no opportunities between the people coming in to confess themselves as the arsonist, people calling me to ask about the YouTube video and asking after Winnie, and rushing to the farm to conduct rounds and not incur the wrath of Joseph.

Frankly, I was starting to wonder if someone had sent a memo to slowly torture me with human interaction until I petered out like an acid/base reaction. Baking soda volcanos have nothing on an introvert subjected to unnecessary human interaction without a reasonable excuse to beg off.

"No, but I think I can help you," he looked at the sidewalk, hiked up his slacks, and sat cross-legged beside me. The blue and gray argyle socks looked mildly ridiculous with his plain white sneakers, but my socks had crocodiles eating frogs on them, so who was I to judge?

"I heard you're looking for my grandparents... and my parents. Or at least you were. Is that still true?"

"Maybe?" I scrubbed my hands over my face and stared at the locked credit union door. Despite it being 10AM on Saturday and the facility supposedly being open until one, it seemed unlikely I'd get a new debit card printed in the next ten minutes, which was how long I was willing to sit here and talk to this man before taking this situation into my own hands.

This situation being my current state of destitution and deprivation at the hands of Amazon. My recurring snack and coffee order had been denied because I'd never updated my card information after canceling the first. I was out of cheese crackers and Oreos.

Though not yet out of coffee, the world was in danger if this wasn't rectified soon.

"Are you planning to rob the credit union?" I looked back at the man. He had laugh lines around his mouth and eyes, dark hair, bright eyes, and a complexion that could have been descended from any country between Asia and Egypt.

"No, I just need Cheese-its," a sigh escaped. "Who are your parents or grandparents?"

"The Jensen's? I'm Justin Jensen, my family and I came to check on my parents' house and the neighbors told me you had asked to be contacted if anyone came back to the house." He looked concerned and interested at the same time. "I told them I'd find you."

"None of the neighbors ever even talked to me," I frowned, and his ears went slightly pink.

"They heard you shouting at Daniel when he got there. They were... relieved you weren't bleeding but not curious enough to risk getting details of the party the night before." His whole face flushed, and I sat dumbstruck.

"I completely forgot. It's been a rough few days."

"That's what I heard." Justin broke into a wide grin and my eyes narrowed.

"Do we... know each other?"

"We do not. I was in the same grade as Seth, but my nephew went to school with you. Robert Kim? Someone tried to call him an offensive racial slur and you accidentally pushed her into horse poop... which the teachers bought because you fell in it too."

The memory was vaguely familiar. I certainly remembered Robert Kim, but I fell in a lot of horse poop accidentally on purpose. Though not as mentionable, I'd had a small crush on his nephew but we hadn't really hung out. The fancy had taken flight into casual friendship when he appeared a bit too flushed after seeing Daniel Kirby in the locker room and gushed about the man's muscular perfection.

Turns out our physical interests in romance were misaligned.

Justin had aged better than Seth... or at least that was what I planned on telling my brother as I mentally reframed Justin as in his forties.

"Do you know where your... parents are?" I decided to start with the homeowners and work my way up generationally. If he said his grandparents were still playing sex slaves in my parent's basement, I was changing my name and moving to Canada... assuming the Canadian government had forgotten about the whole poutine moose incident.

"Yeah, with my grandparents. They'll be home tonight. What did you want to ask them?"

Relief flooded me, two questions with one perfectly ordinary answer that wouldn't keep me up at night.

"The neighbors told you about the fire?" I asked, wondering why he hadn't offered where they'd been or an explanation for their absence after the initial relief at their whereabouts.

147

"Yeah, and that you were accused but then cleared and now you're investigating it. Seems my grandparents and your parents travel in similar circles, and those circles may have been... overlapping."

The man shuddered and I gaped.

"Oh my dog, your parents and grandparents aren't at... like the same *event* are they?"

"No! Geez!" His face went pale, then red, and finally he laughed. "They are at a silent retreat. It was planned before the fire, my parent's solution to spending time with my dad's family without hearing any... details. They don't come up from Florida often, but my parents like to go into their visits with a plan to hear as little about their lives as possible. I got the impression they were pretty surly the night my grandparents arrived. Some sort of incident with locked doors and..."

His ears went pink and I decided the story could end there.

"Where is this retreat?" Spending time with my parents in absolute silence was a creative solution to a problem I'd only recently discovered. Of course, I'd have to give up crunchy snacks and pray the resort wouldn't let them give silent demonstrations.

"Michigan. The thumb of the mitten, as my mom put it. She's sent me pictures." He tried to pass me his phone.

"Dude, no way." I crab walked away from him and the device.

"What? They're just pictures. Meditating, canoeing..." His eyes went up from his phone and he studied my face. "They have clothes on!"

Grudgingly, I accepted the phone and studied the images. His grandparents seemed to have aged well, their grays less prominent in their dark hair, their skin remaining near the bones of their faces and necks. Reluctantly, I tried to pull up their images from that night and sifted through the sea of faces.

In my parent's crowd, the elder Jensen's would have stood out. After getting into the sweats and sitting in the circle, there'd been an open forum of questions. They'd offered advice about the effects of humidity on personal body lubrication and... I'd told them to get something from my pants in the basement when my mom wouldn't let me leave the room. Something... situationally relevant...

"They borrowed my lip balm, which I refused to take back after I saw their banana demonstration," I shuddered and felt my chin drop against my chest. "They probably didn't take my wallet."

"You thought they did?" He looked puzzled and I shrugged as I caught sight of Kelsey coming back across the street. Standing, I brushed my hands down my pants and offered Justin some assistance to his feet.

"Not really, it was just one possible explanation that would cover the Florida matches and my wallet at the fire. But they wouldn't have still been here for the dumpster or the planter fire, and those were also started with matches from a swinger's bar in Florida."

"Which bar?" Justin tilted his head to the side, and I wondered if he had a dog at home.

"Gator Gates." He chewed his lip and I nodded at Kelsey as she opened the door.

"My grandparents own the Gator Gates... Should I call you when they arrive?"

I studied my shoes and then the grime under my nails as I pondered whether or not I actually wanted to see them.

"Could you just have them call me?"

"I thought interviews go better in person? Aren't they suspects?" His head tilted again and I resisted the urge to ruffle his hair and give him a scratch under the chin.

"Yes and no. I suspect they can probably explain the matches, but I also don't want to see anything else explained." Even though I wasn't sure what I meant, he seemed to allow the statement to stand. Likely he too had been on the wrong end of a familial demonstration.

"OK, I'll have them call you." I stuck a hand in my bag and pulled out a piece of paper with my name and cell phone number. Normal professionals would have ordered business cards, but I was neither normal nor professional, so I wrote my number on little pieces of paper I kept in my bag.

"By the way, did you know 'Cyn Sharp Disasters' is a popular search term online?" His question threw me off and I nearly dropped my slip of paper before he could remove it from my hand.

"What?" Kelsey let out a snicker and moved inside. An older couple passed, and a young mother entered the credit union with two of her offspring. I was no longer in a hurry to go inside.

Children were very vocal about how boring they found financial institutions, and my personal feelings toward the place did not need support. At the same time... my gaze drifted back to the man.

No good could come from hearing his words.

"Oh yeah, you're practically internet famous." He turned his phone toward me again, but I waved it off.

"People should be paying me," I grumbled, knowing that if I wanted payment for my humiliation I'd have to post at least some of it myself... or worse: talk about it and allow questions. "How is it that my parents can do naked senior citizen intercourse drawing in the park and remain off the internet, but you get one bull stuck in a building and you end up trending?"

"I think it was your bosses tear away pants that were more interesting," Justin offered and I chewed my lip in an effort not to scream. The last thing I wanted was my name associated with a man in a neon green thong on a farm.

"The internet is stupid."

"Everyone loves the internet until they're trending on it for all the wrong reasons." The man looked sage and I wanted to seek his wisdom, but I doubted his family and life experience differed greatly from mine.

"I guess. If you could happen to get a condensed version of what happened from your grandparents... could you maybe just text me a summary?"

It was a longshot he'd do it, but the senior Jensen's weren't really suspects, not anymore. If they had been gone since just after the first fire, they were out of the picture for the remaining two that were directly linked and the one that might have been a prank... or a frame job. Hard to say.

Also, no one would commit arson with matches from their own bar unless they were incredibly stupid or criminal masterminds.

"Scared they might want to chat about the party?"

"Scared they might try and make me remember the party... or return my lip balm. Also, the banana..."

He held up his hand to stop the words from leaving my mouth.

"TMI. I got you on this one."

The young woman walked out of the bank practically being dragged by her pint-sized humans. Holding the door, I looked back at Justin once more.

"I guess I'll see you later. If you talk to Robert, tell him I say hi." I waved and wandered into the bank to get my debit card reprinted and stock up on snacks.

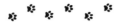

The grocery store was more than I had energy for, but I took my new debit card anyway. Amazon next day was useful only if you could make it to the next day. I pushed my cart through the meat aisle and stared at the chicken breasts.

"Hard to believe that can actually turn into food that tastes good."

Beside me was a man with a dark tan, weather worn face, and clothes that looked second hand. The faded gray ball cap on his head may have once been black, the sports team logo unrecognizable.

"Hard to believe someone looked at a chicken and thought, *huh, that could be food*," I agreed, picking up the Styrofoam package and moving down to the ground beef.

"I've wondered that about a lot of things. Who saw animals nursing off their mothers and thought *let me get a hit of that*?" He grabbed his own package of ground beef and waved as he walked away. Without meaning to, I stared after him with a sudden fear of how cheese was discovered and fixated on his boots.

They had turquoise accents, but he didn't look Native American. Unconsciously, I followed him through the store and grabbed things at random, grateful he needed things only from aisles I actually shopped in. The coffee aisle took my full focus, and I was so entranced reading every bag that when I looked up he was gone, and I tried to shrug off the sense that I'd lost at a game of hide and go seek.

"What am I doing?" I sighed at myself and studied my cart. There were cookies, crackers, chips, meat, veggies, starches... I was probably done after I threw six bags of coffee on top of it and strolled to the dairy case for coffee modifiers, lunch meat, and sliced cheese.

There was easily forty pounds of food in my cart and I was going to have to either carry it two blocks back to my apartment or admit defeat and call a ride share. Neither was particularly appealing, so I decided to flip a coin and decide after checkout.

Declaring my mission to be complete, I pushed the cart toward the front, picking an open register without much enthusiasm.

Unloading the cart, I was surprised by how many bags of frozen vegetables my brain thought I needed. Either auto-pilot Cyn was super healthy, or I anticipated an urgent need for ready-made ice packs.

"How did you end up here? Sweet Pea is nothing like New Mexico."

My ears perked and I glanced over my shoulder to see the man with turquoise accented boots smiling at the young girl with blue highlights popping bright pink bubble gum.

"Oh, we're just passing through," he commented, seeming to notice me watching and trying to take his ID back from the cashier.

"We?" the girl asked and I tried to get a glance at her face.

"My brother and I. We're traveling across the country." He sacked up his groceries and made a beeline for the sliding doors.

Abandoning my groceries for the moment, I tried to run after him and froze in the doorway to see him closing the back door on a faded red hatchback after tossing a half dozen bags inside.

"Wait!" I called out to him, but the cashier grabbed my arm and tried to pull me back into the store.

"Lady, you have to pay for groceries!"

I shook him off and took two steps into the lot, just catching the first two characters of an Arizona license plate.

Chapter Thirteen:
Lean and Mean

"You know how to cook?" Marine Man was sitting, aghast, on one of the two barstools against the counter of my kitchen. While the whole apartment was maybe four hundred square feet, the kitchen was two counters four feet apart. One with a sink and a cut-out for a fridge in the other. Four cabinets on each side and enough outlets for my facsimile of cooking appliances were all that sat in the space directly beside my quasi-living room.

"Yeah, I *am* an adult," I closed the George Foreman on the chicken breast, threw some frozen French fries in the air fryer and a bag of frozen green beans in the microwave. My skin crawled at my declaration, I was so not ready to be an adult.

"What does being an adult have to do with cooking?" He leaned over and took in the ten square foot kitchen. "Everyone I talked to said you can't cook."

"I can cook, I *don't* cook."

"That's not what they said."

"Who is *they*?" I scowled at his gesture of the world at large.

"Well, surprise! I can cook, I just don't. Not for other people. It keeps expectations low and reduces the probability someone will ask me to be a barefoot in the kitchen, knocked up wife. There aren't enough food options in this town to *not* be able to cook. I mean seriously, who lives off of diner food, pizza, and pastries?"

Martin raised a guilty hand.

I climbed off my soapbox and shook the air fryer basket.

"Where is your range?"

"There isn't a range in Sweet Pea, you'll have to drive to Dayton, but they aren't open right now." I lamented my lack of night shooting options. Despite my constant state of tiredness, I preferred to be active at night and asleep during the day.

"No, your gas range? How are you supposed to bake bread and cookies?"

I stared at him for signs it was a joke, but he seemed genuinely concerned there would be no fresh baked dessert.

Resisting the urge to smack him, I poured the freshly brewed coffee on ice and added a pound of flavored liquid sugar to it.

"There isn't one. Hence, I have an air fryer, a George Foreman grill, an instant pot, and a microwave. Can you focus? Are there any stolen vehicles or license plates that match the beginning of the one on that red car? Do you think they stole a bunch of plates with the car to cold plate it?"

The caffeine hit my system and my leg bounced. My whole body felt like it had ants crawling on it: twitchy and restless. I really should have eaten something besides coffee and pizza today, but I hadn't and I needed real food.

It had been a day that didn't need anymore frivolous delays and questions.

After grocery shopping, I'd needed to get Winnie food and human toilet paper. On the way back from Costco in my Lyft, my mom had called and insisted I come over. Her message claimed there was a family emergency, all hands on deck... it had been a lie.

Inside the glass paneled, blue trimmed front door of my childhood home, was a nightmare.

Their great emergency had been a need for finger foods and an "alternate perspective". More than half of their senior swingers' club was there with men and women in their early twenties. Apparently, my parents had retired from being university professors to become adjunct faculty at the community college two towns over. There was a demand for a class on active sex-lives in your twilight years with an open forum for discussion.

My purpose had been to restock the snacks and look horrified at being asked to demonstrate what a "prude" was.

Unfortunately, the Jensen's had arrived and volunteered their explicit stories of the lost evening. While I had learned that they'd brought nearly a thousand matchbooks with them to Sweet Pea to promote their bar, the whole bag had gone missing shortly after they arrived. I'd spent hours with Winnie re-tracing the steps they'd taken the day of their arrival, before I gave up and came home.

Where Marine Man was waiting with a bag of coffee, the report from the fire in front of Mo's, and no fresh ideas of his own.

"You read too many crime novels. No one really cold plates a car." I bobbed my head and shook the air fryer basket, right foot bouncing on the ground. "Are you high right now?"

"Nope. Sleep deprived and over-caffeinated. Also, it's late and I've seen a lot of naked old people today and was questioned about the changes in erogenous zones as you age. Did you know almost thirty is ancient to the average college student? They asked if I needed muscle rub and anti-inflammatories when my knee popped." I dumped fries, chicken, and green beans on two plates and stuck one in front of Marine Man. I threw a handful of green beans and a fry into Winnie's bowl.

"Do you?"

My eyes attempted to murder him, but there was no conviction behind it.

"I always need anti-inflammatories. Muscle rub is obsolete with sticky patches like Salonpas."

Winnie trotted over and gobbled up her treat while the federal agent poked the chicken on the plate in front of him as though it were alive.

"I didn't poison it." I stabbed some fries on my fork with green beans, swiped it in mustard, and ate the whole bite.

"It's just... this was raw meat and now it's food..." He took a tentative bite.

"That's how cooking works. Didn't you get basic life skills in the Marine Corps?" I took a bite of my chicken and chewed slowly. I hadn't put much on it, a sprinkle of garlic pepper and a healthy helping of peppercorns. It was good, not my most spectacular chicken, but it didn't warrant the expression on his face.

I had never cooked for another person before and the look of apprehension on his face was a good justification as for why.

"No... There was a gold digger class..." He ate some fries and green beans. His eating took on speed until he was wolfing the contents down like Winnie at breakfast time. I wanted to feel elated that someone liked my cooking, but I was more disappointed I'd wasted my cooking skills on him. Larry should have been the first man I cooked for and something like guilt mixed with razor blades churned in my gut, stealing my appetite.

Martin the Marine Man Bermudez picked up his plate and licked it clean, effectively stroking my ego free of guilt.

"Geez! Dude, are you starving?"

"No, it's just... I travel a lot. I haven't had a meal that wasn't fried, covered in gravy, or that contained a vegetable, protein, and starch in a long time..." He eyed the air fryer and I dumped half the remaining fries on his plate. "Thanks."

"No problem." I carried my plate to the couch and sat down beside the blue binder. It was the first opportunity I had to look at it and I wasn't sure if I should admit that to him or not. Moving the book to the coffee table beside my plate, I flipped to the summary page of the first linked fire.

An old car in salvage had a small fire in the trunk. Most of the gawkers were quoted as saying they always knew the place would catch fire. Mr. Bright was suspected of starting the fire, since he was the only person who operated and had access to the yard. He was cleared when it was discovered the lock on the fence was dummy locked and anyone could walk in.

Interesting to me was the fire itself. Whoever had started it took a metal hubcap and placed it in the spare wheel cavity, starting the fire inside the metal confines. Mr. Bright couldn't state what the trunk looked like before, but the investigator noted that it looked like the carpeting had been removed, finding clean cut scraps nearby.

Curious, I flipped to the next report and the two after.

Every fire in the town had been started away from anything that would catch and spread. A map of the fires provided by this first investigator showed the fires were always just off the main strip of shops. All of them had been started with matches from businesses around town and all of them had taken little to extinguish, but it was noted that the scenes caused quite the outpouring of curious observers.

The fires in the next town were the same. Designed not to spread, started with matches from bars, and just off the main street in town. Four reports later, the first fire had been during the night, a fair distance from the main street. Each subsequent fire in that town followed the same patterns as the first.

Then the pattern was to always start a night fire before the first daytime fire.

What also struck me was the dates stamped on the reports. He'd just gotten them the day after the Jensen's shed fire.

"That's weird," I said, poking my plate with my fork and coming up blank. I glanced over and saw that I'd eaten my whole plate of food while I read. "The pattern changed. When did you get these?"

I looked at him to see a shrug as he slipped his plate into the sink.

"Picked up copies as I went through town investigating," I cocked my head, examining the stamped dates a second time and let it go.

Maybe he'd needed new copies.

Switching back to the map I'd made, I studied the two towns between which the pattern changed. According to the step by step instructions, the two towns were nearly three hundred miles apart. Every town prior had been maybe seventy-five miles apart.

"Give me your phone?" I held out my hand to Martin without looking at him. He placed the miniature computer in my hand and I looked up the area between the towns. There were three small communities in between and no mention of them in the theft reports or the arson reports. "Why did they skip these three?"

Marine Man looked over my shoulder, studying the map on his phone and comparing it to the map I'd printed.

"Maybe they're named but there's nothing there? Or they're ghost towns?" I clicked on one in the map app and it pulled up a picture. Though there wasn't much besides dust and a handful of businesses, including a gas station and a bar, it was still a viable town with residents. The next two were the same, the third being larger than the first two by at least one order of magnitude but still smaller than Sweet Pea.

"What state is that?" he asked, and I zoomed out until the stretch of highway was labeled.

"Southern Utah." I flipped to the summary. "You don't have Utah here. Did you not contact Utah?"

"I didn't contact anybody. These were brought to us." He studied the map and the path of travel. Again, I questioned why he'd do a public records request for replacement files and not check if there were more just in case. "Did they travel west into Arizona first, cross into Utah, and then hit Colorado?"

"There's only one county in that bottom corner of Utah. San Juan?" I squinted at an image of the labeled counties. "Couldn't you just call them?"

Without waiting for his answer, I searched San Juan County Sheriff's Department and came up with a phone number. Google informed me the non-emergency option was "closed now" and I checked my watch.

It was ten here, so it was... eight there?

Also, still Saturday. So, there was nothing to do until at least Monday. I grabbed a receipt from between the couch cushions and scribbled the number and a note reminding myself to call San Juan County Monday. I started to search the name of the towns with the word arson, just to see if the news had picked up a story he'd missed.

"Did you call the vehicle owner's kid?" I tucked the receipt into the front cover of the binder.

"Yeah... she wasn't very forthcoming."

I glanced up at his face with a raised eyebrow.

"She implied that I was an arrogant jackass who wasn't worth explaining crap to." He stared down at his hands, entwining and releasing his fingers. "I may have approached the conversation wrong."

"May have?" I challenged, abandoning my search and looking up the number to call .

"Did you not get the hint the first time?" A woman practically seethed into the line and my eyes widened at Martin.

"Hi, my name is Cyn. I'm trying to help find out who is starting fires in my town. I'm the one who recommended Marine Man call you." He corrected his name as Martin in the background and I rolled my eyes. "Your dad sold an old red hatchback with Arizona plates?"

She sighed as though I were a pain in her butt and I tried not to do the same.

"Yes. And I hire ex-cons so you think one of them bought the car off my semi-blind dad and started roving the country starting fires."

"No. I think maybe they could know someone who knows someone? You don't sound like the type of person who would hire anyone who wasn't ready to be done with whatever led them to crime in the first place, Ms...." I stared at the folder and blanked.

"Mrs. Adams." I could hear her moving around on the other end, the tap of metal on ceramic. "Look, I'm not sure how familiar you are with Las Vegas, New Mexico, but you have to take what you can get out here. There isn't a lot here and what there is, isn't very alluring to the regular Joes. The biggest building is a detention center. Everyone here knows someone who knows someone."

I fiddled with the pen on my coffee table, trying to frame the next question in an open-ended way that wouldn't offend the Adams woman.

"What sort of charges usually get sent there?" Maybe they'd be known for fire bugs and fans of larceny.

"Mostly drugs and immigration," she responded with what sounded like a shrug. "Ms. Sharp, there's not a lot out here that could, or would, burn. It's hot and dry. Anything that could have caught fire already has been burned by the sun."

"How many people do you employ? Is your shop a popular stop for the recently released? Do you do active recruitment?" I wasn't sure my ultimate goal with this line of questioning, but it would give me an idea of how connected she was to the community.

Instead of answering, she let out a long and exasperated sigh.

"Ms. Sharp, I hire people to fix cars. They come to me, I verify their skills, and I don't ask questions. It's not a business strategy as much as it is a means to an end. Out here, you can't be picky. You hire someone who wants to work and hope they don't rob you blind."

"Have you been robbed?" I nearly leapt at the possibility of a lead.

"No, Ms. Sharp. I'm a decent judge of character. I send away anyone I don't trust."

"When was the last time you sent someone away and they didn't take it well?" I flipped back to the first page of the binder and decided to clarify my question. "Did you send anyone away in August of last year that was especially upset about it?"

Another sigh followed by a shuffle of papers. I heard a file cabinet drawer open and close, something heavy get set on a hollow surface, and a door close.

"August.... August..." She spoke more to herself than me and I waited anxiously for the answer. "Yeah, there was a man in August, his brother worked here. His brother had come from the lock-up but I didn't get the impression the second man had. The Martelle brothers, Ivan and Irvine. Ivan was the one who already worked here, brother showed up in turquoise accented boots demanding a job and accommodations for his lifestyle."

"What happened?" I asked, picturing the man from earlier stomping his cowboy boots like a child.

"I asked him to leave, his brother followed, and a few days later I got a nasty letter in the mail. Handed it all over to the cops and moved on," I could hear Mrs. Adams typing on her keyboard in the background. She had either gone back to work or was attempting to not-so-subtly ask me to leave her alone.

"Sorry, just one last question and I'll let you go. What did the note say?"

The woman huffed out a breath.

"It said 'Everything you worked for will go up in flames'."

Chapter Fourteen:
Foraging

I t is impossible to go back on a promise to the parents of
children.

No matter how tired, busy, or on the verge of a breakdown
you are, parents will not let you cancel taking away their children.
The children themselves may not want to go, but parents spend
months dreaming of when they can pawn their offspring off on
an easily manipulated friend or family member.

Apparently, my wedding gift to Carla and Seth had been
promising them a kid free weekend. To make it extra special, I'd
promised that kid free weekend would be somewhere no one
could see the children's dramatic behavior and contact them to
complain. While I had been assured they would be little angels, I
didn't purchase snake oil or anything labeled "as seen on TV" so

they leveled with me and said I needed to take them somewhere no one would hear them scream. Since the only place I knew for certain it was possible to hide children from Nosey Nellys was in the woods, I'd booked two nights of camping two hours away while Carla and Seth watched. They verified that there were restrooms and running water. I requested a day off of work before they gratefully hugged me.

Unfortunately, I then immediately and completely forgot about the plan.

Forgot until Seth appeared at my apartment at six in the morning with two kids, two kid sleeping bags, two backpacks with their clothes, and a hundred dollars to ensure they would not starve. When I tried to beg off, he'd threatened to replace all of my birth control with Tic-tacs so I could learn the truly desperate measures parents will go to for a moment of quiet.

Then Larry showed up because *he* remembered the plan and I grouchily packed the Jeep Seth had returned. My brother drove off with his new wife in their car, excitedly going on about their relaxing plans at a nearby resort.

Plans that they either still needed to pack for or that didn't require clothing because the trunk was completely empty.

Everyone loaded into the Jeep, and I stared blankly at the road ahead.

"Probably we need food?"

Larry took me back to the grocery store and refused to get out of the car. I meandered aisles and tried to think of child friendly food without risking the kids getting scurvy because I neglected basic nutrients.

"Do kids eat hot dogs and sandwiches?" I asked the woman behind the register. I'd left the kids sleeping in the Jeep, Winnie and Larry watching over them with drooping eyelids while I tried to wrap my mind around the fact that grocery stores were open at this hour.

Who needed to buy food at 7AM on a Sunday?

"What?" She removed an earbud and I tilted my head.

"Do you... just wear those all day?"

She rolled her eyes as though I were an old, obtuse Karen in need of public shaming on the internet.

"Yeah. It's not like anyone says anything I need to hear. Like, if there's a fire, the lights will go blinky or whatever." She scanned the sandwich supplies, the hot dog buns, and condiments. She moved on to the variety pack bags of chips, s'mores supplies, and bags of ice while I considered if headphones would work on the farm to drown out Joseph's yelling.

Probably not, there were no lights to signal fire and we didn't have a visual alarm for when someone was about to be trampled.

"Are you going camping?"

At least my selections were on par with expectation, though I'd admittedly bought nearly all of these same things yesterday for myself. There were fewer vegetables and nothing that needed to remain consistently cold to prevent food poisoning, but my fridge was well-stocked with these same staples.

Normally, when Winnie and I went camping we planned weeks in advance. Food was chopped and prepared, every meal was planned out and hiking trails were looked up. I had never once wandered into the woods without a clear plan for the entire journey, entertainment, food, and relaxation all scheduled down to the minute.

Suffice to say, the Army had ruined my ability to find pleasure in the unknown.

Now, I was trying to throw together a kid-friendly camping trip with no driver's license, prep-work, or ideas on what one did with children in the woods that wouldn't land us on one of those Jackass shows or in the emergency room.

"Yup," I swiped my card and grabbed my bags. She stared blankly at the tray of vegetables on the belt.

"Who are those for?"

"Humans." I scooped up the tray and she blinked. "Maybe a few carrots for my fur child."

"Vegetable platters are gross."

"Good thing you're not coming with me then," I grumbled, hauling everything out to the car. Everyone was asleep and I dumped the ice in the cooler, added the cold food, and stared blankly at the supplies. The whole cargo area was full, but I was still pretty sure we'd need more. I had zero sparklers, pop rocks, or pyrotechnics to entertain the kids and the grocery store was fresh out of glow sticks and tree décor.

"Probably we'll be fine."

Winnie snorted from where she was sprawled half on each of Seth's kids.

"You don't think we'll be fine?"

Larry opened his eyes from where he sat on the driver's side.

"I think you shouldn't take life advice from a sleeping dog. Hop in," he yawned, and I crawled into the passenger seat.

Noticing my cup, I chugged the coffee I'd brought from home. "Got everything?"

"Probably not, but we'll make it work," I yawned back at him and he took my hand across the center console. "Into the woods."

Which unfortunately was an invitation for everyone to start singing.

Six hours later, I understood Lord of the Flies.

Children let loose outside of society were absolutely savage, and Winnie was the kid who led them with violent outbursts to kill the kid with glasses.

Probably I needed to reread the classics and pass on the spicy romance more often, or I'd have planned this trip somewhere with padded walls and no sharp objects.

We'd made it through three renditions of "Into the Woods" with vocal scores somewhere between Idina Menzel and Scuttle before the wee beasties fell back asleep. Sadly, Seth's kids woke up again just before Larry parked the Jeep and immediately started complaining when they burst into the woods like banshees.

"I need to potty!"

"He's touching me!"

"Nature is stupid!"

"There's no cell service here!"

I considered begging Larry to drive away and leave them there. Winnie took off to herd them back into the campsite, and I unloaded the tent. Resigned to the knowledge I wouldn't leave my best girl behind, I started making camp. Larry brought out two sets of noise canceling headphones and stuck a pair on my head.

I knew there was a reason I loved him.

Fifteen minutes in, the headphones were useless, and I needed a cyanide capsule. Winnie stole the tent bag with the rain fly. After I got it back, Sylvia stole a tent pole to joust with her unarmed brother. Erich threw a pinecone at her head in self-defense, which led to a throw down brawl. Both started shouting and throwing bits of nature at each other while I retrieved the tent pole and built our temporary shelter, deciding that the cops could arrest whichever child survived for murder. Winnie took a flying leap after a thrown pinecone and collapsed the tent again moments before it was erect.

I couldn't help it, I screamed.

"I am sending all of you to live on Alcatraz Island!" I shouted but no one could hear me as Winnie began to howl in time to Sylvia's volume eleven rendition of "Let It Go".

I searched the Jeep for duct tape and /or a muzzle, but it would seem I hadn't packed either.

"Should I be concerned about the look on your face?" Larry said, getting out of his camp chair to help me. I'd insisted a dozen times I didn't need his help, but apparently watching me throw a rubber mallet at a tree meant it was time for him to join the children in the "not listening to Cyn" game.

"That depends. How good are you at lying?"

"Not very. What would I be lying about?" He nabbed Winnie by her collar before she could take down the tent a second time. He gave her a treat, faced her head toward a squirrel and watched her take off between two pines.

"You'd be telling my brother his children were eaten by bears and I felt so guilty I couldn't possibly come home." I hammered the metal stake into the ground with a nearby rock. "But really, I will have tied them to a tree covered in bear food and started my community of Sasquatch people in the Midwest."

"What if instead you just take this," he removed the rock from my hand and replaced it with a flask. "And this."

Cookies went into my cargo pockets along with some Cheese-Its and two bottles of water.

"And go for a soothing, drunken nature walk... for the next however many hours it takes you to stop plotting child murders."

Larry concluded his statement by tugging a hat on my head and dousing me with bug spray. I eyed Winnie with the little beasts and shuddered. I never knew fur kids and offspring had so many similarities... and propensities toward chaos.

"Who will keep them from murdering you?"

"I'll be fine," he promised and gave me a quick kiss before patting my butt. "Off you go before you wind up in jail."

He didn't need to tell me twice.

The screams of my niece and nephew followed me up the road. After a quick stop at the bathroom, I took a long hit from the flask and meandered to a brown sign.

"Rainbow Falls, two miles," I read, looking at the arrow pointing to a wooden bridge over a small creek. The path curved between two trees and out of sight, looking like the perfect place to hide from screaming children. "Should we?"

I looked to my side and blinked.

Right, no Winnie. The dog had been too busy playing overlord of the small minions to be interested in hiking.

Without her opinion, I decided it must be a good idea. Another pull from the flask and I started across the bridge with my eyes closed to absorb the sudden quiet. Nature, no matter what I had been forced to bring with me, would always be my happy place. The scent of trees, wind moving through the pine needles... it was magic on earth.

Though I'd forgotten the reservation, a quick check showed most of the campground was still available. The occupied slots were for glampers and not located close enough to the tent spots that the kids would be a bother to those who enjoyed the great outdoors in traveling houses.

With electricity, and television, and private restrooms... Why did people look down on glampers again?

My climb was gentle, allowing my thoughts to wander. I was curious if Sylvia had killed Erich or Larry. More curious how one decided to drive through small towns and start fires. Who benefitted from that? The town, the fire-starters... who really stood to win from burning sheds and the trunks of cars?

All thoughts ceased when the trail took on an upward pitch. I paused to catch my breath and switched from tequila to water.

My thoughts moved to the surroundings and I paused to study the beauty around me.

Ohio only has six types of conifers, and the scent told me these were pine and juniper. Beneath them grew deciduous trees with arching branches that completely shielded the trail from the sun. The heat wave had broken to a mild spring, but in the shade of the trees, it felt colder.

I shivered and kept climbing, staggering slightly from side to side with the drunken exertion.

As I neared what must be the top, the trees grew further apart. Rocks replaced the dirt embankment to my right, scrub oaks and other sun loving trees peppering the surface until I burst into the sunlight just below the ridge. Beside me, the trees cascaded down the side of the mountain in a vibrant rainbow of greenery and I felt my whole body floating forward as I looked down the ridge.

Then quickly backed up to press against the rocks before I tumbled to my doom.

A car door slammed and dirt crunched somewhere above me.

"I still don't understand why you brought that piece of junk," a male voice carried from above me and I tried not to scream at the intrusion.

"It's a primitive fire starter," a second male voice grumbled and a light rain of gravel scattered down the embankment beside me.

"Why would we need a primitive fire starter? We have kerosene, butane, paper, wood... five million things that make starting fires easier than flint with a metal striker," the first voice got louder and another small cascade of gravel preceded the appearance of feet swinging over the ledge. "I mean seriously, you stole it in high school. Move on."

A stream of sunlight glinted off the turquoise accents in the man's boots and I felt my breath freeze in my throat. I was no longer Cheryl Strayed in *Wild*, I was Harriet the Spy, eavesdropping on ne'er do wells in the woods.

"You weren't complaining in Utah when it saved us from freezing to death."

A second set of feet hung beside the first. Tan work boots, scuffed and covered in paint. The shoes were at odds with each other and it felt imperative that I know if the faces matched.

"Utah was over a thousand miles ago. We've evolved, gotten better at eliminating threats. Our skills and talents have grown. Soon, we'll have everything we need to finish the project." The cowboy boots dangled, and the men above went quiet.

My ears strained but I heard no new sounds. What did eliminating threats mean?

Did they just confess to murder?

I inched along the rock, back down the way I had come. A few yards before the emergence, I'd seen a deer path cutting up toward what must be a road. If one of them had murdered someone... I still needed to know if the faces matched the boots.

"I still don't understand why this is so needlessly complicated. We don't need to..." the voice cut off as the trees enveloped me again and I tried to move quickly to the deer path. Mission Impossible played in my head and I held my breath waiting to take the whole thing seriously.

Possibly they are murderers, I thought, moving my feet as quietly as possible and hearing every twig snap.

Maybe they're arsonists, somehow there was no fear.

What if they're both and they see you? The first sense that this might be a bad idea filled my head. Everything was slightly off center and I stumbled on a tree root, scraping open my hand on a jagged rock.

Probably why drinking and hiking are frowned upon, laughing awkwardly, I wiped the blood off on my shirt. Back upright, I let my fingertips drag along the embankment until I spotted the path. It was steep and more of a climb than I was capable of in my current condition, but I took hold of two shrubs and tugged myself up onto a small plateau. Above it was an even steeper slope and I turned around to crab walk up the hill. My hope was it would limit my ability to fall to my death and not see it coming.

In actuality, my feet were alarmingly far away while I was standing and sitting seemed like a safer distance from the ground.

Two car doors slammed and I tried to hurry. No longer concerned with stealth, I let sand and rocks fall on and around me, ripping small plants from their perches as I struggled toward the still out of sight roadway that I had no real guarantee would be there.

I gripped asphalt as an engine caught and heaved myself onto the shoulder of the road just in time to see a red hatchback pulling away from a turnout, flipping a U-turn, and speeding off down the mountain.

"Ugh," I grumbled, staggering down the shoulder until I could see the remnants of what had likely been their camp. A circle of rocks outlined the remnants of a campfire, something sticky coating the wood that was either grease or cooking oil. There was no indication they had set up a tent, just three indents in the dirt a few feet beyond the fire ring.

Wobbly, I sat down hard on a large rock and saw it was perfectly distanced to be a chair for the make-shift fire ring. On the ground beside me was a large branch and I picked it up to poke at the charcoaled wood, contemplating how best to get back down the hill without dying.

The stick caught on the edge of something not quite burned, and I tried to flip it over but teetered headfirst toward the ground. Giving up on dignity, I crawled on all fours to the circle of rocks and stuck my hand in the lukewarm ash and soot, feeling around for the shape I'd seen.

"Why am I not surprised to see you laying on the side of the road with your hand in a fire pit?" A beefy hand dropped in front of my face and pulled me to a sitting position . My eyes roved the previously broken nose of Marine Man and the questions toppled out of my mouth without assemblage.

"Why are your nose broke red car fire match?" I slurred and he shook his head.

"Follow trees waterfall Winnie kids?" My hand closed around a cardboard square and I plucked it from the fire holding it out to the federal agent.

Martin took it between two fingers and studied it hesitantly.

"Matches?" I asked and he nodded, flipping the front of the book so I could see it.

"From the Gator Gates," he confirmed.

I closed my eyes to stop the trees from spinning, and immediately barfed all over Marine Man's shoes.

Chapter Fifteen: Public Nuisance

"Pass me a marshmallow?"

Larry handed me the whole bag and I took one before passing the bag to the kids. Sylvia and Erich each stuffed one in their mouth and then started a game of tug of war with the bag.

"Enough!" I warned them when Winnie was about to join the game. "You will share the marshmallows or you will give them all to me. There is no scenario where you fight, dump them, and Winnie eats them."

Erich handed back the bag of marshmallows and I stabbed one through the end of my pole and toasted it in the fire pit. I tilted my head up and looked at the stars, blinded instantly when a car drove by Larry's veterinary practice. After I blinked at the spots, I looked regretfully at the neighboring businesses just under a mile away.

"They're all empty this time of night. No one will hear you being a responsible adult," Larry murmured into my hair, pulling me down the bench to sit flush against him. My head dropped to his shoulder and I pulled my marshmallow out of the fire and stuffed it in my mouth.

"This sucks."

"Well, you went drunk hiking and those two idiots ate bugs." He rubbed my back but I shuddered at the memory of Sylvia and Erich vomiting when Marine Man dropped me back off at camp. It was borderline a scene from The Exorcist and Larry had already packed up the tent.

"That... I mean... I never had issues drinking and doing something stupid before." I sighed, but I knew he was right. If you didn't maintain regimented hydration and prevent the consumption of inedible forest creatures, everyone would end up barfing. Dehydration had taken its toll on everyone but Larry. The kids hadn't wanted water and were running around like wildebeests and I was too old to be drinking alcohol, doing physical exertion, and practicing poor hydration practices. "Did he ever tell you what he was doing on the mountain?"

"Who?" Larry popped a marshmallow in his own mouth.

"Marine Man, did he mention why he was on the mountain?" Larry rubbed his jaw at my question and I ate another marshmallow.

"Not that I can remember, but we had bigger problems." He gestured to the children who still had small flecks of vomit on their shoes.

"Fair enough. Thanks for letting us crash your workspace."

"Anytime." He kissed the top of my head and we ate another marshmallow each.

The man was a veterinarian, and his primary practice was dedicated to commercial livestock and large animals. He could, and had, treated Winnie, but his cat allergy prevented him from taking on pets as a primary revenue source. His practice, named Dr. Kirby's Critter Care by the deplorable Amber Carter, sat just outside of Sweet Pea with enough of a buffer to be remote but not isolated. The whole center took up a few acres and sat beside a prefabricated shed sales facility and a dressage ranch of thoroughbreds.

No one here believed in horse dancing, so I assumed the dressage place was a front for something else. Rum running maybe. Or fancy tea they smuggled from the bottom of the Boston Harbor and didn't want the revolutionaries to throw back.

Our tent was just inside a metal pipe paddock for horses, the fire pit on the back deck of the facility. Arguably, there was no reason to have a fire pit and a beautiful outdoor space behind an animal center, but there wasn't a reason not to, either.

"If you don't marry Amber, does she get the animal center?" I yawned into his chest and he pulled my ponytail back.

"What do you mean 'if I don't'? I'm not marrying her. I'm marrying you." He kissed the tip of my nose and I squirmed away.

"Yeah, I know. You don't like the legally binding contract, public spectacle deal. But you like me, right?"

"I mean... I love you. But if we get married, your family is my family. Your family is nuts," I took a long drink of water and followed it up with a short sip of Irish coffee. "I mean, yeah, my family is... but yours is worse and your family has Daniel."

He held up his hands.

"No argument, but... we could move? Then they'd be a long-distance family."

"Move where?" I speculated, thinking of all the places I'd lived around the world and struggling to picture Larry in any of them. "It's not like the country is crawling with creepy, moderately well-off men to fund new animal centers in exchange for an arranged marriage to their heinous offspring."

"Guess I'll have to work for someone else then. Maybe we can go to Sunshine, Idaho and I can work at Bellehaven." He rubbed his hand across his stubble and I couldn't help it. I leaned in and kissed him, long and hard.

"Neither of those places are real. I can't believe you read Jill Shalvis for me." He cuddled me closer and a pair of headlights lit up the paddock. A slow-moving vehicle crept up the road and parked just beyond the metal poles of the enclosure. A man climbed out and backlit by the headlights, he was impossible to make out. The figure paused, looking around, before striding easily toward the paddock. His profile angled toward the tent and he gingerly folded in the middle to slide between the poles and approached the tent without noticing the congregation on the patio.

"Stay here," I said quietly to the kids and Larry. Winnie and I moved toward the tent, watching the man, hand raised, appearing to stare at the entrance flap for a place to knock. As I got closer, I could make out the salt and pepper hair in the deep chocolate skin. His rigid posture, and military haircut had me relaxing slightly as Winnie approached him from the side and he looked down at her.

"Are you the guard dog?" His deep voice was stronger than I expected. His hands shook slightly and I wondered if it was fear, Essential Trembling disorder... or something more serious like Parkinson's.

"Not really," I moved toward him and he straightened from where he'd bent to give Winnie a gentle pat. "She's more the welcoming committee. Hard to believe she used to defend this country with those teeth."

"Hard to believe I used to defend it with these hands." He held up one to demonstrate the tremor. "But we all have to move on eventually."

"Except Marines," I scoffed and a loud guffaw bubbled out of his throat.

"Except Marines. Bartholomew Owens," he extended his hand and I shook it. Despite the tremor, his grip was strong and sure. "Call me Bartie. You Cynthia Sharp?"

"Yes, sir," I responded and gestured toward my partner. "Call me Cyn, that's Winnie. She used to be Sgt. Winnifred Pupperson, but I had to take away her rank. It was going to her head."

"My wife wouldn't let me wear my admiral hat around the house for the same reason. Sometimes we all need a reality check," his genuine smile showed off flawless teeth and bright brown eyes. "I'm sorry to come by so late, but I really could use your help with something... well... embarrassing and sensitive."

"How embarrassing and sensitive are we talking?" I asked, head cocked to the side. The man was wearing jeans and a T-shirt with spotless kicks. No way was he into anything weird.

"Umm... do you know what a glory hole is?"

Nothing could have prepared me for my arrival at the VFW hall two towns over.

While normally, men getting their penises stuck in a wall wasn't something I'd personally help with, the idea of witnessing mass male stupidity was too much to resist. Larry had agreed to stay with my niece and nephew, and I got into the car with a stranger to drive twenty minutes and see a sight that was destined to haunt me for years.

"Who? And Why?" I asked Bartie as he pulled up beside what will forever be known as the wall of shame.

"Honestly, Ms. Sharp, I was in the Navy. I've seen dumber decision making in action, but this is the first time on American soil with numerous available alternatives. What do you think?"

There were a dozen men lined up, pants at their ankles. In front of them was a wooden wall similar to the military obstacle course from basic. Every man had his hips pressed against the wall and appeared to be in either extreme pleasure, or extreme pain as each attempted to twist and tug to free themselves.

"I think maybe you need the fire department?" I offered, Winnie sniffing each man's exposed buttocks and eliciting screams as her cold wet nose pressed into their sensitive flesh. "Why can't they get out?"

Bartie rubbed his chin and a mischievous grin crossed his face.

"You know the saying, hell hath no fury like a woman scorned?" I nodded and started to think maybe even if I could help, I wouldn't. "Well that man on the end is married to a bar owner."

I looked at the naked bottom and was not impressed.

Naked hairy butts lined up like that wasn't exactly Tina Belcher erotic friend fiction worthy. Some of the men tried to crane their heads around to see who was there, but most appeared to be mildly comatose. The peer pressure and herd mentality in effect was evident, but I started wondering if drugs were involved.

"She was covering for one of her employees when she heard a woman talking about making out with a man at the VFW. Now mind you, the woman was a retired Marine and she could drink all these boys under the table. When the man's wife inquired, Traci told her how she was dared to kiss one of the men at the bar. That group of idiots all shoved Schmitty forward, the only married one in the group. He tried to decline, said he was married, and the guys taunted him until he gave in and did it. Traci told Schmitty's wife that it was only a dare, she wanted a free drink from her friends and the wife understood. She harbored no ill-will toward the woman."

"But the friends, and Schmitty, needed to be taught a lesson?" I guessed and cautiously circled to the front of the wall. Above what looked to be a bunch of hairless gophers checking for their shadow, was a spray-painted message, *I'll stick my dick in anything.*

"A lesson in humility and public decency were her exact words," he confirmed, nodding up at the message.

"Nice. But I think the fire department can get them out, not sure you need this investigated."

Bartie shook his head.

"It's a volunteer fire department. They have three people, two are stuck in the wall and the third put them there. She got them drunk and suggested a dick measuring contest where they wouldn't have to see each other's... tools. Now she's threatened anyone from letting them out until they've thoroughly learned humility."

"Seems like a lost cause, but what do I know? What's keeping them in there? Glue?"

"Chinese finger traps," Bartie laughed, and I could hear the men muttering behind the wall. "She took a few pictures, paddled all of their asses with a ping pong paddle, and left them."

"Seems reasonable. Why am I here?"

"It's public exposure and we need them out before the sun comes up and children see. Unfortunately, no man in the area has a wife that will let him help them out of their predicament, and every unattached man... Is stuck in the wall. Every town only has married male law enforcement, and all of their wives' support Mrs. Schmitty. Apparently, there is a solidarity issue at stake and the only female Law Enforcement who is obligated to help is Carla."

"OK, well… I'm not crossing picket lines," I pulled out my phone and snapped a few pictures for Mo. No way would she believe me without pictures. "You'll have to wait for Carla to get back from her mini-moon."

"You wouldn't be crossing lines, you have their blessing. After having her getaway threatened, Carla spoke with the wives. They all agreed you could let them out, based on your reputation."

"What reputation?" I needed to do some serious image control if people thought I wanted to touch a bunch of strange men's penises.

"Of being hypercritical and a disaster. They firmly believe you will remind them they're all idiots and while you do it, Winnie will…" A man screamed and I looked to see Winnie nosing his skin snake and growling. "Well, she'll do that."

"Don't put that in your mouth!" I warned her and she flattened her ears to flop down beside me.

"How do I get them out?" Skepticism was replaced with fear as I remembered how finger traps worked. "No…"

"I'd help you, but…" he held up his shaking hand and I took two large steps back.

"Oh dog, no…" but there was no way around it. A dozen faceless hand jobs were in my future and no one would be able to help me.

"Thanks for the soap... are you sure there wasn't any lye in there anywhere?"

Bartie pulled away from the town municipal building shaking his head.

"I told you, you can't put lye on your hands. It's too alkaline."

"I was thinking in my eyes." I tried to rub the visual away but the limp, liberated man meat haunted my mind whether my eyes were open or closed.

"Also bad."

"Bleach?"

"Still no, Ms. Sharp. Besides, would you really want that to be the last thing you saw before you went blind?" He had a point that was hard to argue with, so I shook my head in defeat.

"It's almost three in the morning, do you want to go back to camping or to your home?" He just turned onto Sweet Pea's Main Street and I half shrugged.

"My apartment I guess. I need a shower. I'll hitch a ride back over there tomorrow. I'm not prepared to face Larry after what I've seen." A shudder rippled through me and Bartie's loud guffaw filled the cab of his truck. I felt the pressure in my chest lighten at the sound. "Do you think he'll be mad?"

"That you touched a dozen men's penises and all of them were mortified? Or that you took pictures of it?" When he put it that way, I decided Larry should see the photos I took for Mo and then he can remind me why I need men... or at least just him. The car stopped at the curb to my building and I climbed out with a wide yawn, Winnie grumbling as she followed suit. "Thanks, Ms. Sharp. Our town owes you."

"Thanks, Mayor Owens." He shook his head, correcting the title. "Sorry, thanks Bartie."

"We'll see you soon, I hope," he waved as I shut the car door, flipped the car around, and drove back the way he'd come.

I crouched beside Winnie and took my spare key off of her collar. It was a testament to my dog owner skills that while I was very likely to lose my keys, I'd never lose my dog. It was filthy, coated in dirt and starting to tarnish, but it still slid into the lock and granted us access to the internal office.

Winnie entered first, and I moved behind her, turning to bolt the door shut behind me. In the road was a lone car, cruising slowly and I paused to watch the red hatchback as it passed. The Arizona plate came into view and my exhaustion vanished.

"Winnie!" I hissed, but the dog had passed out. I shoved open the door and jogged up the street. The car made a right, but it was moving slowly. Picking up my pace, I followed it around the corner just in time to see it make a left. When I got to the corner, the car had vanished, and I moved along the sidewalk quietly. There was no engine rumble, no friction indication of tires on asphalt... It was silent.

The car had turned onto Grover Ct, and I realized it was a cul-de-sac. My eyes scanned and ears strained, but there was nothing beside my labored breathing filling the night.

"Can we help you, ma'am?" A man spoke behind me and I turned into the entitled Martelle brother with fancy boots. "You're in the line of this shot and we worked too hard for you to ruin this now."

My fist flew out, crushing the bones in his nose.

Chapter Sixteen: Skepticles

"Get off of me!" I shouted, a man restraining me from behind was breathing heavily. Another minute and I'd have him tired enough to take down.

"You just punched my brother!" Ivan Martelle growled, and I heard a third voice carry from somewhere behind me.

"He said he was going to shoot someone!"

"We don't have any guns, lady!" I twisted against his grip, feeling the sting of friction where his hands gripped my bare forearms. "Are they on their way? She's trying to get away!"

"Let me go before I make you." The steady threat in my voice gave me a moment of alarm. I had never sounded like Liam Nissan, but I wasn't upset that in this instant, it gave me strength. "Last time I'm asking."

Ivan's grip held tight. I stomped on his instep, thrust my elbow back into his gut, dropped to a crouch and swept his legs out from under him.

"What the-" someone shouted and I turned to see four free-standing lamps illuminating the whole street.

A crew of men in black T-shirts and cargo shorts emerged from the shadows. Some were holding electronic equipment, all were wearing headsets, and a paunchy man behind a camera was screaming into a cell phone.

"What are you..." I asked, watching the color shift as red and blue lights joined the work lamps.

"Let her go." Barney's voice came out of the car's PA system and all the men took a step back, but I adopted a combat stance. "Stand down, Cynthia."

His warning had half the men in the area squinting and pulling out their phones. Confusion warred with fear and my face struggled to look in every direction at once.

Barney appeared before me, hands on his gun belt, looking disheveled and uncoordinated.

"You armed, Cynthia?" He asked and I shook my head, seeing the people for the first time and trying to process the words I'd heard shortly before I punched Irvine Martelle in the face.

"You know you aren't either, right?" I inclined my head toward his gun belt and he looked down. Despite having the same name as Don Knotts in the Andy Griffith show, he was a few years older than Daniel. Instead of being lanky and short, he was beefy in a way that lent itself to atrophied muscle and predisposition to calorie dense beer.

"That ain't really an issue so long as you aren't," he puffed out his chest and I rolled my eyes. If he'd been born a decade later, he'd have been named Dudley Dursley... right after his parent's changed their last name to Dursley. His eyes shifted and he leaned in, looking nervous. "Where's Winnie?"

"Why? Do you have a bomb up your butt?" I whispered back, keeping my face serious and concerned. The effort failed and I burst into laughter, coming to when I heard my name on the lips of the cargo short crew.

"It's Cyn!"

"Holy crap, were we rolling when she punched him?"

"Whose channel should it go up on?"

"Man, if only the dog were here!"

My face flamed and I sank to the ground to hide my face.

A new Cyn Sharp Disasters video was imminent and the image quality promised to be ten times better than the others. If this turned out to be what I suspected, I just punched a man over a film shoot and now I would be trending.

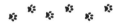

The sun was up, and I had the permanent canvas pattern of a folding chair imprinted on my face.

Once my identity was established, Irvine cleaned and patched up, filming continued, and I was asked to sit quietly aside while they concluded the scene. Though I'd have rather gone home and taken a nap with Winnie, they refused to let me ask the Martelle brothers questions until after they got what they needed.

I was also informed no charges would be pressed if I signed a waiver to have the punch included in their film.

"That's a wrap!"

Startled at the sudden explosion of sound, I fell out of my chair and tried to grab the neighboring chair to keep myself upright. That chair held the waif of an English woman who was hired for accent coaching and rather than keeping me upright, her chair tilted with mine. On her other side was the director and in a matter of moments, all three of us were sprawled on the ground, tangled in chairs and limbs.

"Did anybody get that?"

"Oh man, that's so much better than Irvine getting punched!"

"I got it! Should we upload now or ride the first wave before posting another?"

"Get the hell off my set!" the director boomed, and I shook my head.

"I need to ask questions," I yawned and helped the English woman up. Her hand lashed out and struck my face, then she spun on her heel and stalked off.

If she'd had any muscle, the slap might have hurt. Given that she weighed less than Winnie, it was mostly just loud and humiliating. Ivan and Irvine approached, and with them came the scent of wood fires and soot. They were wearing flannel, boots, and Stetsons that looked well-worn but ill-fitting.

Hand me down cowboys.

"You think we're the arsonists?" Irvine said without pre-amble, taking a plastic bottle of water and drinking deeply. A woman in all black with a cloth apron came over and started pulling liquids, lotions and wipes out of her pouch like a cosmetic kangaroo. Within minutes, the leathery face and sun damaged appearance was replaced with a youthful and mildly ridiculous looking young star.

"I did... but now I think you might be a chimera." I ref-erenced the mythological creature that was composed of so many different animal parts it was impossible to identify.

"Because I can shape shift?" He laughed and I noticed his brother's transformation was less stark.

"It also breathes fire, which means it can't be an arsonist. Like a dragon. If a dragon sneezes and burns down a village, it's not arson. It's an unfortunate by-product of living near a dragon. You don't start fires on purpose, just sometimes you get tired and exhale fire and stuff burns." I nodded sagely and suddenly the whole area was silent, staring at me.

"What?"

"Are you on drugs?" The director was clutching his cell, but it felt unnecessary since Barney was ten feet away, sleeping in his patrol car.

"No, I've been up for... many, many hours. During that time, I got drunk, went hiking, watched my niece and nephew projectile vomit, removed a dozen penises from finger traps in a wooden wall, punched a shape-shifter, and sat through the most boring filming I could possibly have imagined. Dragons and chimeras are more normal than the last thirty hours of my life. How are you always in the same small towns as an arsonist?"

"We... This is the first time we've been in the same place as an arsonist." Irvine took off the worn flannel and pulled on a designer T-shirt. His brother remained as he was, off to the side and quiet in faded jeans and a blue-jean button down. Ivan was staring at his boots, looking somewhere between exhausted and disinterested.

"Ivan?" I spoke to him and he startled. His eyes met mine, and for the first time he truly looked at me and I saw that he wasn't much older than his brother, but his life hadn't been nearly as charmed. "Can we talk... over there?"

I gestured to a sidewalk out of the way, and he nodded. Irvine made to follow us, but I held up a hand.

"I'm tired, I can only talk to one person at a time." He looked put out and pouty, but the director invited him over to watch raw footage of himself and he perked instantly. Ivan followed me to the driveway of a new construction house for sale. All the houses on this street were for sale, and I understood how they could film here in the middle of the night without any complaints over the lights and noise.

Ivan sat first and I gave him a six-foot buffer, sitting cross-legged in the middle of the road to face him.

"That's not safe," his eyes scanned my surroundings and I shrugged.

"So... what is all this?" I asked, not wasting the energy to gesture.

Ivan shifted uncomfortably and I wondered if it was because he intended to lie or because he didn't want to be here.

"We... He... we're filming a pilot. My brother has been doing... not really tutorials, but micro-documentaries on camping, crime, and small-town life. He got the idea and came to New Mexico, cost me my job so I would have to go with him." His voice wasn't bitter, but the resentment was written across his face.

"Are you from New Mexico?"

"Nah, we grew up outside of Tucson. Irvine always wanted to be in the spotlight. Great source of grief for me growing up and continues to be now that we're grown." His shoulders sagged, and he leaned back against the mailbox cemented into the ground behind him.

"Is he also the reason you went to lock up?" I asked and noticed his weary gaze studying me more carefully. The look made me uncomfortable, but it was non-threatening. More the way you'd look at a toddler shouting a curse-word. Funny, but unexpected and still wrong by societal convention.

"No, that was all me I'm afraid." He picked at some paint on the toe of his cowboy boot. "Got into a disagreement at a bar in Las Cruces. Words were said, punches thrown, turned out the guy was a cop."

I winced in appreciation of his predicament.

"But, I didn't mind lock-up. It was only three months, learned a trade and when I got out I found a job."

"At Mrs. Adams's auto body shop?" He nodded confirmation to my question and I waited for him to elaborate, but he held his silence.

"Then your brother came in, threw a diva tantrum, got you fired, and made you go on a cross-country road trip to make survivalist videos?" It seemed far-fetched, but I'd taken my brother's kids into the wilderness so he and his new wife could practice making more.

At least I hope they were only practicing.

"Not really survivalist, but videos. He tried to make it in Hollywood and couldn't. All looks, no substance, and ten-gallons of drama. He got approached to do a podcast, but that wasn't going to get his face in front of a camera. He made a YouTube channel, initially just showing off his 'wilderness skills'", the air quotes were interesting on the man's rugged frame.

"He... doesn't have wilderness skill?"

"Irvine doesn't have any skills of any kind. Despite the face, no one believed he was really a camper so he tried re-branding with a more rugged appearance. We did a lot of test videos in north-eastern Arizona. The red hatchback was mine from high school and it fit the image he wanted. Then off he went, chasing fortune and glory in the fickle age of the internet, somehow getting me to go with him."

"You mentioned small towns and crime?" I prompted, giving myself time to frame the next series of questions. Between what I'd overheard the previous morning and what he was saying now, nothing really fit together.

"That was sort of an... afterthought addition when the nature videos were tanking." He scrubbed both of his hands over his face and let out a yawn. Several of his joints popped and I felt a sense of kinship with this man.

We both desperately needed a nap, a chiropractor, and someone to eliminate our brothers for forcing us into this life.

Though I may have volunteered. I couldn't remember at this point.

"The idea being to go to small towns with crime, or commit crimes in small towns?"

"To visit small towns and film the outdoor sequences, then relax in comfort." Ivan made a face that said he had zero respect for his brother. "Started after he botched a trip in Utah. Didn't bring even half the gear he needed and I ended up using this old fire starter to keep us warm in a snowstorm. Thought he'd quit after that, but he didn't. Some point near Nebraska, we were drawing strange looks in our car when we got to small towns. Talked to some locals, heard about a Bonnie and Clyde team causing chaos in small towns. Took a few months, but we figured out how to follow them. Irvine used the arson investigation to sell his idea to some rich white dude in the area. Convinced him it would be a small-town thriller documentary and he funded it so long as his daughter got a part."

"What do you mean by Bonnie and Clyde routine? What part did you give the daughter?" I had a feeling it was Amber and the haybale boys, though none of it made sense from the perspective of a reasonable human being.

Which Amber and her father were not.

"When we'd find a town they'd hit, the story was always different. A man was seen running from the scene of a fire, or a woman seen running from a theft incident, then the next town it would switch. No one could ever say too much about either, so we made it a cheesy manhunt and linked the two. When we'd fall behind, a suited man would show up asking questions, but he never seemed to get anywhere. They're a modern-day Bonnie and Clyde fire bug team." Ivan didn't look too jazzed about the selling point. "When we hired that guy's daughter, she went... overboard. Had some local boys steal hay that caught fire, drew attention to her father's weed crop, and got us the attention of a national name in reality film."

"So you dropped her, her dad, and her looney tunes antics for a big name and maybe even a bigger check? Were you guys filming on the mountain yesterday?"

He looked at me again for a long moment, but I didn't offer to explain what I'd overheard, simply waited him out.

"Kind of. Set up a tripod in the early morning to film a promo spot and announce the changes to our fifteen YouTube followers." His eye roll appeared only in his voice, but it was painfully obvious. "Got here... shoot, two days after that trash can burned. Thought we were finally going to crack the case and find the Fire Bug Bandits. Now... now we're just a pair of crackpots making idiotic videos. This is the first time my brother has let the cosmetician take off his make-up since we arrived. Said it helped him 'stay in character', but he was secretly filming himself twenty-four seven."

"To be fair, that's probably what you were before. Where did you get the Gator Gates matches?" My question caused his head to tilt sideways, reminding me that I was going to need to feed Winnie soon before she ate all of the furniture in my office.

Again.

"The what now?"

"On the mountain, you started your fire with a book of matches from a bar in Florida for senior citizens who like a little variety in their spice." He stared at me blankly and I considered the psychological ramifications of putting the explanation less delicately.

The man had been through enough.

"How did you start the fire on the mountain?"

"Matches. Found a small pile of them dumped in an alley," he scrunched up his face. "Even though we got here after the dumpster caught fire, I still wanted to see it. We checked it out in the middle of the night, and I found a pile of matchbooks on the corner by the alley entrance. We were running low, so I scooped them up when I saw they were still intact."

"See or hear anyone while you were there?" I asked, but suspected there wouldn't have been much left by that time. It was odd Carla had missed the pile of the incriminating matches, but she wasn't on her A game that day and she'd driven into the scene.

Before Ivan could answer, Barney tumbled out of his car while the two-way radio on his chest squawked out instructions to emergency responders.

"Cyn! We gotta go!" He was running toward me, at least the closest thing to running he could manage, and nearly ate pavement when his toe caught on a shadow.

"I'm working, go without me," I yawned and tried not to look disappointed that he hadn't fallen.

"You have to come, it's your building!" He pulled me to my feet and I blinked at him.

"What's my building?"

"The place that's on fire!" He wheezed, and I ran.

Chapter Seventeen: Not Quite Fired

I t took seven years to run the three blocks back to my building.

Seven years during which I had a heart-attack, two aneurysms, and a pneumothorax. I shoved my way through an elderly couple taking a walk, three kids riding bicycles, and shoved two-dozen citizens out of my way.

The front of my building was cordoned off, police and fire personnel gathering in front while I elbowed my way through gawkers and gossipers. The flimsy yellow crime tape ripped and I burst through it like a Boston Marathon winner, anxious and desperate to see...

"Winnie!" I shouted, yanking on the back of a yellow fire coat. It was attached to a man I couldn't name, and I roughly shoved him against the wall to get to the wooden front door of my office.

"Winnie!"

Inside, the office looked as it always did. Scattered dog toys, coffee cart, battered desk, Winnie's dog bed... but it was empty.

"Sgt. Winnifred Pupperson!" The shout was a desperate plea, and I heard a faint scrabbling of claws above my head. Shoving two uniformed first responders aside, I ran to the open door and up into my apartment just as Winnie reached the top of the stairs. Her bleary eyed expression and lopsided tongue sent my heartbeat skittering to a halt.

Winnie was fine.

My best friend was fine and not on fire. I stumbled up the stairs and threw my arms around her neck, taking a deep inhale of her fur. Small tendrils stuck to my face as the sweat from my run mingled with tears on my cheeks.

Winnie is fine, I told myself. *Winnie is fine.*

Yet the tears persisted even as I reluctantly let her go to inspect my small apartment. Nothing was out of place, the covers rumpled in a perfect Winnie-sized ball. Her food container had been knocked over, but she hadn't been successful with her B and E attempt. I prowled the space, searching every nook and cranny for signs of fire or danger.

There was nothing, so I made coffee.

I alternated between prepping Winnie's food and measuring scoops of coffee grounds into the filter. I added water to Winnie's bowl, I added water to the pot. I sprinkled freeze dried chicken on her food, I sprinkled pumpkin spice into my coffee grounds. I set her bowl on the floor, I pressed start on my coffee maker before falling heavily to the floor.

"I thought..." I started, reaching out to stroke her ear while she wolfed down every morsel in her bowl. "I thought you were hurt."

A stainless steel dog dish slammed into my leg and I watched her brace the bowl against my leg. She was eating in a grid pattern that was both impressive and disturbing and I wondered briefly what she'd do with thumbs.

Suddenly I looked at her. "How did you get up here?"

Despite the night I had, and the many hours before, I never would have left the door to my apartment from the office propped open and the door was spring-pressure close. It had a round ball doorknob, so she couldn't have opened it herself unless...

I checked her paws, but she still hadn't grown opposable thumbs.

"Did someone let you up here?"

She sniffed a circle around the inside of her dish. Then around the outside, confirming that not so much as a crumb had escaped. The precision and dedication to her search reminded me of when she searched for explosives. In her work, and in her meals, Winnie was meticulously thorough about doing a careful search. My partner paced the kitchen in a grid pattern, searching for food until the coffee pot beeped, and I rose gracelessly to consume some.

My eyes fell to the dish rack beside the sink where the last mug I'd drank from usually sat.

The dish drying rack was empty and I contemplated whether or not I'd put it away in preparation for our camping trip. Pulling open the cabinet, I grabbed the first mug my hand fell on. It was an Awkward Yeti comic, depicting heart and brain at a crossroad of adult responsibility and utter nonsense.

A daily struggle in this apartment.

Modified and delicious, the pot was half empty before my brain remembered my office had supposedly had a fire.

"Crap," I grumbled, clipping Winnie's leash on and venturing downstairs.

A quick scent of the air said whatever had burned was neither alive nor still on fire. Winnie followed suit and looked at me, confirming that my weak human nose had been verified by her superior canine one. Satisfied for the moment, I took Winnie down the alley and out into the grassy memorial park that sat in the middle of town. The dog did her business, and we sat on a bench beside the statue of our town's most notable villain: a pioneer who'd slaughtered ten people to steal this land from the native peoples.

We'd only recently reached a point where it was socially acceptable to admit pioneers were murderous jerks... that didn't get the native people their land back, though.

While I wasn't part of cancel culture, killing people for something that was never yours is a crime the world over. Instead of a statue of the murderer, it would have made more sense to have a great big apology rock to the First Nation people whose land was stolen by entitled white jerks.

Another long drink of coffee and I got off my mental soap box. Asking people to take responsibility for the violence and irresponsibility of their ancestors never went well. Sleep deprivation combined with fear for my best friend's life were making me extra cranky and vindictive, not a good combination. One can't change the world if they're too busy shouting at it.

Also, Winnie already agreed with me, and the rest of the town was gathered in front of my building so if I started shouting, I'd just look like a nutter.

My attention shifted from the statue to the three-deep semi-circle arching around the main entrance to my office. Either Daniel or Barney had wheeled over the 10-speed bike to have extra flashers, and the film crew sat just behind the police bike. A dozen plus cargo shorts wearing men were waiting, cell phones poised for another Cyn Sharp Disaster video. Behind them was a handful of shop owners who were waylaid on their way into work. Not much opened this early, and I let my eyes drift to each business like a touchstone.

Mo's was open with a small line.

The bread baker on the next block didn't have a line, but the yeasty air said the production hadn't been interrupted. Marvin's Auto Body Shop was dark, but he showed up whenever he wanted. I paused at the Coffee Cabin, a simple roast shop for beans, sandwiches, and drip coffee served straight up. Mo made sugary works of art, the Cabin made meaty delicacies and Turkish coffee that would keep you up for days and could melt the roof off of a dragon's mouth.

An older woman shuffled into the establishment and I watched for someone to exit. The Cabin was a drop-in on your way to the lumber yard establishment. There was usually a steady stream of flannel clad men meandering in and out during the morning hours, but I didn't see anyone.

Winnie lifted her head and looked at me, but I could only tilt my head in response. Resigned to make sure the Coffee Cabin proprietor hadn't been murdered or tied up by his fetish club and left without water, I dragged myself from the bench and stumbled toward the business.

"Excuse me, ma'am?" An old man in a jaunty cap approached and stood in my path. He wasn't especially tall, but his frame remained upright and un-damaged by age, gravity, and sitting in traffic.

"Yes, sir?" His hand gripped my bicep and he half-turned me to point at Marvin's Auto Body. Winnie poked her nose at the man's pockets, and he stroked her fur without any hesitation. She leaned against his leg as though they were old friends and I tried to get a better look at the man under his cap.

"Do you know if that mechanic has any experience with older vehicles?" Despite the wrinkled and paper-thin appearance of his skin, the older man's grip was casually firm, and I couldn't resist studying his face for signs Hollywood magic was at work. But the skin spots were too irregular in patterning. He was just a fit and self-sufficient older gentleman who'd taken care of his bones.

Maybe there was something behind those milk commercials after all.

"Marvin can work on anything. Cosmetic, mechanical—he's got two decades of experience in this town alone. Have we met before?" Winnie continued to lean against the older man's leg and he didn't appear even remotely concerned. Most people gave Winnie a wide berth, but this man...

"Probably not, I'm just passing through."

The older man shrugged and chanced darting his eyes behind me. Reluctant to hurt him, I gently removed his fingers and turned back to the Coffee Cabin. Outside, the building still looked dimly lit and missing a dozen brutish men. I took two steps toward it when the same older woman stepped out with a bag and a steaming cup of coffee.

Someone must be inside if she had coffee.

She glanced at me and then the other direction and started off down the street, casually sipping and swinging the bag on her arm. After checking both ways for cars and terrifying children on bikes, I trekked over to the Coffee Cabin. Winnie trotted beside me reluctantly as she kept checking behind her for the old man.

My best guess was the man must have kept dried meat in his pants.

At the sidewalk in front of the Cabin she changed her tune. She raised her head straight in the air and let her tail go full helicopter at the scent of bacon and coffee beans. In an effort to live up to the name, Mr. Collarson had used wood panel patterned sticky paper to line the inside of his windows. His wooden front door was modeled after a KOA park cabin door, and the whole effect was very 1980s mobile home chic.

Winnie sniffed the door and pressed a paw on the lower panel. Soundlessly, it swung open and we stepped into the dim interior. While my eyes adjusted, my stomach rumbled, and I tried to eat the air. My debit card was with my cell phone which was at Larry's vet office "camping".

The interior of the coffee cabin reminded me of a curio shop that encouraged loitering. Inside to the left was a long wooden bar, the register on the far left, a space to collect drinks closer to the door. Creating a traffic pattern, a wooden shelf divided the left side of the room, leaving a doorway's worth of space just inside the door and two doorways worth on the other. On the back side of the shelf was a small souvenir shop with branded coffee beans, jars of preserves, and a smattering of tables that generally held truckers wanting to eat somewhere other than the cab of their truck.

"Hey, Mel? Can I have a sandwich? I'll pay you later, I promise!" Though my tone was supposed to be normal, I was practically shouting. "Sorry for being loud!"

Silence followed my apology and I moved closer to the textured wooden slab that served as a coffee bar, checkout counter, and serving station. Butterflies flooded my gut as I realized there was only silence in the shop from the moment I walked in. Behind the counter was empty, the short-order cook station was empty, and the small cluster of tables amidst the jarred jams and the shelves of beans were empty.

"Mel?" I whispered and Winnie pressed her nose to the ground. Nervous and shaking, I peered around the counter, holding my breath.

No dead bodies.

My gaze drifted back up, looking for clues as to the owner's whereabouts. Both of the quick dispense drip machines read full. The coffee scent was fresh, condensation pooling just beneath the rim of the dispenser. Beside it was a plastic pastry case, fully stocked and awaiting diners. I swung open the case and picked up a Danish, the flakey crust soft and pliable.

I stuffed it in my mouth before remembering I couldn't actually pay for it.

I'd just have to keep a tab and leave them an IOU.

Pausing just outside the swinging door into the small kitchen, I decided to knock once while I chewed. Despite the eerie quiet, there was still a small chance someone was in there and planning to murder intruders... or having sex. I had no interest in death or voyeurism. Normally, death would be the least appealing of the two, but not today. I was starving, my hand hurt from punching a man in the face, and I'd seen far too many penises.

Today, death wouldn't be that bad.

The kitchen was empty.

Jene had turned off the grill. A heaping plate of bacon sat on her prep counter, and I popped a few slices in my mouth.

The bacon was room temperature.

Beside the bacon were sausages, egg patties, and bread waiting to be toasted. All of them were room temperature, all of them appearing to have gotten lost and forgotten in what could only be explained as an alien abduction.

Who leaves bacon unless they were also leaving the planet against their will?

"Jene? Mel?" I asked into the pantry and walk-in fridge, but there wasn't a response or any lifeless corpses in the space. Despite the empty kitchen, I still searched the small shop, studying the re-stocked shelves. Three dozen shelves filled with one-pound bags of roasted whole-bean coffee were all perfectly flush with each other and the front of the shelf.

Four columns were missing their front bag.

Winnie fixated on these spots and pointed her head at the register.

"Cyn!"

I turned into Mel as he walked in with Jene and she pulled me into an awkward hug.

"Everyone has been looking for you! They said you barged through the cops and ran upstairs but no one could find you." She crouched to hug Winnie while Mel took his place behind the counter and poured himself some coffee.

"People were looking for me?" I asked, startled out of my intended question.

"Yes, the cops want to know if anything was damaged in the fire. It was all pretty well contained in the area around a metal trash can, but..." her eyes landed on the shelves missing bags of coffee. "Were you shopping?"

"What? No... So these were full this morning?" I asked, and Mel moved back around the counter to look at the display.

"Yes, I face the shelves and restock completely every morning," she ran her finger along the empty space and my frown deepened.

"How long were you outside watching the commotion at my place?" I asked, remembering that I hadn't seen them walk out after the woman had exited with her bag and coffee. "I know it was longer than a minute, the bacon was cold. Also, I owe you money for a pastry, bacon, sausage and some eggs. But I'll have to bring it later because I don't have..."

Jene waved me off and scanned the rest of the store's inventory. Winnie moved along beside her, sniffing each shelf as though she could confirm whether or not it had been touched. Despite not being given a command, she sat twice and nosed Jene to show where else the scent of the coffee thief lingered.

Jene rewarded her with bacon that had materialized from her pocket and I decided my life was meaningless until I also carried bacon in my pocket. Bacon, chocolate and tiny shots of espresso.

"There's also two jars of preserves and a container of honey missing." Her hand touched each spot and Mel rushed back to check the register.

"Someone took two-dozen singles from the register." He started counting the remaining bills and I poked my head behind the counter.

"How do you know that?"

"I start the day with fifty singles. A lot of my customers pay cash and they usually have smaller bills. I go through a lot of singles." He looked up at the tip jar and rubbed his jaw. "Don't think anyone put anything in that yet, but I can't be sure. That's where I get more singles when I run out."

"Did you lock the door when you left?" I asked, spinning in a small circle. The place was still spotless, there was no sign of raccoon invasion, smash and grab, or lockpicking. Winnie nosed Jene's hand and when no more bacon appeared, she sprawled out on the floor and let out a long sigh of depression.

"Probably not, this is Sweet Pea." He looked appalled at my question and I tried to nod but couldn't agree with him.

The people in this town were terrifying.

"So, you... heard about the fire and ran out?" I tried to comprehend the timeline and both Mel and Jene shook their heads.

"Someone came in and told us. Asked us if we knew you because the cops were trying to find you with questions about the fire." He looked to be struggling with the memory. "He was an older man, he had on a newsboy cap and I didn't think much of him. He wasn't a regular, but most of the older crowd go to Suzie's up the road because she gives them free coffee and a discount."

I nodded at his assessment. Suzie ran the diner like a time warp back into the nineteen fifties. From her shift dress to her pen and paper orders, the woman refused to age, and she refused to let her shop age either.

It was likely a Dorian Gray situation, but she was kind enough that I'd never looked for her painting.

"But I don't reckon I've seen him around before, either." Jene let some of her Louisiana upbringing come out and I tried to hide my smile. Despite being able to make amazing Cajun and creole food, the woman prepared only eggs, bacon, and sausage four hours a day and made a mint.

Or at least a mint by Sweet Pea standards, as the cost of living here was negligible.

"Cyn!"

My eyes flashed to Mo in her flour stained apron and wild woman red curls.

"Are you OK?" She patted Winnie down first and then me, as though hoping to slap any injuries out of us.

"I'm fine, why wouldn't I be?"

"I had heard about the fire in your building earlier, but I knew you'd been camping. Except then I saw a news report that a cabin caught fire on the mountain near where you were and I thought... Then Larry called and asked if I'd seen you, but the cops wouldn't let me in and I bribed Chris to go in and look for you, but you and Winnie were gone and he said there had been no medical transport and..."

"Breathe, Mo! Breathe!" I encouraged her and led her to a chair in the dining section. Jene brought her a cup of water and she emptied it in a single drink.

"Right, so Phil said he saw you come in here and he was going to follow to ask you to look into something, but then he was summoned to his shop by a delivery man. He ran into me before another delivery came in and I... I'm just so glad you're OK," she exhaled and collapsed in on herself against the chair.

"Phil? What did he need me to look into? Did you say a hunting cabin burned on the mountain?" Jene brought both of us a Turkish coffee and Mo handed her a five from somewhere. Jene tried to give it back, but Mo made some gesture that said it wasn't happening. It was like a choreographed dance that only food service professionals would understand and I felt like a spy trying to crack the code.

"In that area, yeah. There wasn't much info on the cabin. Phil said he was doing inventory and he's missing some expensive merchandise he knows he didn't sell," she shrugged and my memory drifted to the old lady with the overflowing bag and a glass tree stump dildo. They weren't expensive, I'd bought three when Winnie knocked over a display in front of his shop and it cost me under a hundred dollars, and he threw in an unbroken one so I wouldn't feel cheated at owning three toys I'd never get to use.

He refused to accept I wouldn't use the whole one either, so it lived beside my bed.

"Does he think it was stolen?" I took a cautious sip of the coffee and tried not to choke on the near solid substance that dribbled out.

"He does." She downed the coffee without so much as a wince and I remembered she'd served as a teacher for Teach For America and she was vastly more worldly than I.

"Do you think..." Jene trailed off and I followed her line of sight to the spots where bags of coffee were missing.

"That someone is starting the fires so they can steal stuff?" I asked and we all exchanged a look.

Chapter Eighteen:
Petty Thefts

"Cynthia! Come in!" Phil beckoned me with both arms and I stood on the curb like a statue.

I'd never been inside Phil's shop, The Curious Courtship. Despite owning some of his merchandise, I'd managed to avoid going inside by defying millennial code and forcing cash into his hands so I could run away. Standing in the doorway, Winnie sitting on the ground beside me, I couldn't decide if I wanted answers or to be spared the mental scarring of what may be inside.

My parents were two of Phil's best customers and he seemed like the type to hang pictures.

"Could we talk out here?" He snitched the collar of a young boy trying to sneak past and turned him out into the world.

"What? Why?" Phil thwarted a second boy who tried to topple a rack of periodicals and managed to keep him out at the same time. "What's wrong with my shop?"

I peered past him into the boutique with its soft lighting and upbeat jazz music. Curious Courtship wasn't just an Adult Novelty shop, it was a custom boutique modeled after Paris Fashion week with feng sui. Beside the door weren't mannequins wearing lingerie as one would expect. He had elected to have a wooden work bench setup to display the craftsmanship that went into his glass, leather, and metal-working merchandise. From the outside, you wouldn't necessarily know what the shop was if you didn't know the purpose of the items on display.

To date, Phil's shop had been confused with a medieval torture museum, the craftsman equivalent of the pottery painting facilities, and a farm supply store. Once you put your head past the periodical rack, you could see more obvious adult items, made of lace, silicone, and whatever furry handcuffs were made out of.

I pulled my head back out and watched the large man sashay through his domain with confidence, grace, and sass that I could only pretend I possessed. Deep down, maybe my parents were right.

At some point I'd become a prude and it was mortifying.

"It's just... I have Winnie and she..." he waved off my objection and met a young couple at the register who were holding something black and strappy. "Damn."

Unconsciously, I snagged another kid trying to rush in and Winnie gave her a firm nose to her backside. With an annoyed squeak, she bounced up the street singing "There Once was a Man from Nantucket".

In fifteen years, she'd either be in my parent's living room for the lab portion of sex and society or in prison.

There was no in between with the kids in this town.

Trying to sneak into Curious Courtship had been a right of passage for mid-range cool kids in Sweet Pea since Molly was in school and he opened. The cool kids had nothing to prove, and the losers such as myself had nothing to gain. The novelty lay in the fact that Phil was the town's first openly homosexual man and also the first person to speak openly about sexual intimacy.

Much like my parents, the conservatives of the area wished he would move along as well. There were several petitions that his shop brought down shop values on Main Street and twice as many asking him to open a second one at the other end. Town meetings were strangely divided with one side on open expression of love and sexuality and the other on stuffing all that down for the sake of propriety.

Ironic, as I knew for a fact the town's Republican Lobbyist had a subscription to a lube of the month club from one of the larger online retailers.

Hypocrisy thy name is small town bigotry and politics.

"Come on, Cynthia!" Phil boomed and the couple moved out the front door muttering quietly to each other. "I'll see you both next week at the Biting for Beginners Class!"

They waved at the door and stepped onto the sidewalk while Winnie offered head tilts.

"Biting like... canine work?" I asked, surprised the area would have enough interest in a dog training recreational program. More surprised that Phil's was the coordination hub of the course.

"Canine?" Now it was Phil's turn to tilt his head. His eyes shifted from the departing couple, to Winnie, to my neck, and I felt a single synapse fire. My gut bottomed out and my mouth went dry. Phil was a vampire and the people who just left must also be vampires.

Or maybe werewolves.

"N-never mind," I stammered out and tugged Winnie away from a display of leather goods. Unconsciously, I pulled the collar of my shirt higher while Phil appeared to maintain composure.

"Mo said you were looking for me?"

We'd made it two feet into the store and the cool air felt good on my skin. The yawn that followed was involuntary and I looked helplessly at the Turkish coffee in my hand. It was a Catch-22. I was too much of a baby to drink it and too tired not to. Awkwardly, I pinched my nose and dumped some into the back of my throat.

"What are you doing?" I leapt out of my skin when he spoke beside me and backed into the same rack of periodicals the boy had tried to topple. Phil grabbed it, kept it on its feet, and skillfully redirected me away from any items that were gravitationally susceptible or breakable.

"Huh?" I blinked at him, startled again by the prolonged darkness when my eyes refused to reopen. "Sorry, long night."

"With my merch or with Larry?" He wiggled his eyebrows at me and I swallowed my embarrassment.

"A dozen skin snakes in a wall. Then I accidentally punched a man filming something... It's on YouTube if you're interested," I tried to look casual as I admitted my internet fame was for accidental destruction and assault that only I could make sound reasonable. "You... had some stuff go missing?"

His face scrunched as he seemed to think through his options. Either he wasn't sure he wanted a tired woman investigating or he was weighing the social convention on witnessing someone's live-streamed humiliation in their presence. I took his contemplation as an opportunity to really look at his shop.

In college, porn stores were a dime a dozen. I'd spent a holiday with a friend in Lane County, Oregon, and she had surprised me by taking me to not one, not two, but four twenty-four-hour establishments. All of them had the clinical super store experience of a Walmart, a stark contrast to the red door in the back of Blockbuster you see in movies. In Colorado, the shops had been smaller, but the experience was the same as browsing the racks at a department store.

Phil's shop was cozy. Instead of a clinical sales experience, he'd curated his store. Every item on display had been meticulously placed with care. His craftsmanship and attention to detail evident in every shelf and rack of goods that even I wasn't sure the purpose of. My hand drifted to a sable leather strap with holes punched at various intervals, a metal rod and a buckle along the side of a strap that circled around a longer one.

"It looks like a bridle," I said to no one in particular, stroking the soft leather with a transfixed expression. Phil's work was exquisite, and I couldn't imagine how many hours a single item of his merchandise took to create.

"It is a bridle, dear heart." Phil patted my shoulder and I studied the opening encircling the bit.

"I always thought horse-heads were bigger... I should pay more attention at the farm." I let the straps fall back down and faced the store's proprietor. He'd sucked his cheeks into his mouth and was turning red as he shook. "Are you OK? Do you need... water?"

His composure failed and the boisterous laugh burst from his mouth. The sound reverberated through my body and resonated through the shop as he doubled over and appeared to be between having a seizure and busting his gut. While the melodic sound was comforting, his expression told me something had gone straight over my head like a Jeff Dunham Peanut joke.

"Oh, Cyn, you are so..." he gasped and motioned me toward an unmarked door in the back of the store.

"What?" I looked down at Winnie, but she seemed more interested in the scented squeeze bottles just above her nose height. I picked one up and read the label, Cotton Candy Lube. "Does this taste good?"

Winnie sniffed the bottle and let out a sneeze.

"It tastes like sugar," he took the bottle from my hand and put it back on the shelf. "Personally, I think you need this section over here."

The large man guided me to the end cap that featured dozens of lube bottles in precise columns.

"Are these..." I picked up one and then another. "Flavored after coffee drinks?"

His smile made my eyes go wide and I searched for the price.

"Pick two of your favorites and put the rest back, Cyn," his statement was like asking me to pick a favorite hair on Winnie's head.

"But... Peppermint, pumpkin, cinnamon dolce..." I clutched a fistful from each shelf like a toddler. Phil chuckled and removed six bottles from my hand, leaving two.

Caramel Macchiato and Double Mocha.

"You can't drink them." He raised a warning finger and I nodded.

"Can I lick them off my fingers?"

An older woman harrumphed from the door and I turned to watch Larry and Daniel's mom give me the stink-eye from the open doorway.

"Mrs. Kirby, I didn't know you shopped here." Phil's eyes were practically twinkling.

"I don't! I was looking for you. Please exit this store so I may speak with you." Her clipped tone would have made a lesser woman shrink but I popped the top of a lube bottle and took a long sniff.

"Can't. I'm investigating something." It smelled amazing and Phil just managed to stop me from dumping the bottle into my mouth. "It says edible!"

"Not in large quantities," Phil reprimanded me, Mrs. Kirby loudly clearing her throat to get my attention.

"This is urgent," she insisted but I shrugged.

"I'm too tired to handle anything urgent. I'm working on cold cases." Phil had re-capped my bottle and slid it into my pocket along with two others. "Am I shoplifting?"

"No, dear heart. Let me grab you the list of what was taken and the approximate values." he went through the door and reappeared a second later. "I can't tell you when exactly it went missing, but sometime in the last three weeks."

"The last three weeks?" I asked, studying the value column of the items. Most were nominal, but there were three custom work pieces labeled as RP Bridle, Lined WRBinder, and Mounted Swing.

"I take inventory every three weeks," he clarified, and I nodded, reaching down to rub Winnie's ear between my thumb and index finger.

"What does RP stand for?"

"Role Playing."

I studied his face and he looked to be waiting for me to put two and two together.

"WRBinder?"

"Wrist binders, lined with genuine hide," he beamed with pride and I almost asked for a picture... almost. No matter how beautiful the craftsmanship, the last thing I needed was my parent's hearing I expressed an interest in bondage.

They'd have me registered for whips and chains faster than I could build a new identity in witness protection.

"Were any of these priced physically?"

His face shifted and he concentrated on remembering while I wondered what the point of a role-playing bridle was. The leather cuffs, sure, but a role playing bridle? We were in farm country; you didn't need to role-play horse riding. You could just go ride a horse.

"I don't think so. Most of the custom pieces are for show, people order what they want special. Most of this is just examples of my work," he gestured at the racks and shelves.

Strange that people would come to a store like this for horse tack, even pretend horse tack.

"I've never had a true connoisseur purchase off the rack, and I don't sell to those who don't look well-versed in Pony Play. It could be dangerous."

Again, my niece played pony. The only one who got hurt was my brother's breakables... Maybe Phil wasn't as laid back as he thought.

"Cynthia," Mrs. Kirby was bright red behind me, looking to be pleading for me to come with her.

"She can tell you," Phil continued. "Her family practically runs the pony play scene in Sweet Pea."

"Because of all your grandchildren?" I asked, concerned how anyone could afford a thousand-dollar leather bridle for an imaginary horse.

"No. Now, you have your list. Come with me." She turned on her heel and Phil made a sound like a horse behind me.

"What's that about? She's the one buying expensive things for imaginary creatures to wear." I moved over to the bridle and stroked the strap. "It's incredible, but the imaginary horse wouldn't care if you put plastic over their head."

"No, but her husband would." He patted my shoulder and I stared at the location of the inner circle.

"Husb-" Realization finally dawned and I choked. "No!"

"Yup," he smiled and held the bridle above my head. "This one actually suits you if you're ever interested in learning. Maybe join a different stable, though. Could get awkward fast if you play pony with your man's parents."

The bed dipped and I screamed.

"I won't join your stable!"

My hair disappeared from my face and neck, revealing Larry sitting on the edge of my bed. Attacking Winnie on the couch were my niece and nephew, completely covered in mud.

"Stable?" he asked, placing a mug of coffee under my nose.

It was gone in four gulps, and I felt confident in my ability to sit up.

"You... mom... never mind." I rubbed my face and blinked blurrily at the room. "Where time gone?"

My question ended in a yawn.

"Time gone to nutty town." He mimicked my irregular speech, but I appreciated the simplistic phrasing. "You are in bed.

It is three in the afternoon, and I'm here to bring you back to camping."

I nodded and dropped my head into his lap. The man let out a sound that was suspiciously similar to a neigh and I jumped out of my bed like it was on fire.

"Do you know what they do?" I hissed and the amusement in his eyes was almost as scarring as the knowledge. "How could you not warn me your parents were more regularly at the Curious Courtship than mine were! Your dad has a freaking *bridle*."

His humor died and the pained expression indicated he'd misinterpreted the original question.

"You don't know your parents have a... pony thing?" Larry choked and I patted his back. "Sorry, what were you talking about?"

"My mom and her church friends are outside, praying for your immortal soul." His face was still pale. I crept to the window and looked down to see the church ladies in a ring of handholding prayers. "She said the fire in your office was a sign from God that you must pay for your sins."

"Go get me a set of hollow coconuts. I'm going to Monty Python my revenge," I hissed, but he pulled me back from the window.

"Down, killer." His palms were sweaty, and I gave him a sympathetic look.

"Sorry to ruin your childhood." He cocked his head to the side and I continued shamelessly. "Remember when you found that saddle and thought your parents were getting you a horse?"

"I hate you," he grumbled and handed me my shoes. "Like no dessert for two months, hate you. And I'm not going to do that thing you like with my..."

He cut off when he picked up my pants and the coffee flavored bottles fell out. Larry studied each one, opened the lid and gave me bedroom eyes.

"How did you go shopping without your phone or wallet?" His voice was husky and suddenly I wished my niece and nephew were invisible... or Winnie could be a babysitter. "Did you... *slide* these into your pocket?"

My toes curled and my mouth watered.

"N- no... it was..." my eyes stopped on the list of stolen goods sitting on the counter. "What do you think someone would steal a dozen gel pens for?"

"What color?"

"All the colors," I said, checking the list. Larry wrapped his arms around my waist and studied the list over my shoulder.

"Forget the pens, who wanted to steal four dozen scented candles flavored like unicorns?"

I shrugged and stared sadly at the list.

"It doesn't make any sense. None of these things... except the coffee, chocolate..."

A figure knocked at the top of the stairs and I started at the sight of Barney Fife, wringing his hat in his hands.

"Ms. Sharp... L-dawg," I nearly gagged at the nickname. Neither of these white men had any business using *dawg*. "I uh... I need you to come with me."

"What? Why? To where?"

His hat was nearly invisible in his large hands. Marine Man moved around him and pulled out a pair of handcuffs. I blinked at the quick release lever… why would a fed have toy handcuffs? Was it because he was a Marine?

A Marine would find himself accidentally handcuffed to something without his key on him.

"You're under arrest for battery." He winced at the word and Winnie let out a soft growl. "Look, I'm only here because Carla said if Daniel tried to arrest you, you'd throw him down the stairs and she'd have to charge you with murder. Let's not add to the charges, Cyn."

"OK, I punched that man in the face, but it's on YouTube and they had him sign a release! I saw it! He can't press charges and I can't ask for money in exchange for the use of my image."

Larry gaped but Martin just shook his head.

"No, not the fake wilderness guy. Someone said you attacked their child and then set their shrub on fire." He closed the metal cuffs on my wrists and I growled.

"That little Nantucket…"

Chapter Nineteen:
Time Out

S ome children are over-indulged.

Some were birthed with the genetics of Satan.

Some children needed life to throw them a few curve balls to get their shit together.

Some children... were never going to make it to be adults.

Louisa Mantacore was all of those things, or soon to be... If she didn't master getting hit with curve balls to stay in line, she wasn't making it to adulthood. Both a kindness to society and probably the reason a poor undeserving soul would go to jail for murder.

Maybe I could make a standing advertisement in the local paper vowing to support anyone "wrongfully" accused of her death.

"So, you admit you touched my daughter!" The shrill screech of Ms. Mantacore practically took down the wood paneling that made up the sides of the interrogation trailer. For the tenth time, I wiggled my index finger in my ears checking for damage.

If I went deaf, I was pressing charges and making her and the army pay for my hearing aids.

"Eww," I made the exaggerated vomit gesture and rolled my eyes. "All I did was skillfully detain her criminal contingent from making poor Mr. Phil Phalinx a criminal for letting kids see porn. You should have the birds and the bees talk with your kids so they don't have to learn about it on the streets."

Martin snickered and Ms. Mantacore cut her eyes to him in a look that promised slow and painful death.

He cleared his throat but didn't look terrified in the least.

"My daughter…"

"Is a connoisseur of porn, limericks, and stolen candy the town is too terrified to tell you about." I picked up the ball point pen and rubber band off the floor to spear into the tiled ceiling. "Frankly, I wouldn't be surprised if she set your shrub on fire to murder you. That kid is legit headed down a dark path."

"My daughter's path is not dark!" Her indignation rang honestly and I wondered if she lived life with her head buried in the sand or bought into the positive affirmation racket a little too readily.

"It's not dark anymore, she set it on fire," I answered with a sage nod, and I thought her head would spin three hundred and sixty degrees. "See? That look right there makes me think it's genetic. Have you spoken to a therapist? A priest? One of those pairs of young men in button downs asking if you'd found your lord and savior Jesus Christ?"

I'd gone loopy with sleep deprivation, but even I could see the fear in her eyes.

"Those young men cross the street when they see my daughter," she was practically whispering and a scuffle outside drew everyone's attention to the door.

"Damn-it mom!" The curse carried through the opening interview room door and Mrs. Kirby breezed in with a large handbag tucked under her arm and a flash drive white-knuckled in her hand.

"Don't curse at me again, Daniel Isaac Kirby. Or it will be the last thing you do before I send you on a medical induced vacation," she snapped, and I wanted to applaud.

Also question the fact that his initials were basically *dick*. I couldn't help wondering if that was foresight into his future or a self-fulfilling prophecy. How were all the law enforcement men in this town so aptly named and grossly unqualified?

"Marina, this flash drive not only proves that Cyn was with me all day, but also has a startling number of recordings of young Louisa. That child of yours is a thief, a pervert, and quite possibly the leader of a gang. You need to correct her course or start heavily investing in attorneys and cigarettes."

Marina Mantacore, for her part, looked ashamed. Personally, I think naming a child alliteratively was grounds for an insanity plea, but the woman wasn't the one on trial.

"Mrs. Kirby," she puffed out her chest but deflated at the warning finger. "You can't be serious?"

"I can and I am, Marina." Her statement was punctuated by another scuffle outside.

"I'm a damn deputy! You can't just do-" Larry walked in and shut the door squarely in Daniel's self-righteous face.

"Where's Sylvia and Erich?" I asked and he rolled his eyes.

"In your Jeep. I bribed them with ice cream if they wouldn't set anything on fire for the fifteen minutes it would probably take me to spring you." His eyes fell on his mother and he lifted a brow. "Why are you here?"

"Watch it, Lawrence," her warning voice sent a shiver down my spine. The woman clearly had her Master and Commander voice down.

If only I could get the image of Larry's dad wearing a bridle while she used that voice out of my head, I might make it to 30.

"Miss Sharp, I need your help. My sons are... incompetent in certain areas, and I think you and your partner will be an asset to my cause. Will you please come with me?"

Ms. Mantacore started to speak, then shrank under the older woman's gaze. Mrs. Kirby placed the flash drive in the young mother's hand and started toward the door. Marine Man looked from her back to Larry and tilted his head in my direction. I shrugged and stayed put in case it was a trap.

Larry's mom looked at me over her shoulder expectantly and I shot to my feet.

"Yes, ma'am." Of course, my foot caught on the chair and my head fell toward the table. I stopped the concussion with my hands at the cost of my balance and landed flat on my back looking at the underside of the interrogation table.

"You OK?" Martin asked, fighting down a laugh. I flipped him off but accepted the offered hand to help me to my feet.

"Peachy," I grumbled, shooting a dirty look at Daniel who stuck his head in the door. "You are disgusting."

"What?" He whined and I pointed at the table.

"Buy a box of tissues and stop wiping your boogers on the underside of tables, you child."

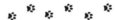

Mrs. Kirby pulled up in front of a plywood barn painted yellow and ushered Winnie and me from her white SUV.

At least, it was styled like a barn. The actual structure was the size of a garden shed. You couldn't fit a vehicle inside, but a motorcycle and lawn mower could sit side by side with ease. Despite the size, it had the white cross beams in the shape of an X, and a wide door that was practically the whole front wall. Two sliding bolts held the door shut, an upper and a lower indicating the door may split in half like the front of a horse stall...

"Oh, hell no," I took a step back and tripped on Winnie. She howled, gnashing her teeth as I barely avoided crushing her with my rather impressive backside.

"Cynthia, do not swear. It's unladylike." Her prim demeanor belied the reason the shed existed.

"First, treating your husband like livestock is way more unladylike than 'hell'. Second, I never claimed to be ladylike... or a lady. I'm a soldier, and soldiers know when to retreat. For the safety of my unit, I'm advancing to the rear." The authoritative tone was diminished slightly by the fact I was on the ground, looking up at her and shamelessly scurrying away on hands and feet.

"Cyn-" A loud scrape came from inside the shed. It dragged along one wall, seemed to thud into another, and a small scream penetrated the walls. Winnie moved forward, scented the air, and released a growl. Following her lead, I hauled myself from the ground and moved closer. A soldier couldn't retreat if someone was injured or needed help. I examined the eaves sitting above the small box that made up the lower portion of the building and checked for signs of damage or infiltration.

The angled top formed a trapezoid, my hand tracing the lower beam just beneath the sandpaper roof. My initial impression of the building was that it was short and shallow, but as I walked toward the rear and stepped back, it was at least two times my height. It took a moment for my eyes to adjust in the sun, but I scanned the landscape for some sort of hint as to what would be prisoner inside.

We were basically nowhere.

Mrs. Kirby and her husband lived in town. The yellow shed sat on a patch of land just beyond the town boundary, shielded by trees. The narrow road she'd driven up wound in what had felt like an unnecessary number of curves. On the inside of the clearing, the road was invisible, and sound was dampened beneath the rustle of pine needles and the hum of avian activity.

It was peaceful.

Private.

"What's trapped inside?"

Mrs. Kirby pursed her lips and gave a small shrug.

"We came out, after I left you." I barely managed to not slap my hands over my ears, but it took effort. "We opened the door, heard the commotion and saw... something. Glowing eyes maybe... or... demons."

Her whisper of the last stole the last of my self-control and I burst out laughing. She was enough of a devout believer to assume demons could be at play, but seemingly not concerned enough to disengage from her potentially sinful activities. It was true testament to the lies people will tell themselves to maintain the image and beliefs they hold about themselves.

The woman stiffened and leveled me with her best death glare. Despite the urge to laugh harder, I held up my hands in surrender and continued to study the joiner point of the roof with the base. In doing so, I made a list of all the ways I would torment the woman by alluding to this should Larry happen to ask me to join his family.

A wave of butterflies rushed around my stomach and I locked the thought in my "don't go there" closet.

Diagonally opposite the door was a small hole. It looked to be chewed into the particle board, roughly the size of a softball with ragged edges indicating it wasn't done neatly with a tool. I pulled my phone from a cargo pocket and shined it into the opening, noticing that even in the heat of the day, the interior continued to be dark and cool. Even on tiptoes, however, I couldn't see much beyond the opening. My phone's light barely penetrated the interior, and I wondered if it was due to the shed's construction or the continuous damage my phone sustained being part of my life.

Possibly both.

"Have you tried opening the door and seeing if whatever it is would leave on its own?"

The glower sent my direction did not answer my question, so I continued to stare until she huffed out a breath and slid back both bolts. While the doors swung open soundlessly, I braced myself for something that looked like my parent's playroom had a baby with my workplace on the farm.

Instead, it just looked like a barn themed bedroom.

There was a bed, hay, a series of nails sporting leather goods, and a wood pellet stove. Cautiously, I poked my head in and looked for a light switch.

To the left was a horse trough and bottles of water, and to the right was the bed.

"Where's the light switch?" I asked, taking two steps inside. Mrs. Kirby clicked something and the room flooded with light bright enough to be a train. My hand instinctively covered my face, just as a hiss escaped the corner of the shed. A weight collided with my arm and raked down, leaving warm, hot blood rushing down my arm. Winnie responded with a howl, her paws clattered on the wooden floor. Another weight landed near my head and I screamed. Blood dripped from my arm and I ran toward where my memory said the door was.

Unfortunately, I missed and collided with the horse trough. Gravity overtook me and I fell backward with a splash, coating myself and the floor in freezing water, the sound of Winnie rushing into the surrounding woods barking her head off served as the soundtrack to my watery agony.

"If you don't stop laughing," I was seated on the stainless-steel exam table in Larry's veterinary practice while he treated the cuts on my arm, face, and Winnie's nose.

"I'm sorry, it's just... you look like a drowned rat and I've never given a rabies shot to a human before." The alcohol swab stung, and I hissed in a breath. If only I'd brought a tranquilizer gun.

That raccoon never would have gotten away.

Right after I bought a tranquilizer gun.

"No woman wants to be called a drowned rat, doctor. Helpful tip if you ever want to get laid again," I growled, and my niece and nephew crashed into the room playing fighter jet.

"Get Laid! Get Laid!" Sylvia shouted and Winnie whimpered, trying to place a paw over her ear. The World War Two dog fight reenactment left the room and I tossed Winnie a treat.

Or at least, I tried to, but I ended up throwing my cell phone on her back just as it rang in a garbled and water-logged monotone that was nothing like the ringtone I selected.

"Cyn's phone," Larry scooped the device off the howling dog and accidentally answered.

"Is she alive?" Martin said into the phone and Larry pulled it from his face. My phone was apparently stuck on speaker phone and I doubted I'd have the energy to correct that any time soon.

"I'm fine, why?"

"Where's the binder I gave you?" He was moving and shifting items around and I heard a sound that reminded me of Tibetan monks. I guessed he was somewhere near my apartment, given that it was Monday. On Monday evenings, there was a learn and move session at the library. I'd seen today's schedule and they had meditation listed as the activity, featuring singing bowls and chants.

Since meditation was sedentary, I figured the regular attendees would be pissed.

"It was on my coffee table last I saw it," I answered, Larry giving Winnie an actual treat and soothing her aches with kisses. The man was going to make an amazing dog father one day. Martin's breath picked up a fraction and a door closed behind him. Something made a sound of distress, something else fell to a carpeted floor and he sighed.

"It's not here," Martin said, and I focused on my phone.

"Where?"

"In your apartment."

"How did you get in?" I asked, but the question felt hollow. I rarely remembered to lock the door and Mrs. Margot had no idea how many keys were floating around the town.

"It was unlocked. I came to get the binder because I wanted to look at the map you made, but it's gone. When did you last-"

Martin was interrupted by a sharp knock on his end and I listened as a woman and man spoke in hushed voices. Martin replied, they said something else and he exhaled in frustration.

I determined he'd pressed his phone to his chest, and no one was whispering, they were just muffled. When the sound remained muted, I smacked my phone on the steel table.

"Can you hear me?" I yelled and Larry visibly flinched.

"Never mind," I could hear him rubbing the stubble on his face over the line before smacking a hard surface in my apartment. Possibly with his head.

He was a Marine with toy handcuffs.

"When can you be back here?"

"What? Why? I'm camping," I lied, knowing that while I would sleep outside, I had zero interest in pretending to sleep under the stars. My plan was to get really drunk and pass out using Larry as a pillow.

There was no research to suggest that alcohol reacted negatively with a rabies vaccine and I was happy to be the first case study.

"No, you need to come do a walk-through of your building to see if anything else is missing or damaged."

"Why?" I asked again, feeling like Mindy in *Buttons and Mindy*. His cryptic demands were annoying and my everything hurt.

"Because the fire in your office was made with that binder and they left you a message," he smacked a wall again and I considered that he may need anger management... or a mild sedative.

Larry's office had a number of sedative options, but no way was I depriving animals of potentially life-saving medication. Maybe my mom had some of her pot brownies leftover... or a spare joint. Though federally, marijuana was still illegal.

"Are you listening to me?" Martin was shouting and I decided maybe the government would look the other way just this once.

"Yes," I lied and he harrumphed so I gave in. "No. What did you say?"

"I said that they burned the binder and left you a threatening note." This time he did bang his head on something.

"What did it say? And stop hitting my walls, they're rented."

Unless the threat was that the note would give me a papercut, I wasn't terribly concerned. While I wasn't stocked up on bandages, I did have a red dish towel, so I was set.

"The note said, 'Mind your own business, or we won't move the dog out next time'."

I stopped breathing.

Chapter Twenty: Getting Serious

"Whoever this arsonist is threatened my dog, Larry!"

I shouted into my phone as I kicked open the fire door at the rear of my building. The call was activated in the front pocket of my pants, where it had been since I jumped into my Jeep and drove away from Larry's veterinary center. He had managed to convince me that until the morning, Winnie was safe and forced me into the back area for more "camping". Every sound in the darkness sounded like an intruder coming to set us on fire. Every shadow, the slowly blossoming smoke from the fire that would end our lives.

At five in the morning, I messaged Martin to meet me at my apartment and slid quietly from the tent. I collected my Jeep keys from Larry's table and drove off just as he emerged into the daylight, swearing.

Then we stopped for two quad shot espressos and a pup cup so I was tired, caffeinated, and ready for war.

"They also framed you for arson!" He shouted as I jogged up the stairs, Winnie padding along behind me. I was listening for sounds of scuffle or injury, hoping that my plan of sending in someone first would have scared off an intruder or forced them to fight with him first and be too tired to hurt Winnie.

"What does that have to do with anything?" I hissed, creeping to the top of the stairs.

Martin was standing at the top, pacing back and forth. He gave me the briefest nod, his phone pressed to his ear, the jeans, T-shirt, and day-old stubble looking somehow more worn and haggard than when he had escorted me to jail the day before. Briefly I wondered if he'd even gone to bed... or left my apartment. I couldn't hear the other end of his conversation, but on this end, it didn't seem the caller wanted much feedback from him.

"Yes," he spoke into the phone as Larry reiterated why I was a day late and a dollar short of caring about this investigation.

"They shoplifted coffee," Larry continued. I marched over to my bed and pulled off all the blankets, then tossed the mattress to reach the hunting knife I kept between it and the box frame.

Then I balled up all the bed linens to take to my mom's house to do laundry because if Martin *had* slept in my bed, they definitely needed to be cleaned . Also, I couldn't remember the last time I'd bothered so they were due either way.

"Again, no one was in danger."

"You've been investigating this for a week and now you care?" I barely heard him as I went to the plastic drawers holding my clothes and removed a taser I had taped to the back. I slipped it into a cargo pocket after confirming it worked by zapping the air.

"They threatened Winnie!"

"You threaten Winnie all the time," he practically rubbed my nose in it. I crouched beside my bed and released the handgun I kept locked in an underbed passcode released bracket.

"She's my child. Everyone knows it's fine to threaten your own children. That's why the expression 'I brought you into this world, I will take you out of it' exists! It's my right as a parent, but no one threatens my kid and gets away with it. Besides, I said I'd stay until morning and it is technically morning. Why are you mad? I followed the rules and now I will defend her with every weapon in my arsenal."

Harder to find was the gun's holster which I vaguely remembered seeing in the bathroom.

"You left her alone in an unlocked building to go punch a man in the face with an arsonist on the loose. Were you concerned then?" his counterpoint stung, but I conceded with silence. I never should have run after a moving car while exhausted and investigating an arsonist. I also shouldn't have been drinking and hiking, driving without a license, or helping Larry's mom de-raccoon her sex stable.

"No, because no one had threatened her!" I went with the lie to make myself feel better.

"So? Someone was threatening to set fire to all kinds of things and you still left her alone."

It was not in the bathroom, so I tried the kitchen.

"No one was threatening to set things on fire, they were just setting things on fire willy nilly! She fell asleep and she didn't want to leave! You know how we're supposed to let sleeping dogs lie!"

"That is a metaphor for secrets and you know it! If you had stayed with her, none of this would have happened." He seemed to miss the point that all of this was happening before I left her home alone, a point I didn't have the energy to argue. I ripped the cushions off the couch and found the holster stuck to the bottom with the Velcro closure of the belly band.

I stuck the gun inside and wrapped it around my waist.

"Fine, I'm the queen of bad decisions. But I repeat, no one messes with my kid, Larry." I hung up the phone and stomped into my tiny kitchen to start the coffee pot. Arming myself had really depleted the eight shots of espresso running through my system and I needed another hit. Martin had stopped pacing and now stood frozen at the top of my stairs, watching me as though I were some sort of circus animal who had just attempted to trample the audience.

"Is there a problem?" I asked him, putting Winnie's tactical vest on her once the pot started brewing. While she probably didn't need the armor, I felt if I was armed she should be at least as dangerous looking. It also looked mostly flame retardant so she would be mildly protected from fire... I hoped.

245

"No, just... Why do you have so many weapons?" His eyes were the size of salad plates and I tilted my head in confusion.

"I was in the Army."

"Yeah but you weren't armed to the teeth when you faced that drug guy." He looked like he believed the two were related, but I didn't see the connection. "You've gone up against an arms dealer, a drug lord, and a murderer with nothing more than your wit and combat skills, but petty theft arsonists are grounds for hauling out your whole arsenal?"

"They threatened my dog."

"Yeah but..." he shuffled his feet.

"They."

"You and Winnie were in more danger..." He held a finger aloft as though making an irrefutable point.

"Threatened."

"Could have been killed..." I looked for a penny or something I could fling to lodge in his throat.

"My."

"Why is this so much more..." There was nothing nearby and I flicked a coffee bean.

"Dog."

The coffee bean missed him by a mile and I wasn't willing to waste another. He seemed to not understand or listen to me, and I was out of patience. For lack of something else to throw at him I ordered Winnie to speak so he'd stop talking.

"Woof!"

The man jumped and banged the back of his head against the wall. Thankfully though, he stopped talking.

"Now that you're done, do you have a second copy of that file?" I asked and he nodded. "Bring it into my office downstairs."

Winnie and I descended the staircase, then the coffee pot beeped. I went back upstairs, grabbed the pot and studied my dish drying rack.

"They stole my coffee mug." I opened the door to my mug cabinet and searched the designs. None were obviously missing and I couldn't remember which one I'd used the morning we left for camping. My favorites were still there, especially the one from Larry featuring me and Winnie behaving like mean girls.

Not that I would admit that I had a favorite coffee cup to my other mugs.

Or talked to my coffee mugs. That would be crazy.

With a sigh, I shut the cabinet and went back downstairs with the full pot of coffee in hand. At the bottom of the stairs, I flipped on the light and gasped.

My office... was destroyed.

The heavy drapes that covered my front window were coated in smoke and soot. Water pooled in the divots of the office floor, soaking into the rugs laid about haphazardly for Winnie's comfort. A metal trash bin sat equidistant between the door, the curtained window, and the wall shared with the library. It had once been stainless steel but was blackened with a burnt ring circling the original area it had burned two feet closer to the corner.

Scorch marks graced the back of the front door and a metal nail had been driven into the wall beside it. Cautiously, I moved closer until I could see that the nail held the note threatening Winnie's life. Beneath it, a perfect scorch from a lit match bloomed above another match book from the Gator Gates, a bar that may have become their calling card after they burned this town to the ground.

And somehow, I'd missed all of this in my hurry to get to Winnie. Looking at it now, it didn't seem possible. If this is what Mo saw...

"Cyn?" Martin knocked cautiously on the back door and I spun on my heel, verifying he was alone and not being lead in by a murderer or a dog abuser. "Why are you holding that coffee pot as a weapon?"

I stared at the pot of coffee still in my hand and then back at him.

"Forgot I was carrying it." I shrugged out the tension between my shoulder blades and tried to breathe. Winnie was on her dog bed with a pig ear. The coffee cart was not damaged or disturbed. My desk...

My feet paused as I looked at the top of the desk and struggled to remember what had been on it. A pad of post-it notes still sat there, a handful of pens, the computer monitor and CPU were accounted for...

"A stapler?" I shifted the contents on top of the desk and the ones just inside around, but there was no stapler. My gaze drifted to Marine Man. "Did I have a stapler?"

He studied the top of my desk beside me with a crease between his eyebrows.

"I think..." his eyes were looking at something beyond my desk and I followed his line of sight to the coffee pot in my hand. "Have you consumed any of that?"

His face was cautious, drawn, and my eyes darted between him and the pot.

"No, why?"

I held it aloft, the light shown through the dark depths of the contents. The color was correct for coffee. My thumb levered open the lid and I took a sniff. Smelled like coffee as well.

"Set it down, carefully," he warned, and I obliged him by placing it on my desk. With equal care, he picked up the pot, carried around the corner and dumped it in the sink.

"What the hell?"

"Look!" He pointed into the basin and I stared down at something solid and dark, getting closer until I was practically pressing my nose against it. "They put something in your coffee! It could be poison!"

Disgusted, I picked it up and showed him my open palm.

"It is a coffee bean, you freaking idiot! Take this upstairs," I tapped the empty coffee carafe still in his hand and shook my head. "Unless whatever you see in my coffee is actively living, I will murder you if you dump it out again. Also, you owe me a new bag of coffee."

Metaphorical tail between his legs, he dragged himself back up the staircase while I filled a container with water to make a new pot. The machine downstairs was identical to the one upstairs, and I grabbed the nearest can of coffee. I peeled off the lid, a subtle click preceding the smell of something chemical. I staggered backward, the lid coming off completely with another click, and the can erupted in flame.

Chapter Twenty-One: Scorched Earth

I nstead f working together, I wanted a fresh look at all the data from a new perspective. Which meant we would assemble our individual understanding of events and swap. Then we could arrange our data with the other person's data and try to assemble a complete picture.

While Marine Man arranged the binder chronologically and incorporated my map, I sat at my desk and compiled the notes of what had been stolen and the possible date range during which it could have been taken. My hope was to come up with a pattern for the thefts and link them to the timeline of the arsons.

Though calling them arsons when my arm had just been set on fire felt very grade school.

"You should go to the hospital," Martin said for the thousandth time and I leveled him with my most imminent death glare.

"You really should," Larry concurred, and I offered him a deadlier death glare. When his gaze moved to the unbandaged arm with the raccoon scratches, I offered him an irritated eye roll.

I got worse injuries from shaving my legs and we both knew it.

My arm was at a right angle, coated in burn gel and wrapped in a soft sleeve Larry kept at the animal center for abrasions on the legs of horses. Beneath the sleeve, my arm was bright red with a half-dozen blisters and singed hairs. As the arm was the only casualty, my face and eyebrows completely intact, I refused their medical recommendations and instead dived into the project at hand.

What was most obvious was that this town sucked at regular inventory and audits.

Second most obvious was that Martin was the slowest worker in the history of partners I had ever had.

I lumped the stolen goods into methodical categories and determined that everything had been stolen within a buffer zone of one week before the first fire through current times, give or take a few days. I also determined all the thefts except those at Phil's fell below the felony threshold for burglary, meaning even if caught in the act it would be a citation at most. It gave me the impression that whoever was committing the thefts had no idea what the value of Phil's craftsmanship was ... and hopefully also not the purpose. My conclusion drawn, namely that Phil's was the outlier in terms of theft cost and the indoor fires in my place were an outlier in terms of arsonist activities, I looked up to Martin for a swap.

Martin had done nothing.

Whenever I looked over at him, he appeared to be studying the papers meticulously. As soon as he thought I wasn't looking, he stared off into space or played with his phone.

"Are you ready to trade?" I asked for the fourth time and he shook his head.

"No, not yet... I think..." he trailed off again just as he had before. Giving up, I fired up my CPU and waited through the startup menu. My background was still the ripped naked man, but someone had edited the photo by adding a rifle in front of his manly assets and I narrowed my eyes at Larry.

In response, he grinned wide and wiggled his eyebrows.

I mouthed *that's for later* and launched my email program. There were a lot of advertisements, a few suspicious job offers and an email from Beth, the armory sergeant I'd worked with closely in Afghanistan.

By worked with closely, I mean she was one of the few women on the deployment and we banded together like rafts in a storm. I smiled and opened her email.

Hey Cyn,

I'm sorry to hear someone is starting fires in your town and it isn't you! That must be so devastating getting one upped like that. I can't be-

LIEVE YOU REMEMBER STEVE BERMUDEZ. DID YOU HEAR THE PINHEAD GOT SHOT IN THE ASS? THEY MEDICALLY RETIRED HIM, BUT I THINK HE'S SINCE BEEN ARRESTED FOR SEXUAL ASSAULT. SHOCKING RIGHT?

NEVER KNEW HE HAD A BROTHER... HE CERTAINLY WOULD HAVE THROWN HAVING A BROTHER THAT WAS A FED AROUND MORE IF HE'D KNOWN. MAYBE THEY AREN'T THAT CLOSE?

THANKS FOR THE CARE PACKAGE AND THE WINNIE PICS.

LOVE AND MISS YOU GIRL, SHOOT STRAIGHT-

BETH

I read and re-read her email, brow furrowing.

"Hey Martin?" I asked, looking over at him. He'd been staring intently at me while I used the computer and he seemed startled when I spoke to him suddenly.

"Yeah? What's up?" He shifted, not seeming to know where to avert his gaze now that he'd been caught. Larry had a Winnie style head tilt and I got the impression that I'd missed something.

"How's Steve? He doing good?"

"Huh?" Marine Man was chewing on the back of his pen. "Who's Steve?"

"Your brother?" I blinked at him, wondering if one day I'd be lucky enough to forget my siblings. "Your *twin* brother?"

"Oh, yeah. Still storming the beaches with the SEALs and stuff like that. Can I borrow your computer? My phone died." He cleared his throat and the device in his lap made a beeping sound as he stood. "My phone's data plan died."

His correction didn't make sense and I stared at him.

"Why were you on the mountain that day?" The question left my mouth before I could examine where it came from.

"What mountain?" He shifted from foot to foot and tried to move closer. As though he forgot why he stood, the man sat again.

"The one... with the vomit... Dude, why are you being weird?" Martin had mine and Larry's undivided attention and he shifted in his seat.

"I just... you're wearing a crap ton of weapons to sit and read files. There's water damage, the place smells like smoke, your arm is fried, and you're acting like this is normal!"

My eyes scanned the disaster area.

"It kind of is..." My phone went off and I checked the display. Twenty-minute work reminder, and Larry's phone let him know the same. "We need to go to work, can you make me a copy of that?"

"That's why I'm acting weird! This shouldn't be normal!" His eyes darted around and he looked suddenly pale. I'd have offered him comfort, but my arm had been burned and he was just being a baby.

When he steadied, I gestured to the binder in his hand as a repeat of my question, and he nodded.

"The library will let you make copies for free. Just leave it with the info desk lady, she'll get it in here." I stood and heard my vertebrae pop in a symphony of percussion that would make Beethoven proud. Martin's eyes were on the holster at my hip when I lowered my arms again.

Interesting... jealousy or fear? Studying his face, I watched him make a conscious effort to look casual and blank. He was really freaking out over something so small as a burned arm and a woman with a gun?

Maybe he was new to the force... I closed my eyes but realized I'd never asked what agency he was with.

"Do you work with Gretchen often?" I asked, remembering him mentioning my one-time cohort and customer from the FBI.

"N-no, just know her from past cases." He shifted the binder without making eye contact.

"Cases you both worked as part of the FBI?" Larry had paused, offering me a head tilt. I gave an imperceptible shake to not say anything. Martin had frozen at the question.

"She's part of the FBI, I was just helping out..." He picked up all his things and stood up. "I'll get you that copy."

"Kay, well... see you later." I moved to the staircase that led to my apartment and Larry followed, leaving the federal agent stewing in his own thoughts as he meandered slowly toward the exit. I pulled my phone from my pocket and sent off two quick texts and searched for any news information on the fires in the few small towns I could remember the name of.

"That was weird," I whispered to Larry as we reached the landing at the top.

"Which part? Where you randomly started interrogating him or when he blew off doing work to stare at you?" He nudged me forward.

"All of it. Who obviously neglects work to stare at people and then acts like he wasn't? Does he think we're blind? And he evaded all those questions." I poked Larry in the chest with my index finger. "That's weird!"

"Not that weird. You are terrifying when you're armed and injured. If all it took to get him to stop flirting with you was a bunch of weapons, I'd have dressed you like this myself ages ago." He nudged me into my apartment.

"He wasn't flirting with me" Right then, an article popped up about a garden shed burning to nothing and destroying thousands in power tools, dated four days after the last small, contained fire in the area. I searched for another small-town name. Again, a structure burned, expensive items inside, no one knew how it started.

"Yes, he was. He tried to kiss you." Larry took my phone just as I read about a warehouse fire two miles from Blueberry Hill, one injury reported and no known ignition source. "Hurry up, we need to make a pit stop."

Despite Larry needing to drop off ointment at his parent's house, we arrived at the farm early. The day had dawned crisp and clear, and temperatures remained well within my tolerable range of 60 to 70 degrees. Horses and goats alike seemed more relaxed in the moderate temperatures, and I found myself excited for the day.

Until Joseph shouted behind me.

"Callie needs an enema, Cyn," he gestured toward the sheep in question. "Since you're here, you can... what happened to your arm?"

"Lost a fight with a coffee can," I shrugged, and he considered a follow up question before choosing silence.

Frankly, I was a bit disappointed.

Donning gloves and grabbing her medicine from the fridge, I helped Callie with her constipation.

"That was disgusting," I peeled off my gloves and turned into Deputy Montalvo, sporting civilian attire and wrap-around shades.

"I've seen worse," I cocked my head to the side remembering how we met. "Heck, you've definitely seen worse. What's up?"

"Not much... I just got off shift but I wanted to talk to you about something." She inclined her head toward the barn and I followed her cautiously. At the indoor arena, she shifted to face me and leaned against the white wooden slats that served as cross beams. Her eyes looked weary and I felt like she was trying to keep eyes on everything at once.

"Are you OK?" Some of her nerves rubbed off on me and I felt a prickle up my spine.

"Yeah... and no. Do you know everyone who works here?"

"More or less, yeah. I mean, we don't all hang out, but they are all good, hard-working people earning an honest living." I felt like a country song despite the truth to my words. "Talking beer on Saturday night, church on Sunday morning... except some of them are agnostic and others Jewish, so Sunday morning is sort of a... metaphor?"

Deputy Montalvo seemed to chew on her cheek and nod.

"Any of them seem... especially destructive? Besides you, anyone have a grudge or an issue?"

My eyes scanned the whole area and I tried to picture the people going about their day. Many of them were here because they loved animals, loved working with their hands. A few were here because it was easy work to get and they had a few recreational hobbies that might be questioned in other occupations, but none of them struck me as dangerous.

"Your face says no, which is why this is weird. That hay the other night, the one those boys stole from here?"

"That they then set on fire and tried to hotbox a whole town?" I tried not to smile at the image of Amber's face when she learned she had "practiced" acting with a porn star for nothing.

Then again, he was cute so maybe she deserved a thumbs up... or maybe...

"Matt and Jack didn't start the fire," her words brought me back and I tilted my head. "I figured they were trying to save their asses, but when their story persisted that the goal was just to frame you for trying to frame Amber in exchange for a glimpse of her boobs, I got curious."

"I don't want to glimpse her boobs," I balked.

"Not you! She said she'd show the boys her boobs in exchange for setting you up."

"Isn't one of them related to her?" Again, I really needed to move before my mom told me it's not incest if you only look.

"Not really the point," she reminded me and I had to argue that it was at least *part* of the point.

"So, that's all my reputation is worth? A quick peek at her peaks?"

"You've never been a teenage boy. My nephew confirms he'd shove his mom down the stairs to see a nice rack, his words." I suspected we might both have formed the opinion that that boy might need therapy, so we said nothing more on the subject. "So, I went back and studied the hay."

She pulled her phone out and swiped to some pictures. It looked like the start point of the hay's smolder, a deep well amidst a sea of inky black. In the center was a small metal cylinder, wrapped in a light coating of ash, beside a pin and what might be a striker.

"What is that?" I asked, confused how young boys would get their hands on something so professional looking.

"Time-delayed fire starter." I blinked at her and waited for more. "That's what the guys in the lab said. You have a semi-flammable exterior that makes a slow burn, releases the catch and a spark burns the fuel in the cylinder."

"How did kids get that?" I marveled and wondered what my childhood could have been with access to such technology. Then my brain flashed back to the news articles, *no known ignition source.*

"They didn't. The hay was supposed to go near Amber's room, but the bale caught in the bed of the truck. They dumped it, returned the truck, and tried to run away. Then the fire spread, and they panicked. Matt dialed emergency, it's in his phone records."

My teeth pulled my lower lip into my mouth and I chewed thoughtfully on the nagging sensation in the back of my mind.

"So... then what was supposed to burn? And why does it look like the device was faulty? Do you think it's supposed to be still partially intact?" I asked her, eyes drifting around at the animals, out into the pasture before landing on the back side of the ice cream parlor.

"I think someone wanted to burn this place to the ground," she confirmed, inclining her head toward the building. "And I think it was supposed to look like an accident, but who would want to burn down an ice cream parlor?"

"There's nothing valuable inside..." I thought, knowing most of the kitchen appliances were antique and handed down through the generations.

"What makes you think the fire would be related to what's inside?" She pokered up and I told her about the articles I'd seen.

"But there's nothing of value in the ice cream parlor, why burn it? Why burn valuable items at all? Wouldn't it make more sense to steal them?"

Montalvo pursed her lips and seemed to chew on her cheek in thought.

"We arrested a man for insurance fraud. Well, the neighboring county arrested a man for insurance fraud. He had all his most expensive weapons in a hunting cabin that spontaneously combusted. Except the investigators found evidence that it was on purpose, the man had three mortgages to support his gambling habit. Though he wasn't in the area at the time of the fire."

I felt my eyebrows draw together. If nothing was stolen, what was this fire a distraction for? Most of those hunting cabins were miles away from each other and secluded.

"Did he say how the fire was started?"

She shook her head.

"He's pleading innocent, no knowledge. We think he hired someone, but this area isn't exactly a hotbed of paid arsonists. Where would he find one?"

My phone dinged and I read Gretchen's response to my earlier question.

"I think I know..." I responded and she glanced at my phone.

Chapter Twenty-Two: Tracking

There was not a spare moment to look into my hunch after Deputy Montalvo left.

Just as her car drove off, a stampede of rabid chickens cut through the farm. The entire flock squawking and pecking at every bit of earth not under an animal's hooves. A pair of brown hens chased a toddler before they discovered chicken snacks in the animal enclosures and decided to eat their way through the livestock's meal.

A decision that ended with Esther.

The donkey kicked one and the others circled poor Esther for defending her legs from pecking. It was an awkward ten-minute showdown while the chickens sized up Esther and Esther... kicked chickens.

It was like watching a toddler sized bully kick down sandcastles at the beach. A chicken would charge Esther, she'd wait patiently for it to get just close enough to whip her butt around and punt it clear into the goat pasture. Though feisty and ambitious, the chickens did not learn their lesson. Another would charge as a feathered foe sailed through the air like a football at the Super Bowl.

"Cyn!" The farm hands yelled, as the fourth chicken went flying and I tried to pretend I was deaf.

Winnie, for her part, stayed far away from the soccer exhibition. Having been kicked by Esther before, she knew above all else to stay away. Having tried and failed to eat chickens on numerous occasions, she elected to hedge her bets and leave them alone as well.

Unfortunately, I was not as lucky.

"Cynthia Sharp, get your ass over here!" Joseph yelled, and I hung my head to trudge toward my inevitable demise, dodging a brown chicken as Esther sent it flying into the wall of the barn.

For all her useful farm qualities, Esther hated men. No one is sure why, though we all had suspicions. This meant Ezzie was the only farm hand who could calm and work with the female donkey. As it was Ezzie's day off, that left me. We had played this game once before, though with much fewer flying chickens, and I spent the rest of the day with an ice pack on my butt.

Thankfully, it was cushioned enough to take the hit.

Un-thankfully, it hadn't been bad enough to get out of future donkey duties.

Or stop me from laughing at "donkey duties".

Joseph swore it was because I was trained to work with animals by the Army. The donkey jaw-shaped scar on his arm said he was a once bitten, twice shy kind of man and I owed him. Which, while true, made me feel like the only expendable female on the farm.

"Nice, Esther..." I cooed, hand outstretched. The gray donkey eyed me warily and I moved toward her head while a chicken charged at my leg. In a demonstration of loyalty to Esther, I attempted to gently nudge it away with my foot.

For which I was clawed, pecked, and eventually forced to kick the chicken out of my way, not managing the same distance as Esther. In my defense, I hadn't wanted to kick the chicken and Esther was a pro. The donkey turned her attention to me and I froze.

"Esther, sit!" I commanded in my best alpha-predator commander voice.

The donkey did not sit, and her look suggested I was on her list.

"Esther, run over there!" I suggested as she sent yet another chicken flying.

I had a sudden urge to play the Angry Birds game, but the donkey did not waver on her decision to ignore me.

"Esther?" I asked, just as the donkey kicked one last chicken... directly into my head.

A claw raked down my cheek, someone screamed, and I was falling toward the ground. I heard the donkey *hee-haw* as something sailed through the air past my chicken covered face. I fought the hen, letting it leave with half the hair on my head.

"Did we win?" I asked, keeping my right eye closed as blood from the chicken scratch dripped down my face. "Is it over?"

A pair of strong arms lifted me off the ground and moved me back quickly, but my one open eye couldn't see the face.

"It's over," he said, and I recognized the voice of J, one of the farm hands who was actually newer than me.

"So, all the chickens have been kicked into the wind?"

"All the chickens... and your cell phone," he whispered, and I nearly collapsed.

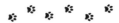

Three hours later, my day done, Winnie and I stood in front of the ice cream parlor. I had a cone of Unicorn Cotton Candy ice cream and she had a pathetic "you hate me" look on her face when I refused to share... or buy her a cone of her own.

"You can't have dairy! I'll get you a treat later," I told her, but the expression she wore said I was being brought up on criminal charges as soon as she learned how to work a phone.

Thank goodness I didn't have a phone for her to learn on.

"Hey," J said, walking up and looking over the pair of us. "You need a ride?"

"Yeah, but I think Larry might come soon," I followed the statement with a giant bite of ice cream and suffered a brain freeze.

"Nah, he just called Joseph when you didn't answer your phone. My wife said she'd clean up your face and do something about your hair if you want to come over," his lopsided smile in the light brown of his face made him look young and smarmy. "Though she might make you look like that one hooker aunt at every Quincenera."

"You have a slutty aunt?" I asked, finishing my ice cream while he led me toward his pick-up.

"Lady, everyone has a slutty aunt in their family," he shook his head and popped open the back door first. Winnie leapt in while I climbed in front and J shut both doors before walking around the front to get into the driver's seat. "If you think your family doesn't, it might be you."

A terrifying thought I was not prepared to examine.

"My wife loves all your YouTube videos, by the way," he pulled out of the dairy onto the two-lane road. "Like, she didn't believe me when I told her I worked with you until that bull got stuck in the shop and I was in the video."

My wound had been cleaned on site, dressed in some of the basic animal first aid supplies kept on hand. It didn't hurt, not really, but the mortification at having my every incident since the release and mass distribution of the video phone, documented and shared, cut deep. As he re-told the story of my accidental international incident in Canada, I wondered what life would be like as someone else. Someone who wasn't an internet sensation for disaster. Someone who didn't have to worry about someone showing up and setting her home or her best friend on fire, someone who...

"Wait!" I held out a hand and J slowed down to a crawl. "Turn left."

Tingles started in my arms and legs when he turned and in front of us was a red hatchback with Arizona plates.

"What are we doing?" J asked, still moving forward. He was close enough to the red car that they may be able to make us out, but I urged him to go faster. I couldn't lose this car, not again.

This was the plate that had stolen my wallet.

"I need to talk to those people," I watched as a wrinkled hand flicked something out of the open passenger window. "Wait! Pull over, I need to make sure..."

I didn't know how to politely convey my suspicions that I was concerned they'd burn down the town by accident while only burning parts of it on purpose.

J angled the car off the road and I ran over to see a matchbook from the Gator Gates laying on the bank, whole and completely unburned. Ahead, the car turned onto a small road between two older farms. Winnie jumped out of the backseat and sniffed the matches, not showing much enthusiasm until a breeze drifted from the direction the car turned.

Her tail went full helicopter and she nosed my hand enthusiastically.

"You know, we're going to walk," I said, deciding J was probably safer moving on than confronting arsonists. "But if you see

Larry or Carla, could you let them know that I may have found my wallet and where you left me?"

J screwed up his face, eyes going from my bandaged arm to the butterfly closures on my face.

"I'll buy you a new wallet," he offered, looking as though I'd asked him to shove me off a ship at sea.

"No... no, it's fine. Just let them know?" I slammed the door shut when he nodded. Indifferent to his looks, I waited until he turned the truck around before I jogged toward the overgrown dirt driveway. Twenty yards in, it curved a sharp left, my view blocked by a tall stand of privacy hedges.

Winnie and I exchanged a look, and she nosed my hand.

We were pressing on.

Despite the urgency at not wanting to lose the car, I felt even more urgently that I didn't want to get shot. We decided to power walk, pausing every half-dozen feet to listen. With my partner's confirmation that there was no engine, shotgun, or shouting farmer sounds, we'd hustle forward to pause again.

At the curve, we rounded cautiously. There wasn't a mirror to alert drivers that someone may be coming from the opposite direction, but that didn't mean the road wasn't heavily trafficked.

It just meant whoever traversed it didn't care about safety.

Without a compact mirror, I stuck my head around the shrub and prayed to dog I could pull it back quick enough to avoid decapitation. Thankfully, the road was empty and dead-ended at a rotted-out cottage overgrown with dandelions and a green substance that was either moss or mold. We darted forward, pausing briefly to listen to the car. The car made the subtle ticking of a cooling engine, and I took that as an invitation to peek into its windows.

The backseat was filled with boxes that had been taped closed. All of them were addressed to places around the country, a return address of a PO Box in New Mexico without a name attached to it. None of the packages were the same size, ranging from shoe box to small moving box, but the handwriting on all of them remained the same. A perfect block lettering with even strokes in a green gel ink.

"Can I help you?" A man called from the open cottage door.

I turned, anticipating a gun or a knife to be pointed in my direction. Instead, there was an older man in gray wool pants and a pinstripe button down. Without the newsboy cap, he was even older than I'd expected. The hair in a ring around his bald crown was stark white, and gravity had taken its toll on the cartilage of his features. He was holding a mug in one hand, his other concealed in the pocket of his pants.

"Yeah…" I said, squinting at the man against the sun setting behind him. "Why the hell do you have my coffee mug?"

Chapter Twenty-Three: Unanswered Questions

I'd expected the man to run.

More, I expected him to deny it or throw the cup at my head.

Instead, he shrugged and inclined his head toward the door.

"Come on in. I'll find a different one and give this one back." He turned and ambled back into the house, leaving the door open.

Winnie wagged her tail and I stared down at her. She bent her head and nudged the back of my leg, but I didn't move.

"We can't just go inside," I hissed, and she nudged my leg.

"They tried to burn down our home!"

She licked my hand and tried to wrap her teeth around my wrist to pull me forward.

"He threatened you!"

She gave up and trotted inside without me. I looked down and all around, but she was gone.

"Why do I never bring a leash for you, dog," I grumbled and followed her to the cottage, hand resting near my taser. Though not the world's most obedient dog in the presence of snacks, she was an excellent judge of character. She'd never once been fooled by gorgeous eyes and a charming smile. The same could not be said of me, which is why I had the taser.

If these people were bamboozling Winnie, they were obviously either deadly or heavily armed with food.

"Hello?" I whispered hoarsely into the open door. My throat had gone dry, and everything was tense and constricted. "Winnie!"

Her nails clicked inside, but the moment I stepped inside, I was blinded by the sudden darkness. My toe caught on something while my eyes fought to adjust and fell face first into something warm and furry.

That howled.

"Winnie! What are you doing?" I said into her fur, blinking repeatedly until I could make out the room.

A hideous floral davenport stood beside an end table with only three legs. In the center of the room was a scarred and battered coffee table, sagging under the weight of packing tape, bubble wrap and boxes.

"We have chairs," a woman huffed above me and I scanned for the source. White house slippers, long flowing dress, gray eyes and greyer hair that could potentially be a wig.

"You... stole a dildo?" I asked, using Winnie's back to help me to my feet. "And a human horse bridle?"

Her cheeks went red and she moved toward a small reusable tote in the corner.

"I... I didn't know what it was. Could you please give these back?" Inside the tote was the glass tree stump, a black leather bridle, and...

"What is this?" I pulled out something that looked like stir-ups attached to a rappelling harness.

Her face got impossibly redder.

"I'd rather not tell you." Her eyes darted, and I dropped it instinctively. "We aren't really a specialty shop and if I'd known the craftsmanship that went into his work, I wouldn't have..."

The old woman wrung her hands and I looked down at her. Standing, the woman barely made it to my shoulder. I spared the ceiling a glance and flinched. It was eerily close and definitely looked like spiders were waiting to drop from it and land on my head.

"What... how..." The old man reappeared and handed me my mug with hot coffee in it. "Did you poison this?"

"Why would I poison coffee? I swear, kids these days are so suspicious. Poison this, kidnap that. We're thieves, not murderers." His eye roll was legendary, and I tried to document the varied expressions he displayed for future use against underaged delinquents... except...

"Thieves? Don't you mean arsonists?" My eyes darted around, but the building seemed to have retained water and looked impossible to burn. "What is this place?"

"An abandoned cottage we rented from the man who owns the farm next door. It's not really his, but he linked the power to his house and shared the WiFi password," the older woman said, pronouncing the wireless internet signal "wee fee", and I tilted my head at her while Winnie nudged the old man's pockets. He sighed and pulled out a piece of jerky, handing it to her.

"Seriously, who the hell are you and why do you keep meat in your pockets?" I was starting to feel like a guest in the Twilight Zone. Not thinking, I took a long drink from the coffee mug. It was warm and just the right amount of sweet. Unlike the last stranger to offer me coffee in their house, the old man hadn't poured whiskey in it, which was for the best.

"Cliff, my wife Bernadette," he gestured to the woman in the floral dress who stuck out her hand.

"Bernie," she corrected as I shook.

"Bernie and Cliff?" I asked skeptically, thinking they must have gotten the generic brand Bonnie and Clyde names.

"Bernie and Cliff Adams," she said, wringing her hands. "I think you spoke to our niece at some point. Her father, his brother, sold us the car but didn't follow through on the legalities. Played dumb when Johnny Law came around, but he knew... always underestimating older folks, you kids."

I scrubbed a hand over my face and killed the rest of the coffee in my mug.

"You stole my wallet from the hospital parking lot," I tried to work up some anger, but Winnie was leaning against Cliff, tongue lolling as he scratched behind her ears. The couple exchanged a look and nodded.

"Can I have my money back?" They shook their heads and I shrugged. It had been worth a shot. "Can I have an explanation?"

Bernie sighed and sat on the mildewy couch, Mr. Adams joining her. My seating options were an armchair with questionable stains, a kitchen chair that could collapse at any moment, or the floor.

Hedging my bets, I picked the floor and set my empty cup in front of me. Winnie lay down and put her head in my lap, nosing the cargo pocket where I kept her treats. I gave her one and found a package of Oreos crushed to dust.

The older couple recoiled when I opened the cookie and crumbs sprinkled the ground. I carefully dumped all the other crumbs into my mouth and gestured for them to speak while I crunched chocolate dust.

"Oh..." Bernie sighed and Cliff squeezed her leg. His touch fortified her resolve and she started again, pulling the wig off her head to reveal a small scalp of fuzzy hair.

"This all started almost a year ago. Two years before that, I was hospitalized: lung cancer and complications due to infections. Worked for three decades, had a comfortable retirement plan and plenty of money... until the bills came. One after the other, the insurance denied this, or I went over our coverage on that. Before I was discharged, the money was gone and our house was in foreclosure."

A tear trickled down her worn face and I watched it move through the creases. Though not that young, she had aged ten years in a sentence and my chest constricted. If this was going where I thought it was, I was more than willing to walk away and let them carry on with their life of petty crime.

"We went to New Mexico to stay with his brother, but he had medical bills of his own. That kid of his does incredible work, but not all of her little ducklings stay the straight and narrow. Most worked hard and she got them fair wages and respectable skills, but every once in a while one would go back in. A bigger man was busted for committing thefts and re-selling the goods on the internet. He stole major items, technology and guns, but managed to make a small fortune in the year he worked. We got the low-down on the gig and started practicing locally. We couldn't steal from individuals, and we certainly couldn't hurt businesses by taking big ticket items, so we... we went small. Things no one noticed until they were long gone and in their new home. We steal items of low value and sell them online."

I nodded at her story, noting the man comforting her whenever her breath hitched. Whatever life they'd chosen, they were in it together and my stomach went squishy at the romanticism. Then I remembered they tried to set my home on fire.

"So if you were committing petty thefts, what was with the fire?" I asked, steeling myself against their adorable criminal faces.

"Well... we discovered in New Mexico that starting fires in small towns was a great way to get open access to businesses," Cliff said with a note of derision. "People are so fascinated by fire and small-town people are desperate for excitement. Utah was the exception, not very nosey about property damage, unless it was theirs. That's when we started the nighttime test fires. This town, though, was the first to actually encourage the fire starting. A nice couple, blitzed out of their minds , gave us a giant bag of matches stating we needed to light up and let loose, and Florida had way more to offer than Ohio. We lost half of them somewhere on Main Street, but we figured someone might find and use them."

"Well you did, and you almost burned down that shed!"

"No, the fire was contained on a paint can lid," he corrected. "It was nearly out before we walked away, and the first neighbor came out. Large man seemed to be just getting home from some-where."

"How did you get my wallet there?"

The man tilted his head and I tried again.

"My first wallet, brown with a dog on it? How did you get it? Why did you leave it there?"

Bernie appeared to give it serious thought and shook her head.

"We found a wallet, but we gave it to the blitzed couple. They looked more likely to know who the owner was... but that was after we left the shed smoldering."

"A whole bottom corner of the structure burned, it wasn't smoldering. And you tried to burn down my building!"

"Burn down your building? Don't be dramatic. We just burned your trashcan and some papers." Mrs. Adams was scolding me and I gaped. "Your door was unlocked, and we walked in. Not certain what was even in there. That dog of yours was sleepy and pawed at a door in the back. We were concerned her owner was dead, so we went up, but it was empty. She leapt on the bed after conning us out of snacks. We went downstairs, took your trash can outside, and started a small, controlled fire."

"Except you didn't take it outside and you burned my entire entry way." I crossed my arms and her frown deepened.

"No, we took it outside."

"You started the fire in my office, by the front door, burning the case binder from your arsons and the matches from the Gator Gates." I pointed a finger accusingly. "Then you left a threatening note for my..."

I stared at Winnie; she'd gotten up to demand affection from the couple.

"Wait. Why would you threaten Winnie?" I asked, the front door swinging open. We turned as a single unit to see Martin, filling the doorway and holding a gun.

"That was me. Get up," he said, leveling the weapon in my direction. "We need to go for a ride."

"Or what?" I asked, standing up and listening to my back pop, but keeping my arms casual. No need to spook the imposter.

"Or I'll shoot you!" he shouted and thrust the gun forward.

"Not with that," I challenged and Winnie let out a soft growl. "I guess you could give me a super spiffy bruise, but if BB guns could kill, Daniel would have a normal number of children."

"How? It's not..." I pointed to the tab on the bottom of his gun that released the CO2 cylinder.

"I hear it's really hard for ex-felons to get guns, Charlie." His face contorted, and I started sweating. My hope had been that revealing I knew his real name, Charlie Darrow, would force him to surrender his grievance. Give up the lie and turn himself in.

The dark glint in his eye said pretending was the only thing holding him back and I'd just opened Pandora's box.

"I see another identity is dead. I was getting tired of that one anyway." His smile showed too many teeth.

"Why don't you sit down, son? We can get you some coffee," Cliff offered evenly, but he and Bernie had moved closer together. They'd seen the same thing I had and it made them nervous.

"I'm not going to sit down and drink coffee, what is wrong with you people?" He thrust the gun toward them and I instinctively edged closer. Winnie stood at alert, teeth exposed, waiting for a command. "I'm going to..."

A sputter came from behind us and we turned toward the kitchen, expecting another shadowy figure. Something was stuck to the back window, making an eerie glow in the twilight. I started to move closer when the man grabbed me, a plastic cuff sliding into place. My wrists were trapped behind my back and he was dragging me to the door.

"Wi-" His hand clapped over my mouth just as a spark bounced off the window and the back half of the building was consumed by fire.

Chapter Twenty-Four: Smoke House

I was dragged from the building, the Adams's sputtering while Winnie's paws clattered on the floor. The entire cottage had filled with smoke, clouding the air and stinging my nose. Warm, wet tears tried to clean my eyes, but the hand over my mouth made breathing all but impossible.

My arms jutted and thrashed, but nothing connected with the man dragging me outside, my feet hitting every step until I was thrown roughly into a car, my mouth free.

"Winnie!" I shouted, choking on snot and smoke as he slammed the door shut. "Winnie!"

Her face popped out of the doorway, leading Bernie and Cliff who covered their mouths with a towel. I flipped around, back against the door, my hand gripping the handle, pulling and shoving at once without success. Charlie climbed into the front seat, and I fumbled with the door lock.

"Winnie!" She made for the car just as he rolled the engine over and gunned the engine, clipping the red hatchback. He flipped a U-turn too wide and sent the back end of the car fishtailing, my whole body slamming against the car door. My head snapping rapidly from one direction to the other sent a wave of nausea through my body. My shoulder spasmed and a warm liquid dripped under the medical sleeve.

The man had popped my blisters.

Dust kicked up, shrouding Winnie and the Adams couple in smoke and sand as we lurched quickly up the dirt drive. Charlie didn't pause, taking a too wide left turn that smashed my head against the back window, ripping off a butterfly enclosure and sending my body hurtling back across the seat as it leveled out.

A small crack had formed in the window.

The driver's eyes were wild. Too much of the whites were visible, pupils dilated in the fading light. His face was red and he was breathing heavily. I watched his eyes, flashing back to the rearview mirror over and over again, buoyed more each time the flames and smoke rose above the cottage and flashed into the night sky.

"Charlie! Come on, just take me back!"

"Don't call me Charlie!"

We were coming up to the main road, and I sat as still as possible trying to anticipate the turn. A fire truck roared down the road, forcing the black SUV to turn right inside of it. My legs bent, I slammed my heels against the window.

The crack widened.

A black and white, lights flashing, was driving toward us. Charlie's eyes went wider and he made a hard right onto a fire road. I didn't have time to position or brace myself, and my head slammed into the window again, sending a sharp pain through my skull. Bright light filled my vision and bile rose in my gut until I heaved onto the floor of the car. Something warm and thick dripped into my mouth and the metallic sting of my own blood sent another wave of nausea through me.

Another bandage from my face had come undone and there was no chance that my DNA wouldn't be all over this car.

Charlie made another sharp turn, the car fishtailing, and he threw it in park. Without shutting off the engine, he climbed out and started moving too fast for my eyes to track. The lights bursting in front of my eyes impeded my vision, but I pressed my back to the seat and tried to line up my feet for another window kick.

Everything tilted and I fell off the seat, just as the back door opened and a strong chemical smell poisoned the air around me. My face was on the floor mat, but the smell wasn't any less strong.

"You are such a pain in the ass," he said, something wet and slippery dripping on me from the seat. "Seriously, who the hell are you? I've been doing this schtick all over the country and now? Drop a random wallet at a scene and then you have to be some sort of Nancy Drew. Now the research I put into making the story believable is what backfires? You stayed in contact with the damn FBI? Do you know what a pain in the ass public records requests are? Getting the reports to make this believable cost me almost $100."

He slammed the door shut and I felt the burn as whatever he'd thrown onto the seat dripped into my open face wound. Eyes watering, my head swam, and I couldn't quite get enough air, but I bent my legs under me and sat back on my heels. My fingers stroked something hard, cool to the touch.

Another burst of light, and I gripped the object for stability, my fingers cutting on the edge.

Hunting knife. I still had my hunting knife.

Deep breath, I rubbed my wrist on the sharp edge, feeling the metal alternately dig into my skin and the plastic tie. Blood pooled in my palms, everything became slippery, but I kept working the plastic and listening for Charlie to come back.

A door popped open.

"Thanks to you, I can't frame those old kleptos anymore." He threw something into the car. It bounced off my chest and landed by my knees. "You couldn't just write it off? I mean I make up the dog poop throwing and you actually did that? Who the hell throws dog poop? Now I have to kill Charlie like I killed Martin…"

He slammed the door again just as the plastic gave and my arms were free. I groped the floorboard for whatever he had thrown, hoping it was a key, worried it wasn't.

Another sound caught my attention… an engine?

I ripped off my shirt and wiped blood from my face, pressing my face to the window and seeing a blue sports car attempting to power its way to the end of the road. My eyes raced around the clearing, was he leaving me here?

An empty tool shed sat with the door waving in the breeze, a red can with a yellow nozzle laying on its side in the doorway.

That looks like a gas can, I thought blearily, and everything clicked.

"Crap!" I choked and grabbed the door handles.

None of them worked.

I climbed into the front seat but the running engine was done remotely. The doors wouldn't open, none of the doors would open and smoke pooled beneath the hood.

"Crap!" I choked, falling back into the rear seat and pressing my feet against the cracked window. Hands steadying at my side, I pulled back and stomped.

Once, twice... it wouldn't budge.

My eyes flashed to the front and smoke was coming into the vents. The world spun around the head wound and I worried I'd lost too much blood.

I slammed my feet again and again until... the window gave, smoke filled the cab forcing a hacking cough that failed to provide air to my lungs. Trying to sit up, my hand slipped on the gas coated seat, and I fell again, seeing a tooth on the floorboard.

"What-" but it didn't matter as the first flame made an appearance under the edge of the hood. A scream slipped from my mouth, and I pulled out my knife to smash the remaining glass and fall out of the window like a rag doll.

I landed flat on my back, vision bursting in bright colors as I scurried from the burning car, hoping against hope that it wouldn't...

The car rose four feet into the air, a plume of fire shattering the remaining windows as it crashed to the ground, and red-hot glass rained down around me before everything faded into darkness.

Chapter Twenty-Five: Red Hot

"That's what she said," I joked, raising my hand for a high-five.

The nurse at my bedside did not give me one. Nurse Sean, the only man in the hospital, besides his husband, who hated me being in the hospital more than I did. A true feat really, as I was the one with the concussion, lacerations, and antibiotic regimen.

"Come on, don't leave me hanging!" I begged the man and he walked out, definitively leaving me hanging.

"You really need to get off the drugs." Larry shook his head from the chair in the corner and I raised an eyebrow.

"You don't think *that's what she said* is an appropriate response to 'that's draining nicely'? I mean come on!"

"He was talking about your gaping wound." Larry rubbed his hands over his face. "I still can't figure out how you managed that."

His hand waved at my legs and my eyes dropped to the sheet. Winnie lifted her head from where it laid across my lap and lifted an ear in his direction, daring him to get her removed.

"Not the dog, I meant the..."

He raised his hands in defense and she laid her head back down.

Stroking her soft fur, I felt the anxiety ball in my gut loosen. I smiled as though I intended to take my secret to the grave, but it hadn't actually been that hard. It turns out that the hospital staff is deeply averse to patients removing their monitoring equipment and bandages to run through the facility like some sort of slasher victim.

An appearance that was enhanced by my yelling, "He's right behind me and I can't get away."

In exchange for my best behavior, which was drastically beneath the normal adult level, they let me have Winnie. If I had been honest, told them that she was the only thing that would stop the panic attacks that ripped through me at the memory of nearly being burned alive, they probably would have let her in anyway.

But that would have made me look weak and I was in the Army, damn-it. You don't ask for help unless you're bleeding and it's arterial, in which case you were authorized to scream.

Everyone had bad dreams, I wasn't special.

"You still aren't sleeping," Larry said quietly and I narrowed my eyes at his audacity. "Your death glare has no power here, Cyn. You need to talk to the psychologist they send in."

"I don't want to." I crossed my arms under my chest and Winnie crossed her paws in agreement.

"Why not?" He crossed his own arms and I jutted out my chin.

"I'll be fine. It's just… processing…" My eyes drifted closed, and a red-hot poker stabbed behind my left eye. "It's just part of recovery."

"Has this happened before?" he asked and I tried to make my face blank but couldn't quite manage it.

"A little, after the incident at the newspaper office," I shrugged and turned to the door as the Adamses shuffled in with a canvas tote and a bouquet of cake pops.

"They said we could visit for a little bit," Cliff said and I smiled when he unearthed a coffee and passed it to me. "I know the sludge here sucks."

I glanced at Bernie and she gave a small smile.

"Strange to be in one of these places for someone else." She leaned in and squeezed my hand. "Did you hear the news?"

"About that sex robot in Japan?" I asked between gulps of coffee.

"Honestly…" Her pointed look had me trying again.

"That Charlie's car careened into a guard rail, and he was apprehended before he made it past city limits?" She nodded and I continued unbidden. "Then he killed himself before anyone could get any answers about the arsons for hire he'd done. Or the fact his name wasn't Charlie, but there is a dead man somewhere named Charlie Darrow whose tooth he threw in the car? Though maybe that man just has a crappy dentist who sells yanked teeth. Or what happened to Martin the Marine Man?"

I rubbed Winnie's head when my heart rate spiked in anxiety.

"They seem to still be working on that, but there was an unidentified body overseas linked to a Marine named Martin... the only ID was a single tooth. The entire rest of the head was gone. The man who died chewed off his fingerprints and his teeth were dentures..."

My voice was a whisper. The man wasn't just an arsonist, he was a murderer and... as yet unidentified. None of it made sense.

"Who kills a man, takes his identity and then makes a living as an arsonist for insurance fraud? Did he really kill those people or was that metaphorical? Killing the fake identity? Are those men still out there somewhere?"

My head ached at the questions, knowing that the answers would be a long time away, if ever.

"Bothers you not to know why," Bernie said for only my ears, and I swiped at the tear that tried to run down the side of my face. "If cancer taught me anything, it's that there is no reason. Not for anything. Sometimes something goes wrong and other people pay the price. I don't think he was well... but he's free now."

"How many people do you think he killed?" My head inclined slightly as another tear followed the first, and she squeezed my hand instead of answering.

"Brought you a gift," Cliff offered, trying to lighten the thick air of guilt and fear that weighed down the air in the room. The mystery wasn't mine, not anymore, but the shadows of their stories would stay with me.

"If it's a tree stump, I already have one." I eyed the canvas bag and he offered me a toothy grin. I couldn't help it, I laughed and felt my chest ease some of the tension.

"Not that," he laughed. "The merchants of Sweet Pea told Daniel nothing was stolen, but we still want to return that to that Phil fellow. His work... he deserves to be paid for his work. Brought you this."

He pulled a small envelope from his pocket and I opened the flap to see a blank card.

"Thank you," I said, not sure what to do but deciding that these past few weeks must have been hard for everyone. Who was I to question why he would want to give me a blank sheet of Kodak paper.

"What- turn it around. Geez! I'm not senile, young lady." I made a face at the 'lady', and he tipped his head in concession. "Fine, pain in the ass. Better?"

I smiled in agreement, knowing a nod would be a stab to the frontal lobe I didn't need. My fingers touched the edge and I pulled out a picture. On the back side was the front section of my office, cleaned and repainted. Someone had put in a new rug and a different desk sat where the previous one had been.

"The desk had an incident..." he shuffled nervously, and my eyes went to his face.

"Forget the desk, you took and printed a picture of my office? Did you print a whole roll or just the one? Don't you have a camera phone?" He rewarded me with a cake pop stuffed into my open mouth and I laughed around the full bite.

"You kids are honestly the worst." He ruffled Winnie's ears affectionately. "I would have texted it to you, but as far as I'm aware, you're technologically challenged. It was a gesture."

"What's next for you?" I sobered at the realization that while they hadn't destroyed anything with fire, they were technically criminals. Altruistic ones, but still criminals.

"We've been exonerated, something about helping a federal agent and ending a nationwide manhunt. We are headed to Florida. Those Jensens offered us a job in their bar, said we'd fit in great." He was beaming, and I swallowed hard at the lump at the base of my throat.

"Did you... Google the bar?" I looked past them to Larry who was laughing around a fist stuffed into his mouth. They spared a glance between us and their expressions were concerned. "Actually, don't. I'm sure you'll be fine."

A scowl covered Cliff's face and I smiled with my hand outstretched for another cake pop.

"This one of those... nudie bars?" Bernie went pale at his question and I squeezed her hand.

"Technically, yes. Clothes are optional for all patrons, but all of them are in your age bracket if that's any help? Also, I think it's illegal to make Naked a uniform without a special license..."

"Oh... that... doesn't sound too bad..." Bernie and Cliff exchanged a look I elected not to read into. "Wonder if there are special classes for people who are a bit out of practice?"

"Oh my, no. No! Goodbye!" I waved them out while they laughed out the door, eager to get to their new jobs.

"Should I be concerned they'll send me pictures?" I asked, Larry getting to his feet and stretching.

"Maybe, but you have more pressing concerns." He walked to the side of my bed, lowering the rail beside me to rest on the edge. My head rested on his chest and I felt a little more tension leave.

"What's that?" I yawned into him.

"You still need to pass your behind the wheel at the DMV," he whispered and captured my lips in a kiss before I could curse him into next Sunday.

Sneak Peek of Book 5: Fetching the Phonies

Chapter One: Flesh and Bone

She is going to get sliced to ribbons, I thought.

The events unfolded like a first-person shooter game. My pale hand clutched the butcher knife, the hem of a navy-blue jumpsuit just peeking into my field of view. A young woman ran upstairs, sweat and blood dripping down her face. Her torn short shorts came into sharp relief just as she fell forward on all fours, her bright red bra on full display as she arched her back to look at the approaching knife. As she rose, the white tank top tore off of one shoulder and her arms pressed the cleavage tighter and still my knife advanced slowly, a menacing swell in music and I felt the tension beside me grow.

"Rawr!" I shouted, leaping toward Mo on the couch.

My best friend leapt from her skin, screamed and upended a bowl of popcorn seeds onto her carpeted living room floor. Her arms and legs flailed violently, warding off the attacker on screen who was as real as the rubber knife that was threatening her. Her face was pale but going near her was too hazardous to provide assistance.

Sensing my inability to stop her, Winnie, also known as the retired Sgt. Winnifred Pupperson, was vacuuming up the salty kernels before the bowl settled. Despite an excellent lineage of top performing working dogs, a German Shepherd father and Belgian Malinois mother, her work ethic was sorely lacking. Not lacking was her vacuuming and gas providing skills, and the two were often related but not necessarily requested. I crumbled into a fit of giggles that shook my entire body. It had been a long time since I'd seen a slasher flick, but they were still as ridiculous as they'd always been. Just a series of poor choices and carefully chosen music.

But watching them with Mo was like taking a child to Disneyland. Half the joy of suffering through this was mocking her secondhand terror.

"Cynthia Sharp, you are the worst person..." The rest of Mo's insult was lost in my raucous laughter. My arms wrapped around my stomach and tears streamed down my face as I slid from the couch to the floor feeling every muscle bunch and release. Winnie bounded over and covered my face in doggy kisses, a mix of salty popcorn with an undercurrent of the salmon in her dog food.

"I hate movie night with you!"

Her exclamation elicited more laughter and her face went red with anger. When I'd arrived two hours ago laden down with snacks, booze, and a streaming password, we fought over what to watch for fifteen minutes until deciding we had to come to some sort of compromise. While I had wanted to watch Elf, hilarious and a reminder of when it was not summer, Mo insisted that warm summer nights begged for slasher flicks. Ultimately, she'd won the movie choice, and I won the snack consumption order of operations. In exchange, she agreed that I could mock it mercilessly if I wasn't absolutely terrified, and I promised to hold her hair back if she puked from mixing nachos and ice cream.

Frankly, she was asking for it because I'd almost been burned alive recently and none of these actors were that good. The woman being chased had clearly been ordered to pose like a Playboy model every time she stopped, and the knife man was far slower than any reasonable murderer in pursuit of bloodlust could possibly move.

Also, I'd been forced to go to therapy, so mocking the faux terror of others was necessary to keep my macho Army woman persona. It was also necessary to convince people not to ask in their calmest voice if I was "feeling OK" every ten seconds.

I was so not interested in discussing my feelings.

Unless those feelings were enjoyment at the mockery of poorly made movies and easily startled friends.

Winnie jumped from my lap toward Mo and threatened to love her to death.

"You and your dog are rotten!" She buried her head into Winnie's fur and made exaggerated kissing noises. She paused and looked up at me with a pinched face.

"Yeah, we are not as rotten as what she rolled in before we got here. You should know better than to stick your face in Winnie fur by now. Absolutely disgusting. Do you have no sense of hygiene?"

"Damn you, Cyn!" Mo threw a marshmallow at my head, missed, and crossed her arms in a pout. Not deterred in the least, I plucked the squishy treat from the floor and popped it into my mouth. Marshmallows had initially been brought out to make indoor s'mores, but Mo's crème brulee torch was out of fuel and when we asked her boyfriend Chris to bring us some, he said we were too drunk to play with fire and to eat the marshmallows raw.

Like animals or something!

Stinkin' firefighters.

"Ew! Do you even know when I last vacuumed? And you accused me of having no sense of hygiene."

"No idea, and I never said I had a sense of hygiene. I can judge you for things while still also being guilty of them," I replied, gliding back on the couch and stuffing three more marshmallows into my mouth. "But probably you've vacuumed since the swan debacle as the marshmallow wasn't coated in glitter, feathers, or rhinestones."

Mo, Mary O'Connor, was five and a half feet of freckles and red hair piled in a bun on her head. Her green plastic cat-eye glasses sat on top of a packaged face mask shaped like a panda bear. The baker and shopkeeper took the look of utter female indulgence to new heights with an oversized Sweet Pea Fire shirt and slippers shaped like dinosaurs. The slippers were a birthday gift from me, the shirt probably belonged to her volunteer fire-fighting EMT/nurse boyfriend who was notoriously curmud-geonly about treating lacerations on my butt.

A non-issue if you were anyone else, but I needed treatment somewhat frequently and his refusal was inconvenient. He made me go to the ER like every other person attacked in a freak incident with spike strips and a runaway tractor.

This after I'd been forced to dress as a swan for their com-mitment celebration and was deprived of leftover cake. There had been four feet of cake and they wouldn't let me have any leftovers for either harboring a stripper or not participating... I had stopped paying attention once the cake was off the table.

Literally and figuratively.

"I'm serious, this is why Larry foisted you off on me you gargantuan..." She pointed a finger accusingly and I clutched my chest in mock offense. Gargantuan, unfortunately, was accurate. At six feet tall and a size sixteen, I'd never blended anywhere in my life. With blonde hair and lavender eyes, I hadn't made much effort since retiring from the Army last year. Specialist Cynthia Sharp, Army MP and well documented world-renowned disas-

ter, was now just Cyn Sharp. A small-town PI, animal technician, and local disaster, who was dating the town's commercial veterinarian, Larry Kirby, and only occasionally causing
property damage.

Weekly is a sort of occasion.

Like taco night, it was something you could count on but
never get tired of.

"No! He *foisted* me off on you because you threatened to
cut out his tongue if you didn't get a girl's night!" I wiggled
my toes in pink rainbow paw print slippers and studied my
short purple PJ shorts and camisole. My face mask was a dog
and as far as I could tell it succeeded in nothing more than
making my face feel damp and smell like witch hazel.

Sadly, witch hazel had zero witch related properties, so I'd
probably still get a zit from the sugar.

"Which reminds me, did you pick his tongue because of
this new trend to please your book nerd?" I continued, standing as Winnie circled, and I accurately guessed she needed
assistance with the doorknob. She pranced to the opened
front door and rushed out into Mo's yard to either do her
business or barf up popcorn kernels.

My money was on the latter. Popcorn kernels were disgusting.

Mo's yard was a wild overgrowth of foliage and weeds.
From the road, you received no indication that a house even
sat there. Trees, bushes, and topiaries hid her front door from
wayward travelers who stumbled into her veritable hedge
maze.

Thankfully, Joseph made Winnie wear a jingle bell on the farm and I could hear her prancing through the garden in search of small critters who would hopefully be wise enough to run away.

"What *new trend*? You please a book nerd by giving them quiet, snacks, and an endless supply of books. If those books are spicy, you make yourself available after," she waved suggestively in the direction of her bedroom as I tuned back in. "For, you know, story recreation purposes."

"Yeah, but I guess the internet doesn't recommend waiting until after. Rather, there's a listicle recommending use of the tongue to offer satisfaction... while reading. You don't even have to put down the book, Mo!"

"Oh my god, that's so rude! How could you not put down the book? What if the scene ends? Do you just keep reading?" She bit her lower lip in thought, and I suppressed a grimace as I heard Winnie rustling through the dry grass, intent on something.

Probably Mo was right.

Putting down the book would have been the polite thing to do.

I made a mental note to have better manners moving forward... maybe. Instead of admitting my faux pas, I barreled on in ignorance.

"No idea, and I don't control the internet! Also don't get me started, Miss 'I read selkie fanfiction that includes pegging'. I read Olivia Dade's *All the Feels*. I know that whatever that is, it is absolutely filthy!"

"Selkies aren't filthy, they live in the ocean! Google it, you narrow minded prude." She chucked another marshmallow in my direction and Winnie leapt through the door to intercept the sugary treat. I beat her to it and she let out a long snort before picking up a long thin chew and carrying it to the center of Mo's living room.

"I did Google it, my computer got a virus and I still don't know what it is." Mo rolled her eyes and I pointed a finger at her chest. "Besides, Mo, you know the only sexy shifters are werewolves and unicorns. Everything else is weird and creepy. Also, if selkies live in the ocean does pegging have to do with pirates who have peg legs kicking-"

"A selkie isn't a shifter," the red head scoffed derisively, cutting off my question about pirates. I could only offer an eye roll since it was probably for the best. The woman who'd run up the stairs on television had been slaughtered on screen in a cascade of fake blood and heaving breasts that were a little too in focus for the purpose of the shot. "Ugh! Why do films do that? Like the woman was just killed, why are we ogling her dead breasts?"

"I don't think we are this movie's target audience," I conceded and noticed something strange about the bone Winnie was chewing on. That something was that I'd never seen it before and had no recollection of bringing it with us.

"It's a slasher flick! The target audience should be anyone with an aversion to a gruesome death who is also fascinated by the prospect." Mo emptied her wine glass, but I was only half listening as I studied Winnie and her new toy. "I mean seriously, this is borderline necrophilia."

To avoid mental scarring, I elected to strike that from my memory.

The woman owned dozens of slasher films and baked while listening to true crime podcasts. If a mysterious series of murders happened in this town, she would either solve it or be the one committing it.

"Did you buy Winnie toys and treats for your house?" I asked, moving closer to the dog and hearing the tell-tale pop of the chew treat losing structural integrity.

"What? No, I just give her people food when you aren't looking. Why?"

The end beneath her left paw was gnarled, a round protrusion coated in dirt. Maybe an antler or a chew modeled after a bone, but the size was wrong for what is sold in stores.

"Do you..." just as I was about to grab her chew, Winnie snatched it up and took off. "Winnie! Get back here!"

My slippers skidded when I chased her from the carpeted living room and into the kitchen. A knee buckled, hyper extended, and my legs slipped from under me. My elbow slammed into the linoleum with force, and I let loose a string of swears that would make a sailor blush.

Thank dog I was in the Army.

Sailors were such unimaginative babies.

"Dog if you don't..." I started as she trotted over, gracefully leapt my prostrate form and pranced into the living room.

Probably for the best, the room was a little wobbly and I wasn't on my threat-making A game.

"You OK, Cyn?" Mo called and I considered briefly if anything felt broken. Arm would probably be fine, butt was well padded, head hadn't hit the ground... good enough.

"Probably," I shouted back. Carefully, I hauled myself the great distance from the floor, my feet getting farther and farther away. It was like looking into a funhouse mirror that was my eyeballs. In the interest of my sanity, I looked around the kitchen until I spotted the open bottle of tequila. "Were we drinking wine or tequila?"

"Both!" She called back and I poked my head around the corner, gripping the wall tightly as the world seemed to spin on a new axis. I was definitely too old to be drinking this much on a school night... or work night.

"Both?"

"Yeah, we started with margaritas and then switched to wine when I tried to convince you to video me doing a strip-tease for TikTok-" I slammed my hands over my ears and started humming. The sound for the latest trend was going to haunt my nightmares with images of bouncing breasts and lime. Winnie, for her part, took her toy to Mo and dropped it on her lap, an invitation to play.

"Who's a good..." she started, face suddenly going pale as she picked it up with her thumb and index finger. "Where did she get this?"

"That's what I asked you," I moved closer to it, trying to identify whatever her teeth had dug into that became startlingly white without the layer of dirt and other deposits. It had long thin strings that, combined together, accounted for its shape and density.

Mo rotated the chew in her hand, analyzing it from all sides and realization dawned as she screamed in time to the newest on-screen victim.

"Oh my god, your dog killed someone and brought me the femur!"

Then she may have passed out

About the Author

E. N. Crane is a fiction author writing humorous mysteries with plus-sized female leads and their furry friends. She is one of two authors under the Perry Dog Publishing Imprint, a one woman, two dog operation in Idaho... for now. My dogs are Perry and Padfoot, the furry beasts shown above. They are well-loved character inspiration in all things written and business.

If you are interested in joining my newsletter, please subscribe here: https://e-n-crane_perrydogpublishing.ck.page/578ed9ab37or on my website, PerryDogPublishing.com

You will receive A Bite in Afghanistan, the prequel to the Sharp Investigations Series, as a thank-you for joining. I only have one newsletter for mental health reasons, so both romance and mystery are on there! If you only want one in your inbox, follow

Perry Dog Publishing on all socials to stay on top of the latest news... and pet pics.

Made in the USA
Las Vegas, NV
10 December 2024